A PROPOSAL

"You're afraid of marriage," he said, coming up behind her.

She turned around and knew that on any other occasion she would have laughed because there he was, standing in that stupid pink bathrobe that made him look like a pink teddy bear. But inside she was quaking, and didn't know why. "You have no right to tell me what I might or might not be afraid of. It's none of your business," she ground out, knocking back the rest of the drink.

"We have somethin', you and I," he said softly. "And I mean to see this through."

"Why? What does it matter?"

"If ye don't know by now, Laura, ye never will."

Tears pricked her eyes and all she could say was, "Please leave. I'm sorry, it's very late and it's a two-hour drive back to town, but please leave. And here, take this with you." She held out the ring, forcing it into his hand when he didn't automatically take it.

Cupping it in his fist, he turned and walked away, stopping at the base of the stairs as he asked, "Do ye not feel anything for me at all, then?"

She couldn't answer that. "Just go. Please." It was so hard to stop shaking, to withhold the tears that threatened to fall.

Lumau Publishing

Mulligan's Dream: Print Edition
© 2018 by Sonia Gay

Cover image © Photographee.eu
Book and cover design © 2018 by Sonia Gay and
Lumau Publishing

ISBN: 978-0-9958376-4-5

Lumau Publishing
lumaupublishing@gmail.com

MULLIGAN'S DREAM

Book One of the O'Farrell Legacy

S. M. Cross

For Mom

ACKNOWLEDGMENTS

There are many people who are to be thanked in the creation of this book, going back to my mother, who always believed in me. Although no longer with us, she is a guiding spirit and someone I talk to a lot.

Thank you to my readers, to Lori and to Patricia, to Susie and to Leah. You all praised my work and then pointed out the errors. I listened and want you to know that your efforts are much appreciated.

To Robert, without whom my journey to Ireland would not have uncovered nearly so many splendid corners tucked away in a very verdant, ancient land. Your stories have enriched not only me, but this work, and I treasure each and every one. To the staff at the Castle Inn B & B in Killarney, who were always kind and helpful through my lengthy stay, and to Kieran at the Vodaphone store, who gave me technical advice. I now remember to turn my devices off and on again before panicking.

To the people of Ireland, all those I spoke with, who told me stories and made me feel at home; to my friends who kept asking when the book was coming out; and lastly, but not least, to my family, without whose support and tolerance through my manic writing sessions, with your agreements to feed the animals while I was working to get this off the ground and general acceptance of my weirdness, has always buoyed me up. And to Marcelle, who very generously gave of her time to help get this off the ground, all for the price of a dinner. Gotta love friends like that!

Thank you, all.

Celtic Dreams

by S.M. Gay

I'll tell a tale of Ireland's blood
Where love and turmoil grow.
Where Cupid's bow hath touch the hearts
And vanquished every foe.

***

A tale of Hank, so strong and true
And of his love, fair Laura.
Of broken hearts and broken dreams,
Of mending lives with honor.

***

So hark ye now and learn the tale
Of Ireland's children, free.
Of lives and loves, of romance sure
And O'Farrell's Legacy.

MULLIGAN'S DREAM

Chapter One

Laura Foster stood at the window, gazing out at the fluffy flakes of snow drifting down from a leaden sky. It was late afternoon and soon darkness would shutter the view of the trees, their branches heavy with the recent snows. It hadn't stopped for two days and she'd given up shoveling the driveway. Her car, a light SUV, was parked under a carport, the likes of which looked as if it might collapse from the weighty pile of white stuff but for the slant of its roof. The metal roofing material released most of the built-up snow to slide harmlessly off to the side, where it continued its fall down a small embankment into the clearing at the side of the cabin. There was no wall at the front, no garage door to keep the snow from blowing into the carport, building up until it clogged the opening. It would take her days to dig out, she reflected.

This cabin was her retreat from the world at large. Her busy job kept her mind occupied during the week, but on weekends, she liked to escape the pressures from town and take the two-hour drive up the mountain to her cozy hideaway.

Normally, the drive was peaceful and scenic, the road winding through newly plowed access ways to the back country where the cabin was situated, overlooking the broad valley below. At the moment, it was impossible to see the valley, or rather, distinguish it from the mountains of snow around her. She'd never seen the stuff so thick.

Her mind took her back to another time, the year she and Erik, her husband of twelve years, had put the finishing touches on the cabin. He'd been standing in the kitchen, paint brush in hand, a big smile on his face. "Whaddya think, babe?"

She remembered gazing around at the distinctly orange paint, unsure at the time if she liked it or wanted to throw up. But he'd been so proud of his handiwork, she forgave the fact that he was color-blind, and for all he knew, was painting the walls beige. To him, everything looked like some kind of muddy brown so really, what difference did it make if it was orange or beige?

"I can tell you're at a loss for words," he'd smirked, laying the brush carefully in the now empty paint tray and walking toward her with that swagger he always used when wanting to be playful.

And playful they were. He'd pulled her into a hug and then bodily carried her to the sofa where they celebrated the absolutely last thing they had to do in the cabin. She remembered the feeling of his body on hers, the strength in his upper torso, his powerful pelvic thrusts as he ground his penis into her body, taking her over the top to a climax he shared. Whatever she'd thought about the paint color went straight out the window into the dark night. She didn't care. He'd fulfilled his promise to build her a cabin in the woods and it was everything he'd said it would be. A half loft, it was compact but with every convenience of their place in town, right down to the en suite bathroom and soaker tub.

Too bad he hadn't stayed faithful. Shortly afterward, she'd found out that he not only loved her well, but also every other woman he came into contact with.

Finding out about his infidelity had been pure accident. She was supposed to go to the mountain straight after work. He was supposed to already be there. Instead, she stopped off at home to pick up a few things and walked into a free-for-all in her bed. Erik's ass sticking high in the air, his balls tight as he thrust enthusiastically into the object of his affection, accompanied by the woman's encouraging words. "Yes, Erik, oh, yes!"

Her best friend.

The sight stopped her cold, but only for a moment. Having had dogs that were prone to poking their noses where they weren't welcome, she came up with the perfect solution times ten.

Retreating before she was discovered, Laura went back to the hallway, grabbed the vase of flowers from the sideboard, checked that there was still water in it, and remembered to her delight that she had filled it that morning with enough to last for the weekend. It was full. Marching back into the room where Erik's balls were hanging, bouncing to the accompaniment of his heavy panting, Laura threw the contents of the large vase, flowers and all, directly at the point where his dick was embedded in her best friend's crotch.

The lovers both gasped in shock, first at the water and then at the sight of Laura standing there.

She'd turned and walked away without a word.

He hadn't contested the divorce and she'd taken him for everything he had.

Including the cabin. Despite the fact that its builder had been a two-timing sonofabitch, she loved it. It had been her haven then, and it remained that way. She'd since painted over the orange.

A low, rumbling noise could be heard, bringing her back to the present. She identified it as the snow sliding off the carport, a sound she'd heard more than once in the last couple of days. At this rate, the little clearing at the side of the cabin would be like a swimming pool in spring, so much snow would be contained within its boundaries.

She turned away from the window just as headlights passed her driveway. It was Henry Mulligan, better known as Hank, who owned the cabin farther along. Hank was originally from Ireland, and like Laura, had fallen in love with the mountain and the valley below. But as far as she knew, Hank and she were the only ones who made the trek up the mountain in winter on a regular basis. Most others who owned cabins on this side of the mountain came only in the summer or over Christmas holidays when the skiing was good and time allowed for a long, leisurely drive, a drive too long for most families on a regular weekend. It wasn't just the time involved; it was often the conditions. Laura had blessed her SUV more than once, with its 4-wheel drive and gutsy engine. If she had a regular sedan, her mountain retreat would be something to look forward to only in the absence of snow.

She peeked out the front window and sighed in frustration at the depth of the snow in the driveway. At this rate, she wouldn't be going anywhere tomorrow. She'd be digging out.

That wouldn't be so bad, she thought as she turned toward the fully stocked pantry for something to make for supper. There was food aplenty, and the electricity was still working. The emergency generator was available for backup, just in case, and that was all that she really cared about.

Out of curiosity, she picked up her cell phone and was reassured when she heard a dial tone. So, add communication to the list of continued services. It was all to the good.

Still, glancing once again through the now darkened window, the only light she saw outside was coming from the lamp over the wing-backed chair. It partially illuminated the view, not enough for clarity but certainly enough for Laura to know that if the snow did not stop by morning, just seeing anything out the front window would be a challenge. It was slightly reassuring to know that Hank was up here. She didn't know him well, only to say hi, really. But she knew he had a bobcat with a blade that she could borrow if she got desperate. The two- or three-mile walk to his place from hers wasn't advisable at night but it was a refreshing and picturesque stroll in daylight hours.

And if she was lucky, maybe she could invite herself in for a taste of his…

Another rumble interrupted her thoughts, a loud one this time, like the roar of…what? There really wasn't anything to liken it to. It was loud and the ground shook slightly and then the realization hit that there had been an avalanche, not uncommon a few miles away where the mountainside sloped directly into the valley. But this wasn't few miles away; it seemed much closer.

She braced herself, holding on to the back of the chair while the vibrations rattled objects like a small earthquake. A few moments later, it stopped, and shaking her head, Laura went back into the kitchen to scout out some grub, thankful that she, at least, had not been in its path.

***

As soon as the first chunk of snow flew past his windscreen, Hank jammed his foot on the brake. More boulders of snow crossed the road in front of him, blocking access to his cabin. He thrust the truck into reverse as rapidly as possible, steering it wildly as he tried to avoid the worst of the slide.

A chunk of hard-packed snow hit the passenger door, knocking the truck off track. Another hit the hood at the same time as one hit the passenger window. The truck shook as it careened drunkenly on two wheels before finally coming to a halt on its side, slamming Hank's head against the door. The grunt of pain that burst from his throat was completely involuntary, and as he shook his head to clear it, his fingers felt the bump that had instantly formed. "Feck!" The truck continued to vibrate as snow hammered into it and over it. His head hurt like he'd been hit with a brick and he couldn't think straight.

The next thing Hank noticed once the motion stopped was that it was suddenly quiet. The music he'd been listening to had quit. His adaptor must have been pulled from the speakers. But more than that, the truck engine had stalled. Not that it would have done him any good with it being on its side, but it was cold out there and the interior was nice and warm. He turned his head toward the passenger door and saw only snow.

"Ah, feckit!"

The stain of white powder was everywhere and then he realized the airbag had deployed. He couldn't remember it doing that but the evidence was in front of him. It was now deflated and hung limply from the steering wheel like a used condom.

Pushing the nylon material out of the way, Hank struggled to release the seat belt and debated his next move. No one knew where he was. If he didn't find a way out himself, he'd either suffocate or freeze to death, neither of which was an appealing option. He fumbled around for his cell phone. It had been tucked into the cup holder, which was now empty. It had to have been flung somewhere, but where? He only hoped he could find it before he stepped on it.

For a brief moment, the green hills of Killarney seemed a welcome thought, albeit a very long way off.

It was a thought that was quickly banished by the mountain he knew on its friendlier days, today not being one of them.

Well, faint hearts never won any battles and right now his objective was clear: get out of the damn truck—he'd long ago stopped thinking of them as lorries. If there was as much snow as he thought pushing on the passenger door, it would be crazy, if not impossible, to use it as an exit. He'd have to push the door up and doubted he could even do it with all the weight that was piled up on it.

Hank stretched his arm and gave it a brief try. Obviously, the strength of one arm was not going to do it. The door remained stubbornly closed as if locked.

Twisting his body, he could see the rear window and wondered if he could fit through the thing. Christ, he'd bash it out if he couldn't fit through it because to do nothing was to invite death and at thirty-three, he wasn't ready to do that yet.

"Ye crazy bastard," he said to himself, "look what ye've got yerself into. How the feck are ye goin' to fix this one?"

A little more wriggling had him facing the small window at the back of the crew cab. Maybe he could open it, despite the snow behind it. "Jaysus feckin' Christ, how the hell am I to get through that shite?"

He looked around for his gloves. They'd been on the console between the two front seats and now he rued the fact his hands hadn't needed them while driving. He found one on the driver's side door, it's dark shadow darker than the window it was lying on.

Feeling around with his hand, he located the other one, not far from its mate. Okay, he had gloves. Things would be fine.

It wasn't easy but he managed to pull them on and get himself into a position the likes of which had never occurred to him in all the years he'd had his truck. He put his feet on the driver's door, leaned over the side of the seat, and attempted to slide open the small back window. The realization that he couldn't be effective from his current position was obvious with his first attempt. There was nothing for it but for him to crawl into the crew cab and get up close and personal with the window.

He shuffled his foot, trying to get his leg into a better position with which to push himself upward when he heard the unmistakable sound of a cell phone being crushed. It was a sound rather like stepping on fine gravel, he mused as he cursed himself for being such a fool. If he'd left it in his glove compartment where he normally put it on long drives, he would still have it. It would be safe. For a very brief moment he wondered if it would still be useful and then gave his head a shake, a movement he quickly regretted as his vision wavered and a jolt of pain shot through his skull, reminding him that all was not well within his cranium.

A few moments later, the cell phone's whereabouts and condition confirmed and sweating from the exertion of hauling his six-foot frame around the confined space of the truck's interior, he was finally positioned in front of the window. Able to get both hands on the latch, he pulled upward and felt the window give slightly.

"Come on, ye wee bugger," he swore as he pulled harder.

He gave up with a grunt, waiting for the pounding in his head to subside. There was no way this window was going to make it easy. And now that he was in the back seat, he was powerless to do anything else but pull on the wee bugger some more. Which he did, to no avail.

"Ah, feckit," he swore again.

Angling his lean frame, he managed to manoeuver himself back into the front seat, feet on the driver's door and assessing the back window with squinted eyes.

"Alright, me son. I hate to do this to ye but ye've given me no choice in the matter."

He lifted one leg, squeezed it through the gap between the two front seats, took a deep breath, and aiming at the window, kicked with all his might.

The window held as pain radiated up his leg and into his thigh, not to mention the pounding it caused in his skull. It felt like all the Furies of hell had decided at that moment to throw a party inside his head.

"Feckin' Christ!"

He stood motionless as the pain died away, and regrouping for another kick, took a deep breath and struck again. This time the window gave slightly and before the pain could achieve its apex, he struck again, ignoring the signal his brain was trying desperately to relay.

A fourth kick and his leg went through the window, lodging in the hard-packed snow outside the truck. He wanted to throw up.

Hank stood a moment, breathing heavily, the pain in his leg and thigh registering as a dull thud while that in his head thumped furiously. His vision swam dizzily as his breath came in gasps and he felt wetness on his cheek. A tear. The pain had been so bad he'd teared up. Well, wasn't that just ducky! He'd been reduced to tears from a bump on the noggin and now his foot was stuck in the back window of his truck.

Pulling his foot back into the truck was proving to be more difficult than he had imagined, encased as it was in the snow outside. He wondered how long it would take for the heat of his body to turn the little cavern around his leg to ice, making it a nearly impossible task to extricate it?

Once again, ignoring the soreness and occasionally wincing at a fresh stab of pain, he managed to shift his foot back and forth, creating a small open area around it.

He had no idea how long he'd been at it.

An urge to simply close his eyes and sleep was cut short before he could put it into action. He couldn't relax in his current position. It was impossible. And now, with his foot stuck out the window, he was in a worse predicament than before.

Using his hands to support the underside of his leg, he lifted his knee, wriggled his foot some more, and was finally able, after much exertion that left him sweating profusely, to pull his leg from the battered window.

It had been tricky. Not only had his leg been stuck in the snow outside, it had also been wedged within the window opening.

His heart was beating so hard it felt like it was going to jump out of his chest, but at least his foot was free. And that begged the question of what to do next? Could he get himself through the opening?

A rough assessment gave him his answer. "Ye're feckin' clueless," he mumbled. The window might lead to freedom but he still had a mound of snow to dig through.

Rummaging around in the back of the crew cab, he found the folding spade he kept there for emergency use, and if this wasn't an emergency, he didn't know what was. Locking its short handle into place, he dug into the first bit of hard-packed snow, chipped away until he could get a chunk free and then deposited it on the driver's door. If he ever made it out, he'd get the truck repaired and detailed.

What felt like hours later, he'd made a small tunnel that he thought he might be able to get through. The unfortunate part of that was the accumulation of snow now piled inside on the door of the truck and covering most of the driver's seat . He'd had to deposit it somewhere.

Being sandwiched between a block of snow behind him and a block of snow with a short tunnel in front did not do anything to bolster Hank's spirits. If anything, it overwhelmed him.

Slumping down as far as he could, he wedged himself good and tight and closed his eyes. Maybe he just needed to sleep a bit.

His eyes shot open. He didn't know if he had slept or only dozed but he was cold and stiff and his head was thumping persistently.

Raising the shovel and pushing it to the end of the short tunnel, he angled it upward and began to dig. A few strikes later, it gave on an upward thrust, and as lighter snow deposited itself in the tunnel, he scooped it away and began the arduous task of hauling himself through the narrow path he'd dug, finally sticking his head out into the cold, dark night.

Inhaling deeply, he thought that freedom never smelled so good.

Chapter Two

A distinct thud repeated itself and finally roused Laura from sleep. In her dream, she'd been doing home repairs, hammering a nail into the wall, the thud of the hammer banging the nail home in perfect time with the thud that awakened her.

A repeat of the pattern and then a muffled shout, as if someone was calling her, was enough to wake her fully. Turning on the light and throwing a robe over her nude body, she quickly descended the stairs to the main part of the cabin. A glance at the longcase clock in the corner showed it was not quite three in the morning. Hardly a time for visiting. So if not a visitor, then who? The clock's ticking was the only sound in the cabin. It echoed off the hardwood floor, and briefly, she heard the wind blow snow at the window, grainy bits like pebbles on the frozen glass. Otherwise, there was no other sound. Maybe it was her imagination, run amok on a cold winter night?

Just in case it wasn't, she needed a weapon. Too bad she'd never owned a gun. She could sure use it now. The poker by the fireplace was the closest thing she had to hand, and Laura grabbed it as she made her way to the door on shaky legs.

A muffled shuffling on the deck could be heard through the door and another thump on said door was proof enough of someone outside.

"Who's there?" she called through the thickness separating her from the possible intruder.

"It's me, Hank Mulligan, from up the road. Can I come in?"

"Hank?" What on earth would Hank be doing pounding on her door at three a.m.?

"Please, I think I'm hurt."

Hank the Hunk, hurt? Laura couldn't believe it. He was a mountain of a man, all brawn and Irish good looks with a head of black, curly hair and a grin that went from ear to ear. Not to mention his eyes, as blue as night, and that included the stars.

A grunt came from the other side of the door and then the unmistakable sound of someone falling against it. Laura dropped the poker, and with fumbling fingers, undid the lock and swung it wide.

Hank fell sprawling onto the floor, flat on his face before giving way to another grunt.

"Up. You have to get up and move so I can close the door," gasped Laura, her bare feet registering the cold from the snow being deposited on her floor. It blew in gusts around her toes, the cold draft making its way up her body, naked beneath the flimsy robe she'd thrown on.

The mound that was Hank moved slightly but it was obvious he needed help. Grasping him beneath his arms, she slid him, rather easily for all his bulk, along the polished wooden floor until she could close the door and keep the snow and winter cold at bay. The fact that it was snowing harder than ever barely registered as she took in Hank's appearance.

His head was bare but for the curls frozen in place and quickly melting, depositing small chunks of liquefying ice on her hardwood floor. His bomber style jacket was torn and so was his pant leg. And was that blood she saw through the gap?

Leaning over to help him up, she met his eyes, those midnight blue eyes, and was lost. How on earth was she supposed to maintain any kind of composure and help him out if all she could think of was jumping his bones? Her ex hadn't been able to help himself, he'd said in his defense at their divorce hearing. He just had to have those women. Maybe this is what he felt, she thought as her nipples hardened in response to her mind's wanderings.

"Laura? Can ye help me a wee bit? Me arm's stuck and I haven't the strength to move it."

She saw instantly that he'd fallen partially on his side and his arm was indeed stuck at a funny angle, not to mention that every time he tried to help himself, he slid on the polished wooden surface. "Oh, sorry. Here." Laura grabbed his arm and heaved, rolling him over in the process and landing flat on his chest. "Oh…"

His head hit the floor and Hank emitted an involuntary grunt, first of pain and then of pleasure as his lovely neighbor landed flat on his chest, her eyes, those lovely green gardens filled with golden lights, staring into his. Even closer was her mouth, the perfect rose-colored lips, ripe for kissing, shaped in the "Oh" of her expression.

Hank didn't move other than to peel off his gloves. He needed to warm his hands, they were so cold and stiff. But more than that, he wanted to touch her.

It was a mistake. As soon as his cold hands connected with her skin through the thin robe she wore, she shot off his chest as if propelled by a cannon ball.

"I'm sorry," she exclaimed, pulling her robe more tightly about her nude body.

Hank could tell she was nude. Not even a thong could be hidden beneath that robe. The silken fabric with its glossy sheen fitted her smoothly, every delicious curve outlined for his benefit, whether she intended it or not.

"Warm. I need to get warm. I'm so cold…been out there for hours…" It suddenly dawned on him that he was cold, a thought punctuated by the involuntary chattering of his teeth. "Christ, I'm beginnin' to sound like a feckin' woodpecker."

Laura laughed and then, her face showing the compassion he somehow knew her capable of, said, "I'll go run a bath for you. Are you badly hurt anywhere?"

She'd been gazing at the gap in his pants. Through the thawing process inside her house, he was only just coming to the realization that he'd cut his leg. But just how badly it had been cut, he didn't know. Maybe it was just a scrape. "I don't think I'm badly hurt. I'm too bloody cold to tell."

Nodding and giving his body a cursory glance, she folded her arms around her waist as if that movement could protect her from his curious eyes and went up the stairs to where he presumed the bathtub was.

Her absence gave him a moment to take stock of his surroundings. He'd never been inside the cabin before but the windows that went from the floor of the living room to what he'd surmised, and now knew to be the ceiling of her bedroom, provided a spectacular view to the outside world. Often, due to the sun on the windows, it was impossible to see inside. With no one around, she needn't fear any light from within exposing her. The drapes he'd seen across the top floor ensured her privacy when she wanted it.

He could hear water running and so began unzipping his coat and peeling it off. It was ruined but still serviceable for the time being. Both sleeves bore the evidence of crawling through the busted out window of the truck, showing several small rents in the fabric and a large tear that ran from the shoulder down the side seam of the right arm. He vaguely remembered feeling it catch and then hearing it rip but he hadn't reckoned on the resulting damage being so extensive, and at the time, he hadn't cared. He just needed to get out of the truck.

Tossing it over by the boot rack, he then struggled to pull off his laced-up boots, but the laces were tightly tied and wet, difficult to undo with half frozen fingers.

He was still fumbling with them when Laura came back

down the stairs to tell him his bath was ready.

"That'll be lovely, darlin', but my feet are still stuck in my boots."

"We could cut the laces," she offered. "I think I have spare boot laces here somewhere. I keep spares of almost everything."

"Well, I'm not so sure I want to cut these. I'd hate it if ye didn't have more and at any rate, I think I can get these…" His voice trailed off as a waft of her perfume invaded his senses as she bent down to inspect them herself.

"Here, let me give it a try. I have skinnier fingers and longer nails. You never know."

Her long, wavy locks fell over her shoulder, several shades of gold and light red mixed in and creating the most gorgeous mosaic he'd ever seen. And why had he not noticed before? Was he blind? In all the years he'd been coming up here, this delectable dish was in his grasp and he'd been blind to it all!

Not really, he corrected himself, remembering that up until last year, that sleazebag of a husband of hers was here, too. He didn't know the full reason for her divorce but he'd seen Erik Foster in the bars in town, seen how he'd sidle up to whatever lady happened to be by herself, and in nine out of ten cases, walk away with the woman on his arm. It didn't take a rocket scientist to know what was going on. What Hank couldn't understand was why any man would want to leave someone like Laura. If you were looking for a goddess come to life, she was surely it.

Her hands were sure and capable as they struggled with the wet laces, lovely manicured nails and delicately tapered fingers working their magic.

"There," she said, spreading the laces so he could pull his foot out.

He bent over to ease his foot from the boot and couldn't help but notice the creamy line of her breast, exposed as it was as her robe shifted with her movements. There was an immediate response in the region between his legs, and despite the chill that had engulfed him, he began to sweat.

"Here, luv, if ye wouldn't mind…I'd appreciate ye holdin' my boot while I pull."

She did as he asked, leaning over and holding his boot with one hand at the top and the other at his heel while he slid his foot out. Her breasts swung freely beneath the robe, the two globes almost within arm's reach and certainly within line of sight.

"And the other, too, if ye wouldn't mind."

"Of course not," she said, looking up and smiling as she took hold of his other boot in the same fashion.

A moment later, his feet were clear and he was rewarded with a view of her heart-shaped face, the long milky column of her throat, the cleavage of her breasts as she sat like a geisha in front of him, the belt of her robe loose and exposing more of herself than he was certain she was aware.

"How's your leg?" she asked, as if suddenly aware of the silence that had ensued.

His eyes instantly averted, he glanced at his leg, at the tear in his pants running midway between his knee and his hip. "Can't say for sure 'til I've got my jeans off."

Nodding, she said, "Well, upstairs and into the bath with you then. We'll get you warmed first and then see what it's like."

As if it knew it was the subject under discussion, his leg began to throb as did the bump on his head. "Have ye any pain killers?"

"Pain killers?" She thought a moment. "I might have something. How about acetaminophen?"

"Aye, that'll do. Anything to stem the pounding in my head."

"Your head? Oh, I didn't notice."

"Nah, it's in my hairline, not that ye'd see it. But it's there." He rubbed the spot and felt the goose egg sized lump.

"Yeah, it's there alright."

As if he'd invited her to do so, she leaned over and reached out her hand and he felt her fingers lightly work through the damp hair until they came across the lump. "It's pretty big, alright. If you think you can stand, we'll get you that bath and something for your head, too."

Her position was nearly his undoing. Were he a less sturdy man, he would have swooned at the sight of her breasts. An inch more and they'd be in his mouth.

It was almost too much. Hank wasn't sure he could stand at the moment. The effect of her on his libido had that member visibly standing at attention, straining at the zipper on his jeans. Said jeans were also damp and clung coldly to his skin, reminding him that he was rather in need of that hot bath. It was uncomfortable in many ways. "Right. I believe I can stand if ye'll give me a hand up."

She stood at the same time as he made his attempt but he hadn't been aware of the puddle his boots had left, and as he put his foot flat on the floor, it slid out from under him. Since he was holding tightly to her hand, she had no choice but to follow the downward motion of his body, the result of which was Hank back on the floor with Laura landing on top.

It was the loveliest sight, he thought as his mind replayed in slow motion her robe falling away, the silk belt finally losing its tenuous knot, allowing the robe to fly open as she fell.

He couldn't remember the last time he'd had a naked woman on his chest and that meant that it had been far too long.

"Oh," she gasped, trying to pry herself off him and cover herself at the same time.

"Oh, darlin'," he breathed, "don't cover yourself on account o' me. I've never seen anythin' so lovely." His words seemed to stop her and she froze in midflight, her hands straddling the expanse of his chest, her legs across his hips, and the tip of his penis through his jeans only a layer of clothing away from what he now knew was his ultimate goal.

"I, uh, I," she stuttered as his hands encircled her face and brought it down to his. She came willingly as if this had been the plan all along.

Their lips met in a tentative kiss and then his tongue found hers and he was doomed. Doomed to probe and taste and suckle for all he was worth.

Of their own volition, his hands pushed at the shoulders of her robe, felt the softness of her skin. He nearly came in his pants.

Laura didn't know what had come over her but this man was akin to her own personal god. He'd come in from the cold, sensing her need for human warmth and companionship on a night that had started out feeling so isolating and the closest she'd ever come to being afraid on the mountain.

She didn't care how he got here, only that he was here. How could he know that he had been the object of her desire since Erik had shown his true colors? This man, this gorgeous hunk of flesh, was on her floor and fate had thrown her on top of him. Laura wasn't unaware of the bulge in his pants or the position she found herself in, breasts plastered against his chest with only his shirt in between. It hadn't occurred to her when she grabbed her robe that it was the one made of silk, the one whose belt came undone of its own accord. She'd been in a hurry and grabbed the first thing she could once she realized there was someone at the door.

And then his hands were pulling her face toward him and she went, mesmerized by his eyes, by his mouth, open in invitation.

The first touch of his lips to hers was like a magical elixir that pulled her in and made the real world disappear. She hadn't noticed that he'd pushed her robe from her shoulders or that her hands had found the zipper to his jeans, fingers fumbling madly, trying to undo the clasp at the same time.

Laura felt his hands on hers, flipping open the snap with ease, felt his breath give with the release of his flesh and the way he pulled her tightly to him as her fingers touched the silken tip of his penis and the bead of moisture that had leaked out.

"Oh darlin'," he breathed, "if ye keep that up, we'll never get off this floor."

At the moment, Laura didn't care. She'd stay on the floor forever if it meant she could have this man. She shifted her body, felt his penis touch the curls between her legs and then her skin. So close, they were so close…

"I haven't any protection for ye," came the voice, pulling her from her dream.

"It's okay," she heard herself say, "I'm on the pill."

"Oh, well, if you're not worried then," he said and ran his hand along her thigh.

"You aren't carrying anything are you?" Please don't let him say he is, came the thought in her head.

"Carrying? Oh, ye mean am I sick down there?"

She could only nod. Oh, his hands were doing wonderful things to her. How could a butt massage feel so good?

"Sweetheart, I haven't had sex in so long I've begun to think I'm a hermit. So no, I don't believe I've anything for ye to be worried about."

Relief swept through her as she gave in to her desire and slid farther down. The rounded head pushed against her vaginal lips, the wet tip slid against her before zeroing in on the tunnel she offered.

"Ah, my darlin', when I climbed out of that snow cave tonight I had no idea I'd be finishin' it with' a beautiful woman on my flute."

Laura only barely registered what he'd said. Something about a cave. Oh right, wasn't that what some people called a vagina? And did he say "flute"?

It didn't matter. She was having the most glorious time of her life!

Angling her body upright, she impaled herself farther, heard his sigh of ecstasy as it joined with hers.

His hips lifted and dropped slowly but she could tell he was still encumbered by his jeans. Regretfully, she slid off him and turned to push his jeans from his legs.

All Hank saw at that moment was her vaginal crease, ripe and glistening with juices, and he had to have her. At the moment he didn't care about his jeans or anything else, so grabbing her hips, he pulled her toward his mouth, licking his lips at the very idea of tasting her.

She hadn't given up on his jeans and as he took his first taste of her, he felt one leg work free of the damp clothing. It was all he needed. In one great thrust of his tongue, he dove into her cleft to the depths of her tunnel and heard her cry out in surprise. She stayed in that position, ass up and head down while he drank her juices and feasted away.

But Laura had plans of her own. No sooner had he started suckling at her than she took him in her mouth. Hank was hard pressed to concentrate on what he was doing. She had him coming and going, both sensations incredibly erotic, and he knew that if he didn't pull her off, he'd come in her mouth, a move which may or may not be welcomed by her and he certainly didn't want to upset things at this stage of the game.

"Your leg needs tending," came the voice from his nether regions.

"Feck it. I don't care if it falls off. Swing 'round me, luv, and let me have ye proper like."

She made to move but indicated with a nod of her head the direction they should take. "Upstairs. Let's get you cleaned up before we continue."

Hank looked down at his swollen cock. He didn't think he could walk anywhere.

"Ah, lover, let's finish here first. There'll be more lovin' later as well. I just don't think I can walk anywhere at the moment."

Her eyes fastened on his penis, standing as upright and solid as one of the stately pines on the mountain. "I can take care of that for you."

Chapter Three

Laura's lips engulfed the tip of Hank's penis as if she were sucking on a lollipop. In, out, the suction was almost his undoing but when she touched the very tip with her tongue, it was all he could do to stifle the urge to shoot his load right then and there.

She pulled back, torturing him as her tongue flicked across the tip and then settled into the crease, to lick at the pre-come as it seeped out.

By this time, Hank was beside himself. All he could think of was how much he wanted to be inside her, and as much as she seemed to be enjoying what she did, if he didn't act now, there would be no time for second guesses.

His arms were wobbly from digging his way out of the truck, the muscles sore and spent. But that didn't stop him from picking her up and flipping her around so that she was sitting on him once more. The surprised look on her face stayed only for an instant because he took his cock in hand, found her sweet spot, and thrust hard, as far as he could go.

Just as quickly, her face registered delight, her eyes closed and her head tossed back, those long, burnished tresses tickling his legs as he thrust into her.

She breathed a sigh that could only be interpreted as ecstasy, and he joined her as he felt her inner walls tighten around him. It was all he needed as he came, felt his penis hit the tip of her cervix time and time again as her vaginal walls gripped him hard.

Hank thought he'd died and gone to heaven.

Laura slowly raised her head and looked down at him with sex-softened eyes. "Oh my gawd that was good!"

She leaned forward to lie on Hank as he stroked her bare back and caressed her smooth buttocks. A rumble started low in Hank's stomach that he couldn't hide.

"Are you hungry?" she asked, looking up from her spot on his chest.

Suddenly the world began to spin and Hank chuckled at the timeliness of his hunger pains. "Yeah, I think I must be. I was heading up to the cabin around five or six when the avalanche took me out. It's taken me this long to dig out and come here."

Still impaled on his cock, she said in surprise, "So that's what you were doing banging on my door. I wondered why you were out there. I thought maybe you'd gone hiking and got lost but it didn't make sense, and then things happened so fast…oh, you poor man!"

Hank saw her look him over as if seeing him for the first time: his tousled hair, the scrapes and bruises, the snow, now melted, littering her floor in small puddles and droplets here and there. "Yeah," he said, "it was no deadly craic getting out."

"Deadly crack?"

"No fun," came the explanation, ignoring the fact that she hadn't realized he'd said an Irish word and wasn't speaking of drugs.

She raised up slightly, touched the tips of her love-swollen breasts to his chest, causing all sorts of wonderful feelings that he was at a loss to describe, kissed him full on the lips, and then drew back slowly. "You know what you need to do, honey. You go slip into that tub and I'll get some food for you."

Hank felt his cock begin to harden once again. "I can think of other things I'd rather do."

He'd slipped out of her vagina and she turned to stroke him with her hand. "Maybe, but you'll fade to nothing if I don't feed you first and I'm just not willing to let this end quite yet."

With that, she stood, beautifully naked in the glow of the light from upstairs, and with an outstretched hand said, "I'll help you into the tub and you can at least get warm."

Hank was going to argue about needing to get warm but he realized, in some part of his brain as he began to come off the high she'd had him on, that he really was chilled, even if parts of him hadn't recognized it yet. So prying himself off the floor and kicking off the jeans that still hung on one leg, he followed her upstairs, admiring the shape of her arse as he went.

She showed him into the bathroom and helped him out of the rest of his clothes, then said, "It's all ready for you. Have a good soak while I get that food."

The tub was large enough for two as he lifted one shaky leg over the side and into the water. The temperature was perfect, a little on the hot side, just as he liked it. He eased his six-foot frame into the bath, leaned back, and sighed with a release of anxiety he hadn't known he'd been feeling.

He could hear Laura downstairs, putting his clothing in the washtub and pulling out pots and pans as she made him something to eat. He was finally beginning to feel warm through and through and was grateful that his leg wasn't hurt too badly. It was only a superficial cut and would quickly heal.

He laid his head back and slipped down into the water, closing his eyes and mind to the moment at hand. How he'd ended up here was a miracle. When the avalanche first hit, he was sure he was in a death trap, doomed to stay in the truck as it got colder and colder until he eventually suffocated or froze to death.

The entire time he was digging himself out, the one

thought that kept intruding was how was he going to survive getting to his cabin? It was another mile or more along the road at least and even when he got there, he'd have to light the fire. And he remembered thinking as he left earlier that day to go to town for groceries that he needed to chop more firewood. There was plenty there, it just needed to be split because the stack, as it was, would be burned through in a couple of hours.

Once he was out of the truck, it was clear his cabin was both too far and the avalanche too treacherous to try to climb across, especially in the dark. The only option was to go back down the road to Laura's and hope she'd forgive him for disturbing her. Only he hadn't bargained on the fact that it took him so many hours to dig out, or that he was so tired from his exertions that he actually fell asleep at some point, waking up cold and shivering.

At least I woke up, he congratulated himself. Many wouldn't have and would have died then and there. As he slogged through the deep snow, trying to stay in the now vague tracks from his truck and falling over too many times to count, he could only focus on Laura, on her glowing eyes, her kissable lips and luscious body, and think that, of all the things he wanted most in life right then, it was her.

And how was he to do that, he'd wondered, when they hadn't even had a date because he'd been too busy or too nervous to ask her out?

Stumbling up the road through knee-deep snow, trying to stop his teeth from rattling in his head, he'd thought that of all the people who'd ever existed, how did it come to be that they were the only two on the mountain at this particular time? Hank was a big believer that if things were meant to be, they would happen, and this was certainly one of those times when he hoped to hell he was right.

The aroma of something wonderful was tickling his senses and then he realized that, whatever it was, it was coming closer. His stomach growled in anticipation at the tentative knock on the door.

"Can I come in?" she asked.

"I thought ye'd never return," he grinned when she poked her head around the opening. "I'm nice and warm now but a little cuddling would be nice."

She pushed the door open wide and entered the room bearing a small tray with a bowl of soup and buttered bread. Two beer cans stood beside the bowl and she grinned as she set the tray on the bathroom counter. From the cupboard at the end of the tub, she pulled out a tub caddy and laid it across the water in front of Hank, and settling it into place, put the tray of food on top.

The soup smelled heavenly and Hank's stomach rumbled loudly. He lifted one dripping hand from the tub and went to pick up the spoon when Laura stopped him.

"How about indulging me in a fantasy?" she asked.

Hank, never one to turn down an offer, especially not after what he'd witnessed of her so far, merely smiled his acquiescence.

"I'll feed you, you just lie there and soak. Bread first or soup?"

Hank wondered at her fantasy. If that's all she wanted out of life, who was he to ruin her fun? He was going to enjoy introducing her to his kind of fantasies as he relaxed and enjoyed the moment.

By the end of the bowl, Hank was full. The bread, she told him, was bought fresh from the bakery on her way home and the soup had been left over from the day before, and did he mind that it was left over?

"You bought fresh bread and did ye make your own soup?" Hank asked as she removed the tray and put the caddy away.

"I cheated. I used one of those dried soup mixes in the grocery store," she explained as she removed her robe, exposing every inch of her glorious frame. "Scootch over,

I'm not finished with you yet."

Hank made room for her in the big tub, not a hard thing to do with her slender frame. From his view, looking up as she stood before him, his only focus was on her globes of delight, the nipples pert and ruched, and her patch of curly hair, as reddish-gold as that on top of her head and so close to his face he could smell her juices.

Despite the temperature of the water, Hank got hard.

As Laura stood over him, all she could think of was how fate had blessed her this night. Never in her wildest dreams did she ever think she'd get Hank the Hunk in her home, let alone in her bathtub.

As she knelt down in front of him, she couldn't fail to notice he'd gotten hard once again. What a man! Surely it was an invitation, and as she lowered herself down, she felt him slip inside her. She lifted and lowered herself again, feeling the walls of her vagina press against him as she moved.

Hank sighed and closed his eyes.

Laura picked up the soap and built up lather in her palms that she began to massage into Hank's chest, gloriously free of any chest hair and glistening from the sheen of oil in the water. His pecs were well formed, the nipples flat with hard nubs that she delighted in rubbing between her soapy fingers.

Another sigh and a slight movement from his hips were Laura's reward.

She soaped him well all over his chest, under his arms, and down his torso, following a slight trail of hair that began below his naval and grew to the spot where they were joined. A thrill laced through her and Hank moved some more.

Laura sighed.

The next thing she knew, Hank had taken over the soap and was doing his own bit of lathering, rubbing her breasts lightly, tweaking her nipples and splashing them with water to take away the soap. And if that wasn't enough, he put his lips to her breasts and began to suckle, eliciting feelings deep inside.

"This isn't quite enough, is it?" she said matter-of-factly.

"I don't know what ye mean," he remarked between mouthfuls of breast.

"I need you to fill me."

"Mm-hmm."

"On the bed, not here." She felt desperate, as if she would never find completion in the bathtub.

Suddenly, she was lifted up, held in Hank's strong arms as he stood, her legs clasped tightly around his waist.

"Hang on, me darlin', whilst I get us to the bed."

He winked at her as she clung to him and he made the few steps to sit on the edge of the bed, Laura still impaled on his cock.

"How the hell did you manage that?" she asked, full of wonder that after all he'd been through, he could still manage such a feat.

"Must be all that wood choppin' and haulin' I do to keep my house warm," he grinned.

Laura was completely taken in by that grin and captured his mouth with hers. His tongue invaded her; she welcomed it and responded with an invasion of her own.

She felt herself go forward, following Hank as he leaned back, and then, suddenly, he was on his back with her on top. He was still inside her, pumping slowly, building up the momentum once again.

Unable to resist, she left his lips to suckle at his nipples and heard a groan of delight from his delicious mouth. That mouth that had done such wonders for her and now she was repaying him in kind.

Her tongue laved at his hard nubs.

Hank's pelvis sped up.

Laura took one nub into her mouth and suckled hard.

Hank grabbed her buttocks in both hands and held her tightly while he pumped.

A thrill shot through her and Laura rose up, tossing her

head and arching her back.

Hank grabbed one nipple with his mouth, teased it with his teeth and then suckled hard while the pressure in Laura built to an all-time high. Although he'd already made her come that night, Laura was delighted that she could feel herself begin to climax again.

Hank thrust harder, faster. He'd let go of her breast now and was concentrating on pumping, his facial expression that of either extreme pain or extreme pleasure. If it matched hers, then pleasure it was.

Laura felt her inner muscles contract, felt the heat build in her breasts, felt her nipples tighten with desire and then it all exploded in a million stars. She gasped her climax and could hear Hank, echoing her moans of delight while he shot his load deep inside her.

He lay on the bed, completely spent, with Laura still on top of him. A little wriggling on her part and some coaxing to get Hank to shift just a little enabled Laura to pull the quilt up over them both. Hank's arm went around her, pulling her close beside him, legs entwined to spoon together before they both fell deeply asleep.

Chapter Four

The winter sun was high in the sky when Laura opened her eyes. The last thing she remembered was falling asleep in Hank's arms, but as she reached for him beside her, all she felt was a vacant spot, not yet cooled.

Arising, she donned her silk robe and went downstairs to see Hank putting his clothing in the dryer. Suddenly shy, she eyed his naked frame, wondering how she could feel shy when they'd shared so much in the past few hours. "I guess we should have put them in the dryer before going to sleep."

Hank smiled and turned the machine on before striding toward her. Putting his arms about her waist, he kissed her lips gently. "Ah, darlin'," he said, rubbing her back and caressing her buttocks through the silk garment, "I'd love to stay and have more of you but I've got to see how bad things are. I've got to see if I can get my truck out of the snow."

Laura nodded. It was too much to hope that they would just hunker down for the duration. "Is it still snowing?" she asked.

"Yeah, it's still coming down, but lighter now. I think it'll stop soon. Looks to be some clearing to the south."

"How about I make us some breakfast while your stuff dries? I'll get you something to put on in the meantime."

"What? You don't like the sight of my nads hangin' out?"

She laughed gaily and was surprised at how comfortable she was feeling with him once again. "I just thought your nads might be getting a little chilly."

He rubbed her neck with his face and held her close. "I've got all the warmth I need right here."

She couldn't resist and slid her hands down over his butt cheeks, felt the muscles tense beneath her touch and his penis shift its spot where it touched her stomach.

"Keep doin' that, my love, and ye'll get more of what ye had last night."

"Mm," she sighed. "As much as I'd love that, I think I need something to eat first. How about some grub?"

"Alright, if ye insist."

"I do. And there's another robe upstairs. I think you can get it on."

While Laura went about making breakfast, Hank retrieved the robe, presenting himself in the kitchen once again.

"I'm not sure that pink is your color. You look a little like an overgrown teddy bear," she giggled when she eyed him. He'd struck a pose, looking something like a weight lifter engulfed in pink fluff.

He sighed in resignation. "Ah well, I may look a wee bit strange but it's definitely warmer than wearin' naught at all."

As they sat down to breakfast, Laura realized just how little she knew of him. Oh, she knew he was a good person, knew that others in town spoke highly of his character, but what did she really know about Hank Mulligan?

When she questioned him about his arrival in Canada, Hank shook his head.

"That was a long time ago," he began. "I arrived here when I was just twenty, lookin' for something I could never quite find. I'd married a sweet Canadian girl and come here with her, only to find that I wasn't her ideal man after all. We fought all the time, mostly about money. She had some dream that I would make her rich, although how she thought that of a boy from Killarney, I'll never know. I'm a hard worker, but when there wasn't work, there wasn't much I could do about it and she didn't seem to appreciate me doin' odd jobs. Seemed she thought I should be able to be the contractor, not just the pennyboy. After nearly five years of a non-relationship, we called it quits. Her family felt I'd married her just so I could get me citizenship but that wasn't it at all. I thought I truly loved her and would have done anything for her, but time proved me wrong."

"So then what did you do? You were divorced at what, twenty-five?" Hank nodded and chewed on his next mouthful. "Seems you've done a lot in the last few years or so."

"Mm-hmm," he said when he'd swallowed and washed it down with coffee. "I met a fellow who built log homes to sell overseas. He taught me about building, home construction, all kinds of things. He was a generous fellow to boot. Put me up in a small caravan in his back garden and showed me how to live, Canadian style. It was him what helped me build my cabin up yonder and him what got me established hereabouts. Now when people need somethin', I'm here to do it. I can repair anythin', and while I don't make enough to say I'm wealthy, I do make enough to make ends meet and give me a wee bit extra. Life's grand, eh?"

Laura grinned, "It is," she agreed, falling in love with his delicious accent.

"Well, that takes me to now, where at the tender age of thirty-three, I think I've found what I've been looking for. So what about you?"

Laura wanted to ask what he'd been looking for but was caught on his last question. Groaning and pushing her hair back from her face, she said, "I'm afraid my story is just as grim as yours but in a different way. I met and married my true love and we were very happy. He built me this cabin as our hideaway and in fact had just finished it when instead of driving straight here after work on Friday like I usually did, I went home. I'd forgotten something and went there to get it. When I walked in, I could hear sounds from the bedroom and when I got close, I could hear a female voice say to my husband, 'Yes, Erik, oh ,yes!' That was when I stopped and peeked in the door to see my husband's balls slapping against some woman's cunt while he fucked her on my bed! I was so angry I grabbed the first thing I could think of, a vase on the hall table with some flowers in it. I chucked the contents at my husband's ass end, flowers and all. The resulting shriek was worth every drop. I'm just sorry there wasn't a rose in the bunch," she finished, and couldn't help the smile that creased her cheek.

Hank was chuckling as he downed the rest of his breakfast. "Remind me not to piss ye off!" he said finally.

"Well, the bastard deserved it. And then I found out that he'd been doing that every week for as long as we were married." She felt her face grow hot with the anger and humiliation she'd felt and speared her fingers through her hair while gripping her coffee mug tighter. "I thought he was faithful, just working late on Fridays in order to be able to come up here without worrying about being called in on the weekend. But no. I heard that he had several women, one of them someone I thought was my best friend. So I took him to court. He didn't contest it as there were a few paramours he'd pissed off who were only too happy to be a witness for me, and I walked away with a nice settlement and this place. I know he loved this place but so did I, so I figured for everything he put me through, I deserved to take away from him something that was equally as precious. This cabin. And I never regretted it!"

She felt near tears but sniffed them back. She hadn't cried then, so why did she feel like crying now?

Hank was amazed. This gutsy woman who had given him such pleasure had been cheated on by some scum of a husband who didn't deserve her at all. The next thing he thought was that she was free. It was something he'd wondered about for some time because he could remember her coming up here with her husband and then, one day, the husband stopped coming. But she hadn't appeared as if she were in mourning, and then he'd seen the guy in town. So he was quite sure there had been a rift, he just hadn't known if she was truly single or not.

And now he did. She was every man's fantasy, or at least his. And she was free and ripe for the taking. Hank Mulligan, ye lucky bastard, he thought to himself. If ye go carefully, ye can spend the rest of yer days with this woman. So brave and so sweet. And smart, too!

He covered her hand that held the mug with his, wanting more than ever to kiss her tears away. His penis was having second thoughts about just hanging around, but before he could act on anything, she withdrew her hand from his as if embarrassed by her tears and turned away.

Rising from the table, she began to clear up the dishes. It was abrupt but, clearly, the conversation was over. So, while she puttered in the kitchen, Hank went to retrieve his clothing. The awkward moment passed.

One look outside told him it would be a while before any road clearing equipment got to them and he really did need to check his truck, and even more, get to his cabin so he could feed his cat.

"Laura, me dear, I may be needin' to borrow some things from ye," he called from the laundry room off the kitchen.

Laura appeared in the doorway just as he was hauling on his jeans. His shorts cupped his manhood, molding it and his nads into a neat little package and he saw her lick her lips as if in anticipation of a feast. Her eyes hadn't left his crotch the entire time it took to draw his jeans up over his ass and pull up the fly.

Shaking her head and clearing her throat, Laura said, "Sure. What is it you need?"

Her green-gold eyes were an invitation he chose to ignore although it took most of his strength. "Snowshoes."

"Snowshoes?"

"Yeah, I was hoping ye might have a pair I could borrow. I have to get to my cabin to check on my cat. The poor thing's likely hungry by now."

"Oh," she gasped, "you have a cat! I had no idea or I wouldn't have waylaid you. I mean…"

"It's alright," he said, having slipped on his t-shirt and finished tucking it in. "If I'd had the presence to remember the poor wee beast, I'd have said something. As it was, all I wanted was to be warm. And there you were, hot as ever and willing to share your heat. How perfect was that? I think, once I tell him, my big tomcat will agree it's what I needed to do."

He pulled his work shirt from the dryer and pulled it on over his t-shirt, then sidled up to Laura and pulled her close. "And if ye have a second pair of those snowshoes, ye could come with me to my cabin and hang out there for the week. I don't think we'll get out of here before then."

They both turned to the front window where daylight flooded the room. The snow was heavier again and Laura's SUV could not be seen, nor could the driveway. He felt her sag in his arms and gave her a questioning glance. "What is it?"

She stepped out of his arms and rubbed her face with both hands, then ran one of them through her still tousled hair. God but she was gorgeous!

"Oh, nothing. Just that yes, I do have snowshoes. My ex and I loved to snowshoe up the mountain. It's a fabulous view from higher up. So, I do have two sets and one might even fit you."

"Then what's the bother?"

Without batting an eye she said, "They're in the shed," and pointed toward the back of the cabin where snow was piling up as deep in the backyard as in the front. The shed, or what could be seen of it, was quite a distance to the rear of the cabin, its red metal roof a prominent point against the gray and white backdrop of mountain, forest, and snow.

Hank sighed in resignation. "Well, it's sure we'll not get anywhere without them, so if I have to dig my way to the shed, then so be it. I'll just be needing a shovel then."

He looked at her expectantly.

"No shovel?"

"I'm thinking," she said. And then, "Oh, I remember where I put it." She went to the front door and opened it to a wall of snow, three feet high, filling in most of the doorway. Releasing a small shriek, she jumped back as snow tumbled into the room, landing on her bare feet.

"Out there?" asked Hank, getting used to snow blocking his way.

"Uh-huh," she answered, nodding at the same time. "I use it to clear snow from the porch and down the steps to the driveway and sometimes along the driveway when I need to. I've got a big snowblower for when it gets worse but I can't haul that all the way up the stairs and onto the porch."

Hank slipped his boots on, aware they were still wet inside from all the snow of last night. "You wouldn't have some plastic bags, would ye?" he asked hopefully.

"Yes, those I do have, and close by too," she grinned as she pulled a couple out from behind the laundry room door. "Here you go."

Taking the bags from her, he slipped a foot into each one and then back into the damp boots. "Ah, grand. That'll work just fine for now," he said as he hefted his jacket on. Pulling on his gloves, he scooped the snow from the floor and flung it outside before doing a karate-style kick to knock the short wall of snow away from the door. "It's not as bad as it looks up here," he said, making his way along the wide porch to where he could see the handle of the shovel sticking up. "I think the wind blew this up here. Doesn't seem to be doing that anymore."

Retrieving the shovel, he made his way to the front door but Laura wasn't there. "Laura?" he called, and from upstairs heard her reply.

"I'll be right there."

He closed the door after banging the snow off his boots outside, and taking the lone shovel, tip-toed to the back door carefully so as not to drop more snow, and waited for Laura to appear. When she did a moment later, he couldn't help the smile that spread across his face.

"Well," he grinned, "you've got to be the prettiest little lumberjack I've ever set eyes on."

She was dressed in a plaid work shirt, not unlike his, tucked into jeans that fit her delicious curves. He watched as she made her way to the closet at the rear and pulled out a set of lined coveralls. "Here, see if you can get into these," she said, handing him the tan-colored garment while she pulled out another for herself.

As Laura did up her winter coveralls, she turned just in time to see Hank still struggling to get the coveralls he had donned done up. A well of laughter erupted when she realized just how muscular he was compared to her ex. "Oh wow, there is no way those are going to fit past your waist!" she exclaimed.

"Ah, maybe not, but my jacket will cover the rest and my legs will be drier than last night. They'll do for now." He managed to slip the shoulder straps into place after extending them as far as he could, leaving the zipper gaping open from his hips up. He pulled his jacket off the hook where it had been hung to dry, and tattered though it was, it would have to do. Shrugging it on, he could read her mind. "I have a better one at the cabin. One with no tears or holes. This'll be fine until then."

"Okay. If you're not concerned, then neither am I." She led the way out the back door and pointed to the shed about fifty feet from the back door. "I keep seasonal stuff in there mostly, but the snowshoes haven't been used for a couple of years. I'd forgotten we had them so I sure hope they're still okay."

"Right. It's off we are, then," said Hank and thrust the leading edge of the shovel into the snow.

All Laura could hope for while watching Hank and the shovel make slow but steady progress toward the shed was that the snowshoes would be serviceable. She didn't want to be the one responsible for Hank losing his cat.

"Remind me come summer to move your wee shed closer to your house," Hank said in an out-of-breath voice.

Laura shook her head, even though Hank wasn't watching. "I don't think you can; it's pretty sturdy." And then the thought hit her that he was projecting into the future. A future that seemed to include her. How delicious!

It had taken them what seemed like forever but couldn't have been more than five or ten minutes to dig their way to the shed where Hank began the chore of clearing the doorway. Laura flopped down in the snow and leaned back, letting the fluffy flakes coat her cheeks and lashes to slowly melt away. It wasn't cold out, just snowy, and Laura relished giving in to her childhood memories for a few moments.

The next thing she knew, a huge weight pushed her farther into the snow and she opened her eyes in surprise to see Hank on top of her, his handsome face mere inches from hers, his lips descending to kiss, and kiss they did.

Laura's mouth opened to his, the snow bed gave a little and then firmed up. He was so warm, even through all that clothing, and she clung to his bulk, suddenly regretting the layers between them. Her legs splayed. She wanted him there, inside her, and her hips started to gyrate against his pelvis.

"Ah, Laura, me luv, this will never do." He raised himself off her and pulled her up with him to stand before the cleared door of the shed. "Time to see what's in your wee shed," he said, brushing the snow from her shoulders and back.

There was a look in his eye, a twinkle of…what? Regret? Well, Laura thought, nodding at his suggestion of opening the shed, she regretted it too. Regretted they weren't back inside so she could have him again. It was hard to ignore the moisture that had already built between her legs.

The frozen hinges gave and there was all the stuff Laura remembered, like a time capsule had been opened on her past. She remembered why she didn't go in there unless she absolutely had to. All the summer things, the pads for the chairs and lawn swing, the lawn mower, the gardening things, all things she and Erik had bought together for their little hideaway in the mountains were there before her, reminding her. Things they'd enjoyed doing together, like building the rock garden and putting in the fish pond.

She brushed the memories aside, acknowledged for the first time how much they hurt and reminded herself that Hank the Hunk was in the shed with her; that they'd been intimate in a way that she and Erik had never achieved. Erik had been an okay lover and she'd been fine with that. Or thought she was. But Hank? O. M. G! She'd never had anyone in her past that could rival Hank. He was as good as his reputation claimed.

And that stopped Laura cold. He had a reputation. That meant that she was possibly just another conquest in a long line. How many women back in town drooled over Hank the Hunk? How many had tasted his wares?

Hank was sifting through the summer things she'd never bothered taking out so all the winter things were stored behind it. Poor foresight on her part, but then, who knew she was going to need snowshoes when they hadn't been used since before she and Erik divorced?

"Aha!"

Hank's triumphant roar and manly grunt as he lifted the first pair of snowshoes to daylight brought Laura out of her slump. She took them from him as he passed them to her and tossed them into the cleared area outside the shed. The second pair soon followed. "Okay, I think that's all we need in here," said Hank, eyeing the rafters, walls, and shelves of her "wee" shed. Said shed was a ten- by twenty-foot outbuilding and had been sometimes used as a shop on rainy summer days when wood needed to be cut while they were building the house. The side door was like a folding garage door and could be opened to expose the entire side of the shed, unlike the man door they had entered at the front. Wee, indeed!

Hank was inspecting the snowshoes, checking the rawhide laces and noting that everything seemed in good condition. He looked at Laura, feeling like a true mountain man, and winked. "What think ye, me darlin'? Are ye ready for a trek?"

She laughed and refrained from saying, "Aye," although it was on the tip of her tongue. Instead she nodded. "Let's head out," and taking the smaller of the pair, placed her feet in them and did up the laces.

Chapter Five

Laura led the way to the front of the house, through the woods at the near side where, in months devoid of snow, a set of stone steps hugged the log walls. For now, covered in snow, the steps were like a rolling trail that helped them avoid the deep cavern on the opposite side of the house where the carport roof let the snow slide off. The snowshoes, while ungainly at times, kept them above the deep drifts and in short order had them on the roadway in front of the impressive log structure.

"Wow," said Laura, looking back at her house, at the depth of the snow all around. They could barely see the upper structure for all the snow in front of it. And it was still coming down.

"Shit!" she swore, and then quickly apologized for her profanity.

Hank just grinned. "What's up?"

Shaking her head, Laura ground out, "My cell phone. I left it inside."

"Not to worry," said Hank in a matter-of-fact way, "I've a phone ye can use when we reach my cabin. And sure no one's going to be calling us yet. Not until tomorrow when ye don't show for work."

She couldn't help but see his point. Who would call? Her parents were across the country in their own little world, comfortable and carefree and completely ignorant of the goings-on in their daughter's life. And that was how Laura liked it. Any friends she had knew she came to the cabin, and as Hank said, wouldn't be worried until she didn't show up at work. Was her life really that empty that no one would know if she were safe or not? It was a sobering thought.

"Come on, then, the day's wasting away," said Hank, leading the way.

Shrugging off the inevitable, she adjusted her jacket and followed his steps down the road. "We should have brought water."

"Yeah," he answered. "Should have made a list before we left, too. It was rather premature, wasn't it?"

"Our leaving?" At his nod, she answered, "Yup. It was."

"Ah, but we're havin' our own wee adventure and it won't take us any time at all to reach my cabin."

All Laura could do was nod. The snow was still coming down, and if not for the fact that the road had been plowed just the day before the snow began falling, she knew they could easily lose their way. As it was, the roadbed was like a trough with high, snowy sides too tall to peer over. Similar to a tunnel without a roof.

A lump appeared in the road ahead and Hank stopped suddenly. "Ah, and there she is," he sighed.

"What? I don't see anything."

"My truck," he said, feeling almost broken at the sight of it. Or rather, the inability to see it at all. It was just a mound of snow under another mound of snow. Not even his escape route could be detected without closer inspection and Hank had no desire to be caught in a trap.

With that consideration in mind, he pointed to the upper side of the truck where it seemed safer to navigate their way around it.

"The snow will be hard packed here," he said to Laura, "I'm not so sure about down there and I certainly don't want to start anything off again."

They eyed the path the avalanche had taken and made a wide berth around the main channel of snow and into the bush where the trees were thick and provided some leverage.

"It's not too bad through here," Hank said, huffing his way along, feeling the sweat build up beneath his jacket. "Ach, I could use that water we didn't bring," he joked.

The guilty look on Laura's face showed all too clearly how bad she felt.

"Ah, me darlin', don't fash yerself. 'Tisn't yer fault, ye know. I wasn't so brilliant either if the truth be told." He stretched his arm out and ruffled the hood of her jacket.

They continued on and finally, well into the afternoon, saw Hank's cabin come into view. "I must admit," he confessed with a voice almost out of breath, "'tis a sight for sore eyes."

"And parched throats," said the tired voice beside him.

They shared a heated glance before they started toward the cabin, only to be halted in their steps by the sight of a bear snuffling along the ground between the cabin and where they stood transfixed.

"Now what?" whispered Laura.

Hank couldn't answer. "You're the true Canadian here, I'm just an import," he whispered back. "What are you supposed to do when you meet a bear?"

Laura looked sideways at Hank the Hunk and suddenly wondered how he'd coped all these years in this isolated cabin. "Haven't you ever seen a bear before?" she asked.

He shook his head. "No. Not like this, anyway. Mostly from the truck with them far away. Just how I prefer to view wildlife."

"Are you a chicken?"

"What? Chicken? No, I, uh, I just don't fancy myself dinner for yon bear." Really, did she think he'd run from such a creature? He might sit down and wait for it to move off but he wasn't such a fool as to go charging at it to try and hurry it up.

"Why don't you go scare it off?" asked the hushed voice at his side.

"Because I value my hide," he answered.

"It's a black bear. The avalanche likely woke it up early. I don't think it'll hurt you."

His eyes met hers in a questioning glance, one eyebrow raised and the other eye slightly closed. "If you're such an expert on bears, why don't you go scare it off?"

"I guess if I have to I will because I don't feel like hunkering down here until it decides to leave. What's it after, anyway?"

Keeping one eye on the bear, he said quietly, "I'd suspect it's hungry."

"Maybe," she agreed. "But you don't have any garbage outside, do you?"

"No, nothing a bear would be interested in."

"Such as?"

"Such as an old crank case, some spare parts from an old truck, a couple of tires. That sort of stuff."

"Sounds like you have a junkyard in your yard."

"Not a junkyard, spare parts. There's a difference."

"Sure. Well, I'm getting cold just sitting here, so if you aren't going to scare that thing off, I will."

Before Hank could stop her, she got up and plodded toward the bear, waving her arms and yelling at the top of her lungs, "Hey, bear! Hey! I'm talking to you! Go away, bear!"

The bear stopped what it was doing and looked her way. It huffed.

Laura stopped her plodding.

Hank froze. Oh, kee-rist, he thought, she's done it now. And before he could think twice about it, jumped up, and as fast as he could on snowshoes, ran past Laura, yelling at the top of his lungs, "Aaaaaaaaaa!"

The bear paused but Hank didn't stop. He picked up the first piece of loose something he could find and flung it at the bear, missing it by a mile. "Aaaaaaaaaaaa!" he yelled again and was relieved to hear a second voice join in the chorus.

The two of them joined together and rushed toward the bear, yelling and throwing things, mostly dead timber sticking out of the snow. The bear, wisely realizing it was outnumbered by crazy beings, turned tail and ran off, never stopping to look back.

They halted several feet short of the steps to the front door, breathing heavily and propping themselves up on each other. The adrenalin that had them rush headlong into a potentially disastrous situation was wearing off.

"That was likely the singularly most stupidest thing I have ever done in my life," breathed Hank, gasping his words out between great gulps of air.

"Probably," agreed Laura, equally breathless.

Hank looked around the cabin and noted the snow was less deep here than at Laura's. Her cabin was completely exposed from all sides, but here a copse of dense trees provided coverage, and as they drew closer, it was evident the snow was easier to navigate.

They removed the snowshoes, a move Hank immediately regretted as he put his booted foot down, not expecting it to plunge hip deep. "Ah, feckit," he muttered under his breath. "Jaysus, Mary and Joseph."

He glanced across at Laura, who was having a hard time containing her laughter. "What?" he asked. "Have ye never seen an uncoordinated eejit get out of snowshoes before?"

"Do you need some help?"

She was still laughing and he couldn't help but join in. "Oh, right, if you'll just take my hand and pull, I'm sure I can get myself out of this."

She leaned over, holding out her hand to grasp his, bracing herself as best she could by hanging on to the railing of the front steps. Hank grabbed her hand and hauled.

Laura's hand let go of the railing, sending her sprawling on top of Hank, in a reverse of their earlier position back at Laura's.

"Mm," murmured Hank, "I rather like this. Except my leg's still stuck."

Laura laughed, a delicate trill that lightly echoed on the clear afternoon air. "You're crazy, Hank Mulligan, do you know that?"

"Mm-hm, so I've been told before," he agreed and gave Laura one of his cockiest grins. "But if ye like, we can continue this inside once I've fed Figaro."

"Figaro?"

"Yeah, my big tomcat. The name seemed to suit him at the time."

"Oh, I thought maybe you just liked opera." She nudged her knee into his crotch.

"Do that again and we'll not be away from here for a while."

She repeated it.

Hank felt his body react, like electricity running from his toes to stand the hair up on top of his head. Christ, but this woman did things to him!

He squirmed and her knee met the bulge in his pants again and this time he answered back, lifting his hips as best he could with one leg stuck in the snow and the other splayed out in front of him.

A twinkle appeared in her eye and a small dimple in her cheek made itself known as she grinned up at him. "This is the most amazing fantasy ever," she exclaimed as he felt her hands draw the already partially opened zipper of the coveralls down as far as she could. Removing her mitten, her hands fumble with his pants and then the sensation of cold air hit him, only to be covered quickly by a moist warmth.

Holy mother of God, was she doing that now? Yes, she was! He lay back in the snow, captive to her ministrations as her mouth took him in, as her tongue laved the length of him and licked the tip sending delicious sensations directly to his brain.

He arched toward her, felt her take him wholly in, right to his balls. Good God, Jaysus save me, he thought. And before he could control it, felt the pressure build. "Ah, darlin', you might want to stop right now before I let loose," he warned, trying to sit up but finding no purchase to support his hands.

The head in his crotch moved. "Not a chance. I'm going to milk you dry."

He rolled his eyes closed and gulped great gasps of cold air. Her mouth, her tongue, her lips literally sucking on him as if he were a giant lolly, and then a cry rent the air and he felt as if he lost consciousness, panting, gasping, and then coming back to earth, opening his eyes to see her grinning up at him. Only after that did he realize he was the one who had screamed.

"Bingo," she said, grinning from ear to ear as she tucked him back in and covered him up.

Chapter Six

Hank felt weak, lying in the snow watching Laura pull herself off him and straighten up before holding out a hand to assist him to a sitting position. "You're feckin' magic, ye are," he exclaimed, taking her hand, and this time, feeling the support she provided, enabling him to pull himself out of the snow. A look passed between them that told Hank she was enjoying this interlude as much as he was. Her little plan of taking him whenever and wherever was exposed, and if he wasn't careful, he was going to be exposed more than he wanted to be. She'd tucked him in but the zip was still open and he'd be falling out again soon if he didn't do something about it right quick.

After he adjusted himself and did his pants up as much as he could, they cleared a path through the snow and up the few stairs to make their way to the front door. It had no lock and so gave easily as soon as he lifted the latch.

At her questioning look, he only smiled. The house was as Irish as he was.

Laura couldn't help but stare in wonder at the black iron latch that opened the door, like some great piece from a medieval castle straight from the heart of Ireland. And once she stepped inside, the novelty of the place continued on.

The long wall to the left of the entry was solid stone, at least, that's what it looked like to her, like something out of a Celtic manor house. It was home to a stone fireplace and hearth that stretched out into the room, engulfing the leather sofa opposite, which was covered in a variety of furs.

And if she wasn't mistaken, that looked like an iron fob to one side of the hearth. As she gazed around the room in the dim light from the row of windows, complete with leaded glass that lined the front wall, she could see the trappings of an Irish hideaway. Part castle, part cottage, it was anything but mundane.

Before she had time to take anything else in, a huge orange cat sidled up to her leg, meowing and purring at the same time. Gasping in surprise, she realized it was only Figaro and bent to pet him. The fur on his back where the different oranges blended in swirls was coarse to her touch but under his chin, where a patch of white coated his throat, his fur was as soft as a rabbit's. And Hank hadn't been kidding, the cat was huge, his back almost to Laura's knee.

"Ah, Figaro, me lad, ye'll be wanting yer grub, ye wee moggie."

"Moggie? I assume that means 'cat' in some kind of language," laughed Laura, "and as for 'wee,' well, I think that cat is anything but 'wee'." She saw the cheeky grin that Hank gave her and the wink that accompanied it as he dropped everything to lie where it was to get food for Figaro.

She removed her coat and snowpants, hung them on the wooden pegs by the door, and then lifted Hank's outer trappings to do the same. She liked how he had dropped everything to see to the cat before he'd thought of anything else. Even her, said a voice in her head, which she chose to ignore right then. Look at the circumstances, she chided herself, the cat was hungry. It's his responsibility to feed it. It's only right, she finished up, shutting off the voice completely.

And then it didn't matter because he came back to where she was standing, pulled her into his arms, and began to kiss her senseless. And then…

"Hank?"

"Mm," he muttered, his voice coming from somewhere behind her ear. He was doing scathingly lovely things to her but…

"I have to go pee," she blurted out, and he immediately stopped and looked at her as if his mind was having trouble switching gears.

"Oh, of course! I'll show ye where it is, then."

She followed him past the open-concept room that housed the living room, dining room, and kitchen, into a hallway with the bathroom entrance just before the entrance to another room she took to be the bedroom. He flicked on the light for her and patted her rear as he left her to herself.

The bathroom didn't look modern. It was like the rest of the house from what she could tell, a little bit of old Ireland tucked away in the woods in Canada. The fixtures were modern but everything else about the room screamed Irish Cottage.

And she loved it. From the rough-hewn timbers that framed the large mirror over the vanity that was surely hand-crafted, to the lights in antique sconces that were electric but looked old-fashioned, as if they were gas. She saw something on a shelf, an actual gas lantern, and wondered if it was for those times when the generator ran out of fuel, or maybe a romantic touch was needed. She tucked that thought away for future possibilities.

The finishing touch in the bathroom seemed to be the tap that resembled an old pump, done in a very dark bronze, and she laughed to herself when she touched the pump handle and the water automatically came on. Oh, wouldn't Figaro just love that, she thought.

As she left the bathroom, a warm glow could be seen coming from the front of the house, as was the unmistakable sound of crackling logs. And there, hunkered down in front of the massive fireplace, was Hank, feeding another split log into the flames. Warmth emanated from the fire, engulfing the room in a cozy glow as night descended outside.

It was breathtaking. Laura stood transfixed at the image before her: Hank tending the fire, Figaro, now sated, rubbing his head against Hank's legs and purring louder than the fire was crackling. She closed her eyes, imagined herself in this very tender scene. Hank and her together, and Figaro curled up near the fire.

"I see ye found you're way back." Laura opened her eyes and saw that Hank was standing next to the fire. "Are ye maybe a bit hungry? It's been a while since breakfast." His eyes reflected the glow from the fire, but as he took a step, Figaro yowled and the mood was broken.

"Shite! Fecking cat!" he exclaimed, tripping and catching himself before he hit the floor.

Hands splayed out before her as if that would help Hank at all, Laura gasped before breaking out in gales of laughter.

"Ye thought that funny, did ye now?" he asked, sending her a look from a narrowed eye beneath a quirked eyebrow.

"I'm sorry," she giggled, "but if you had seen yourself, you would have thought it funny too. He didn't hurt you, did he?"

"Figaro?" At her nod, he said, "Nah, I just enjoy the feeling of teeth and claws sinking into me ankle."

"Oh, I'm so sorry, I didn't mean to laugh. It's just that, well, it was funny." She went over to him where he had one hand leaning on the back of the overstuffed sofa and the other rubbing his ankle. "Do you want me to take a look? I have first aid," she offered.

"First aid," he laughed. "Yon cat might need first aid by the time I'm finished with him, thankless beast that he is."

"Well, if you had your tail stepped on, I'm sure you'd lash out, too. I do believe the poor thing had his pride injured, not to mention his tail." She cast a quick look at the cat that had since found a perch on the front windowsill and was busy washing his paws.

"Humph," said Hank, obviously not impressed. "I'm crushed that ye'd give more sympathy to my attacker than to me, the injured party." He gave the cat one last look before heading into the kitchen, and not bothering to turn on the overhead light, opened the fridge and hauled out a large pot to put directly onto the stove. A moment later the burner beneath it burst into flame and the aroma of a hearty stew wafted past Laura's nose.

"Oh my, that smells heavenly," she sighed, watching as Hank pulled out what appeared to be homemade bread and began slicing off pieces to put on a plate. "Did you…I mean, is it…"

"Homemade?"

She could see the hint of a smile in his cheek. What couldn't this man do?

And then he dashed her hopes. "No, not homemade. But I did get it at the bakery, so it's kind of like it's homemade. You know, like yours," he said, referring to the bread she'd bought at the bakery, too.

She went to stand beside him, took in the aroma of stew, the almost-fresh bread, and him. He had a distinct scent that filled her nostrils and intoxicated her. She wanted to get closer, taste him again…

"Here," he said, jolting her out of her scent appreciation by thrusting the plate in front of her. "You put that on the table and I'll bring the stew."

The table, as she had noted on her way to the bathroom earlier, was a heavy round edifice, the top of which looked faintly scarred and was a good three inches thick if she wasn't mistaken. Supported by a large, central pedestal and four feet across the top, Laura was sure it would kill someone if it ever fell on them.

Hank brought utensils with him and they sat in great wooden chairs with carved backs, the pattern of which Laura was sure she'd seen somewhere. As she sat down, she remarked on them. "They're so unique," she said.

"Yeah, well, it was me what did them. It's an Irish knot, Celtic if ye will. A never-ending knot that ties families and people together. Very spiritual."

"Does this pattern have a specific meaning?" she asked, running a finger along the rounded edges, swearing she could feel an energy emanating from the wood. His energy.

"I tried to do a Dara knot, but it didn't quite turn out so I made my own. Each chair is a wee bit different. I'm no craftsman, eh?"

The chairs were a marvel; all four had slightly different patterns like variations on a theme. Almost identical, but not quite. "Well, craftsman or not, they are amazing." Just like you, her mind finished for her.

The stew was hearty, filled with small chunks of beef amid cabbage, potatoes, and other vegetables. It was exactly what Laura seemed to need on a day such as this. They were dining by candlelight and the glow from the fire. It was as romantic as anything she could ever imagine.

"Will ye need anything back at your house before morning?" asked Hank, dipping a large slice of buttered bread into the broth before popping it into his mouth. A small drop of broth lay just below his lip and it was all Laura could do to refrain from licking it off for him.

"No," she managed and mentally thought of what she really did need. Underwear, her toothbrush, face cream… and then, "Tomorrow's Monday, isn't it." The thought was like a dash of cold water on her face.

Hank nodded in confirmation, finishing his mouthful. "Yeah. If ye need to get down the mountain to work, I can take ye."

She wished he hadn't said that. Up till now, she had every excuse in the book not to show up at work, but now? Well, it was a tough choice she didn't want to have to make.

"How on earth could you get me down the mountain? We can't snowshoe our way down, it's too far."

"Aye, but I have a snowmobile that'll do it. I can get ye far enough that you could get picked up and taken home if that's what ye want."

If that's what she wanted. It was very much not what she wanted. Would it be too forward of her to ask if she could stay? Just a little longer?

"I, um," she hesitated, not certain how to go on, and a quick look at Hank told her he knew she was wrestling with her decision. His eyes crinkled as a grin spread across his very Irish features. That black-on-black hair, the navy-blue eyes, and a devil-may-care grin across his broad face held her spellbound. "You know, I think I'll just call in to work and tell them I won't be in until the road gets cleared. Is that okay?" She didn't know why she was asking if it was okay. She could go home to her own cabin just a couple of miles down the road. The road that took them half the day to snowshoe along.

But there was the snowmobile. She and Erik had had one, as did most people who played in the mountains during winter. It was the one thing she didn't care that he had taken. But Hank had one, so she wasn't stuck here if she'd rather be home. Or if Hank wanted her gone.

"So you can spend the night and no bother about having to be somewhere in the morning?" he asked, finishing his stew and the last slice of bread.

"Oh," she suddenly remembered. "I don't have my cell phone with me. I'd have to call in."

"And my own cell phone is in a terrible state of disrepair, I'm afraid."

He looked a little sad. No, annoyed, that was it. "Why? What happened to it?"

"Ah, well, it was dark when I was crawling out of my truck and my foot found it before I did. The whole thing is smashed to smithereens; I don't think it's in any kind of operatin' condition. Besides which, it's still in the truck. I couldn't have grabbed it, even if I'd wanted to. But there is the landline if you're desperate to call in." He nodded toward the back of the house where she assumed his bedroom was. She hadn't been bold enough to check out the room when she left the bathroom earlier, although she'd wanted to.

She nodded. The phone was a good idea. Then she thought of the snowmobile he said he owned and asked about it. "I assume it has a light on it but I've never liked snowmobiling in the dark; and with the avalanche, I don't think it's safe to travel in these conditions."

His eyes darkened, softened. "No, I wouldn't recommend it." He rose from his chair and held his hand out for hers. "Let's go sit by the fire."

Chapter Seven

Hank pulled her close against him as they stood before the fire. A quick glance told him the logs would continue to burn for a while yet before he had to put another one on. Maybe later he'd let the furnace kick in and save him the trouble of having to interrupt whatever they might be doing in order to stoke the fire overnight. Overnight. He sent a silent prayer of thanks heavenward for this magical time out of time.

And then he turned his attentions to her, to this wonderful woman who had rescued him, given him sustenance, and breathed new life into him. For truth it was that he'd not felt alive for over a year before that night. Then suddenly there was an avalanche, a get-out-or-die situation because he had no doubt that if he had done nothing, he would have frozen to death or suffocated, neither of which seemed like a good option to him.

The mile-long crawl to her place, the times he'd fallen and was too tired to get up, only to remember that he was still alive and wasn't ready to go yet. The knowledge that he'd more living left to do prodded him awake, kept him moving until he collapsed at her front door and into her welcoming arms.

The fact they'd made love like rabbits had nothing and everything to do with now. He couldn't get enough of her; had wondered how he'd lived until now. How had he made it through each day without her by his side? She was magical and beautiful and he wanted nothing more than to have her again.

She seemed more than willing, albeit tied to her responsibilities in town. He liked that about her too, that she wasn't willing to abandon everything at the drop of a hat. She thought about it, weighed the options, and in the end, realized that she needed to stay. At least for now.

Her fingers crept beneath his t-shirt, smoothed the skin across his back before moving to his chest to caress his pecs, find his flat nipples and bring them to tiny peaks beneath her incredible ministrations.

He sucked a breath in through his nostrils, felt her lift his t-shirt from his body, he a willing helpmate in the act until he stood shirtless before her. Her tongue licked at one nipple, then moved to its mate and laved it well before suckling like the wanton she was. She was insatiable, his mystical woman, and no Irish lore could have invented one more perfect for him than her.

He reached to pull her shirt off her but she traveled a path with her tongue down the center of his stomach, past the gap of his jeans where she'd already opened his fly. His manhood sprang out, happy to be released once again and before he knew it, she had him in her mouth and was gazing up at him with a look that spoke volumes. Eyes glazed over in rapturous delight, she had plans to suck him dry once again, he was sure. He felt her moist lips around him, felt her tongue on the slit at the tip, and was nearly undone. His nads tightened in response.

Backing away from her took every ounce of his being. He wanted to be there, to let her take every drop he had to offer, but he wanted to have her completely. Quickly divesting himself of his jeans and tossing them out of the way, he then grabbed the sheepskin from the sofa, and laying it on the floor before the fire, gently urged her down onto it, pulling her shirt off over her head and undoing the clasp of her bra before cupping her breasts in his eager hands.

Bending over, he took her mouth with his, slid his tongue inside to tango with hers, knew she wanted this as much as he did, and slowly withdrew to kiss her chin, her throat, the valley between her breasts, those lovely mounds that glowed golden from the fire. His lips kissed her ruched nipples, his tongue tickled them until she moaned her pleasure. He teased each tight bud with his teeth and then suckled them like a newborn babe. For at that moment, he felt newly born, a man brought back to life once again.

He felt her squirm beneath him and helped her remove her jeans and the bit of silk she called underwear. Her scent wafted to his nostrils, and if it was possible, he felt himself grow harder.

Sliding down her wonderfully fit body, he settled between her legs to taste the nectar that was driving him wild. His tongue dipped between the folds of her sex and she gasped appreciatively. Gently, taking her little nub of pleasure between his teeth, he held on to it, teased it with his tongue, and then thrust his tongue deep inside her when he felt her begin to writhe beneath him.

"Hank, please, oh please," she breathed, holding his head between her hands, pinning him right where she wanted him, where he wanted to be. "Don't stop, don't…" and then, "Oh, yes! Yes!"

He held her steady as she bucked and gyrated beneath him and held her close as she came back to earth, eyes dreamy with sated desire.

"And now for us both," he whispered into her ear as he positioned himself inside her legs, his cock at the ready and both of them naked on a sheepskin before the fire, just like the Irish tales of old. She was wet, so slick when he slid into her and felt her intake of breath, felt her arch beneath him and her legs go round his waist, anchoring him there. She was on fire, she was love incarnate. She was his, and as he began to slide slowly in and out, she looked up and grinned, mischievously carefree.

"You are amazing, Hank Mulligan. Completely amazing."

Her eyes closed in a lover's daze, slowly, such an expression of complete enjoyment on her face that Hank was nearly overcome with emotion.

"How did I get to be so lucky?" he whispered, more to himself. But she overheard and smiled.

"I could say the same thing," she breathed, so quietly he almost didn't hear her.

Her body began to move with his and he felt her inner muscles grip. Increasing his pace, he was holding back although he could feel the tension building at the base of his spine. His nads were like steel globes, hard rocks that urged him on, his flute, deep inside her, the feeling of friction while going in and out, in and out.

Her breath quickened, light gasps that came through lips swollen with kisses. She arched into him, grabbed his ass with a grip that belied her feminine state, and pulled him to her in cadence to his thrusts, gripping her legs more tightly about his waist, holding him there.

Thrust he did, felt the muscles tighten across his arse where she held him in a vice-like grip and at the base of his spine as he thrust into her velvety warmth. Felt the tension in his shoulders, his biceps, up the back of his neck where droplets of sweat leaked from his hairline, adding to the moisture he felt building up across his forehead. The heat from the fire only added to the heat they were creating, an intimate inferno that only they shared.

In, thrusting in before pulling out again but not quite completely from her silken depths before thrusting in and in again. The tempo increased, her breath matching his thrusts as did his. Faster, harder, until she cried out his name, his life force pouring into her as he lay spent atop her, still joined. Still one.

His breathing slowed as he slipped to her side. He could have slept then. Almost did. But the fire needed another log and he didn't want her getting cold lying naked in his living room.

He rose from her body, kissed her nipples and then kissed her mouth. "Wait here," he said, and reached for another fur to cover her with.

"I'm feeling like something out of a medieval romance novel," she murmured with a love-roughened voice.

Hank turned his face toward her as he finished setting the log into place. "Ah, you're the stuff of dreams, Laura." As he moved to lie down beside her, an electronic trill split the darkness and he swore, "Shite!"

"Is that your phone?" asked Laura as it trilled again.

"It is," he said, clearly annoyed at the intrusion, and moved off to the back of the house where it could be heard on the third ring.

Laura lay on the makeshift bed, eyes closed, dreamily sated by the light and warmth of the fire. From the bedroom, at least that's where she assumed he was, she could hear snippets of his conversation. "How much?" and then, "Fuck it, Siobhan, if you think I'm paying you that much!" and then, more quietly, "Fine. I'll make sure you get it this week."

All of Laura's good, easy feelings about this man just slid into the mire. He was paying somebody some money. And not just any somebody. A woman. But he didn't seem to want to pay this Siobhan person as much as she apparently wanted. At least, that was what she'd overheard. And then the last few words she heard were "paternity test," or so she thought.

Pulling the fur over her shoulder, wanting to hide the fact that she'd overheard anything, she curled toward the fire, pretending they were still in their fantasy world. She didn't want to wake up to now. She wanted to be back there, in the cocoon he'd created.

Laura felt him slide into the makeshift bed behind her,

caress her shoulder, kiss it and move his hands to cup her breasts, pulling her closer to spoon in behind her.

"Is everything okay?" she asked, thinking that it would be alright to ask such a thing because he did seem a little vexed.

"Oh, yeah, naught to worry about."

He nuzzled her neck beneath her hairline.

"It's just that it sounded a bit intense."

"Nah, it's fine. Don't fash yerself."

"Fash? That's a funny word."

"It's Irish."

"So I gathered."

"Where were we?"

"I think you're on the right track." She nuzzled her bottom against his groin, felt his penis shift and grow, and decided that no matter what skeletons Hank had in his closet, she was going to leave them there.

Chapter Eight

It was early morning, dawn not yet broken and the room still shrouded in darkness. Laura had just woken up and although confused at first, soon remembered where she was. More importantly, who she was with. She turned her head slightly to see the outline of Hank's profile on the pillow beside her. He was amazing, this new lover of hers, and she felt her body quicken with desire at the memories. So many memories in such a short time. She resisted the urge to reach out to him lest he wake up because she wanted time to observe him first, just for a little while. He was sleeping so soundly, not quite snoring, his short straight nose with its rounded tip outlined by the bit of light reflected off the snow outside and casting a shadow across cheeks and chin, dark where his beard had grown in overnight.

Hank didn't have curtains on his windows—didn't need them, he'd said, for who would be peering in those windows anyway? Bears? She had laughed and agreed. Maybe it would only be bears because a person would have to be pretty desperate to be a Peeping Tom around this forest hideaway.

As she lay watching him sleep, the realization dawned. Light. From the moon. It had stopped snowing and today there would be sunlight. It would be like a magical wonderland out there, all that new snow and bright sunlight. But it would also mean that her fairytale romance was over.

She sighed at the thought. She would have to go back to work tomorrow, Tuesday, not that they would miss her much

62

today. She doubted if many people would be able to make it in to work today anyway. The snow had blocked more than just her road, she was sure. No, it was the proper ending to her fabulous weekend, an ending she had no part in making. It wouldn't be her fault that the real world would intrude as it always did. Her marriage had been a fairytale and it had ended. That's what fairytales did. They ended, not always happily ever after like in the movies. The old-fashioned fairytales, the real ones, were often parables with sad endings. The Little Mermaid didn't really get her prince in the original version. No happily-ever-after there for her.

And there wouldn't be for her, either. She had no doubt that Siobhan, whoever she was, had a firm grip on Hank, no matter how pissed off he'd sounded at her on the phone. And what was that about money? Extortion? Or did he truly owe her? And had he really mentioned a paternity test? Was he hiding away up here from something, or someone, to get out of paying child support?

Well, that wasn't her problem. She wasn't in this forever, although as a lover, she knew he'd spoiled her for anyone else who came along. No one could top Hank the Hunk, of that she was certain.

Said hunk rolled over, put his arm across her, his hand automatically finding her breast.

"Mm," he said. "How long have you been awake?"

She hadn't realized he was awake himself. His eyes were still closed as if he, too, were fighting to keep the fairytale alive. "Not long," she answered. "It's stopped snowing."

"Mm," he said again. Her man of few words was now kneading her breast, running the tips of his work-roughened fingertips over her nipple, sending shockwaves spearing down her body to the central core between her legs.

"Oh, that's delicious," she said, wondering how she would ever survive without him when the fairytale ended.

A chuckle was his response, just before he came over her,

spreading her legs with his knees and easing himself into her.

Now it was her turn to murmur, opening her legs wider to take him deeper inside, sighing her pleasure as he began to move. "How do I love thee, let me count the ways," he quoted and she couldn't help but giggle at that.

"Keeping track?" she managed to get out as the addictive sensations began to build.

"I've lost count," he admitted, his breathing heavier as he continued his ministrations to her breast. He'd begun to lave her nipples and suck on them as he placed his fingers on the sweet spot of her mound, now slick and responsive to his touch.

"Mm," she sighed into the darkness, "don't stop, that is so…" She arched her back beneath his touch, began her own movements, mirroring his rhythm as if his fingers weren't hard enough or fast enough.

Hank's hands abandoned her sweet spot to pull her closer and hold her there. A moment of panic, an irrational fear that she wouldn't make it. Irrational, yes, because she immediately felt her insides tighten around him. The pressure built. She couldn't speak, could only vocalize the passion she felt, crying out loudly when she came, feeling him come inside her, the pulsing of his cock rhythmic against her inner walls.

Stars exploded behind eyes closed tight with emotion and then she was floating, falling back to earth to sleep again, warm and comfortable in his arms.

Hank looked at the woman sleeping within his embrace. How had he ever lived without her? It wasn't just sex, though he knew that to be a big part of it. It was her bravery in the face of the bear. Or was that foolishness? Whatever it was, he loved that about her as he loved the fact that she hadn't screamed and bashed him on the head when he fell into her living room that first night. It was what some people might have done. She was practical, tough when she had to be yet so soft beneath him. He couldn't believe it when she cried out her climax. Feckit! He'd thought he'd hurt her but she'd urged him on, not with words but with her body, her insides gripping his cock so tight he thought he'd died and gone to heaven. She'd learned to play his flute so well, not just with her box but with her mouth, too.

No one ever in his lifetime had taken such pleasure in oral sex with him as she did. When she attacked him outside the cabin, he'd been a prisoner to her wanton desires. At first, he wasn't sure what she was about, but when her hot tongue licked the length of him, he nearly shot his load right then and there, so surprised was he at her boldness. Surprised and delighted. No, he didn't think he'd be letting this one go.

Daylight was beginning to intrude. The room was slightly brighter than an hour earlier; shapes in the room were taking on definition. Laura had been right when she'd said it had stopped snowing. The moon was setting, the sun taking over, and soon he'd have to deal with the wreck his truck was and get his cell phone replaced. Luckily, he still had a landline. They could call out if they needed anything.

Siobhan's call last night had been ill timed. It had almost put a damper on their lovemaking but Laura seemed okay with his dismissing it as nothing. In fact, it hadn't been nothing. It had been everything. His little bubble of security in the backwoods of Canada was beginning to crumble. His old girlfriend, the one who had clung to him like shite to a blanket and who wouldn't believe him when he told her it was over, had found him. He knew she would find him sooner or later as she had, less than three years ago. It hadn't surprised him because her last words had been a threat she'd pulled off. I'll find you and make you pay, she'd said. And he, cocky male that he was, thought it to be nothing but the ranting of a woman scorned. And the story of a child they'd conceived together could possibly be true. She had emailed him a photo of a birth certificate with his name in the spot reserved for the father of the child. Then she'd sent photos of a girl that looked to be about thirteen or fourteen, the age she would be if what Siobhan said was true. The girl even looked like him. A little. Okay, she had the same black hair and blue eyes, but so did a dozen kids he'd grown up with. Killarney was rife with black-haired, blue-eyed people. And that was where the similarity ended.

So she was blackmailing him for his paycheck; had guilted him into giving her more money each time she called, stating the daughter he'd fathered needed clothing and food. And then the girl had been sick and needed medicine. Siobhan had lost her job; the list kept growing.

Hank didn't doubt the part about her job. Jobs, food, and rent were an often fickle existence in Killarney—or anywhere in Ireland, for that matter—especially for a single parent. If you had a job, you could almost afford both rent and food, if you were careful. It was hard to make ends meet sometimes, but throw in a kid and only one income…well, it wasn't hard to imagine the hardship. He'd seen his own mam die too early from trying to hold down jobs to get enough for rent and food. His da was a low-life who stayed home only long enough to get his wife pregnant. Shortly after his sister's eighth birthday, his mam kicked his old man out and told him never to return. All he did was drink and beat up Hank. Although he'd been a mere lad of ten, he still remembered his mam's words. "You son of a whoremonger! Ye've got some nerve comin' to me after being with her. Get out and don't ye dare darken me doorway again. I hate ye, Henry O'Farrell. Do ye hear? I hate ye!" She'd broken down after that and sent him and his sister to bed. They never got dinner that night.

For years afterward, he wondered what she'd meant by her words; but not until he was old enough did he begin to understand that his da had other women.

By the time his sister, Meara, reached the tender age of fifteen, she'd left both school and home, setting off a chain reaction with her disappearance. She'd shown up a year later, pregnant, looking for a place to live. It was sad. She'd stayed only long enough to burn a hole in whatever savings they had and then left again to follow the bastard who got her that way. To this day, Hank had no idea where she might be. He never saw her or heard from her again after that.

It had left his mam broken. She caught pneumonia that winter and never recovered. He'd been just eighteen, working at whatever job he could find and not bringing much in. She kept putting off going to the doctor because she knew they didn't have money for medicine. Hank abided by her decision until one night her breathing got so labored he couldn't stand by anymore. By the time he got her to the hospital, it was too late.

After the funeral he sold off everything they had, put away every penny he earned by living cheaply and nearly getting himself into trouble along the way. But he managed to put together enough for airfare and a few dollars extra and flew to Canada to be with the girl who swore she loved him and couldn't live without him. A Canadian girl who had met him while he was guiding tourists around the county. They were so in love that they married only a month after meeting.

It was all sunshine and roses at first and Hank knew a kind of stability he'd rarely experienced. They had a roof over their heads, food in their bellies, and even money left over for clothes and evenings out now and then. It was a good life, for a while.

He couldn't have said when things changed. People talked about the "seven-year itch" but theirs seemed to fall after five. Although he'd worked all day, she harangued him about earning more money. She wanted the things her friends had; he wasn't her idea of a good husband anymore. The simple life that had seemed so good at first was no longer enough for her. It seemed to him that the novelty of having an Irishman in her bed and all the romantic notions she'd harbored had worn off.

His citizenship had come through mere days before she announced she wanted a divorce. It was the best and worst time of his life, all rolled into one.

Months later, he saw her in a BMW with a man who was old enough to be her father. Maybe he was? Hank had never met her parents because she said she never wanted to see them again. Fair enough. So he surmised that perhaps she'd found the kind of relationship she claimed to have wanted and was happy with a man, albeit one old enough to be her da, who could give her the kinds of things Hank could only dream of.

Laura wouldn't be like that. Somehow Hank knew that she was not a material person. Oh, she loved her cabin and had fought through her divorce in order to get it, but he'd have done the same thing. Only there hadn't been anything to argue over in his own divorce. They'd simply parted ways and he'd moved on.

And here he was in the cabin he'd built with his own hands, and a small business as a handyman-cum-carpenter keeping him afloat, and all in less than eight years. Laura knew all about him, or about the kind of work he did anyway, and hadn't let that stop her from having a relationship with him. She didn't seem to mind that he wasn't a millionaire or even very wealthy. And she loved his cabin. She'd said so.

He kissed her cheek lovingly, watched the corner of her lip curl up in a smile, and snuggled down beside her. Pulling her close, he closed his eyes and let the past go. He was here now, with Laura in his arms. He would make this work and worry about Siobhan another time. It was only money, after all.

***

"Tell me about Ireland," she said, after they'd got up and made coffee. The fire made them cozy and warm, seated as they were on the leather sofa, furs laid out randomly, the dim light of morning piercing the leaded windowpanes.

"Ah, it's a magical place at times, wonderful, green as green can be everywhere, any time of year. Sheep and cows dot meadows of green, the mountains are smaller than here, but no less grand for all that. And the lakes have fish of all kinds, so thick ye can scoop them out with yer bare hands," he said, a smile on his face at the images he was creating for her.

"I'd believe it all, except for the fish," she added. "Somehow, thick as they might be, I don't think you can really catch them with your bare hands."

"Ah, maybe not, but it's a challenge, and I've yet to meet an Irishman that didn't take to a challenge."

"It does sound lovely, though. Are there castles?"

"Castles? Yeah, there're castles, but not the kind ye might be thinkin' of. Ireland's castles are more like fortresses built to withstand invaders, not house the nobility. There were manor houses for them, the chieftains who ruled the clans. The fortresses are plentiful, to be sure, but few are much more than broken stone walls with cows and sheep grazing where people once lived."

"That sounds sad," she said, sipping the hot coffee, feeling the liquid warm her inside. Hank was seated beside her, his arm across the back of the sofa just above her head. He stroked her hair every now and then as if she were his cat, who was now ensconced in front of the fire, washing himself.

"Well, many things about Ireland are sad. 'Tis an unfortunate land with many riches, only none as can make the people wealthy overnight. War and strife have left their marks and although I think it's better now than it was, whatever life I had there is nothing compared to what I have here."

"Still, I'd like to see it someday, maybe explore the castles, such as they are. Do they have other things, like Stonehenge?" she asked, casting a sideways glance at him through her lashes.

"Oh, there are stone forts, low round things, and stone

rings, none so famous as Stonehenge, but all very mystical all the same. We've no more a clue as to why they're there than they are about any of the stone rings in Britain. They say they were created for this or that, but no one really knows for certain. It's all conjecture."

She snuggled against him, took a quick glance outside and noticed that the sun was suddenly gone. Sighing into him, she remarked, "Oh crap, it's snowing again," and felt him crane his neck to peer out of the window.

Kissing her forehead, he agreed and said, "All the more reason to hunker down here another day. The snow pack is getting heavy and we don't know when another avalanche will occur. I wouldn't want to chance getting caught again."

"You might be right," she said, placing her coffee mug on the small table beside the sofa before turning into his embrace. "I kind of like it here."

"Ah, my lady love, it would be grand if ye stayed as long as ye liked." His hand strayed to her breast and down along her side to cup the roundness of her butt.

"Oh, that does feel good," she admitted, wriggling to lie alongside him and encourage him on. She'd never been so bold with anyone, not even her ex, and she couldn't understand how Hank brought out the wanton in her.

"Turn this way," he suggested and as she did, he slid both hands inside her pants, massaged not just one butt cheek but both before working his fingers toward the slit between her legs.

"I don't know how you do it, but I can't keep my hands off you," she breathed between moans of pleasure. Her own hands were exploring inside his pants as well, finding his balls, stroking the length of his cock, wishing they were naked so they could get at it again. But her mind had stopped working. Hank soon had her panting, and somewhere in the recesses of her mind she recognized that her body was suspended, her entire being focused on the climax that was rapidly building.

Moments later, she felt herself spiral out of control, felt his fingers inside while her muscles contracted around them.

As her climax subsided and she floated back to consciousness, she came to the realization that he had done it on purpose, that he hadn't expected to come with her. "Wait," she said as he tucked her shirt back in to her pants, "I haven't done you, yet."

"Ah, darlin', there'll be more later. Right now, I'm afraid I need to split some logs or yon fire might just go out. And then where would we be?"

"What happens when you go into town? Don't you have a backup?"

He nodded matter-of-factly, black curls bobbing, "Oh yeah, but the furnace is not as romantic, eh?"

Raising an eyebrow at him while casting a look at the blaze, she had to agree. But chopping wood had never been her strong point, hence the propane-powered fireplace in her own cabin and the poker that was just for show. However, if they wanted the romance to continue, wood it would be.

"Okay, let's go chop some wood." She scrambled to her feet, held out a hand to help him up, noticing that he was a little slower than normal. The bulge in his pants appeared to be the culprit. "Told you I should have done you."

He looked embarrassed, she thought, and suddenly felt bad about bringing it to his attention but he just laughed it off.

"Ah, it's the effect ye have on me. I don't mind it so much." He straightened up, shifted his clothing, and led the way to the back door. "All the wood is out here," he said as they donned their coats and boots. "I don't think the snow is that bad out the back door. It's more sheltered there so it shouldn't be too bad to get some wood bucked up."

They spent the next half hour splitting and stacking until Hank said he was certain they had enough to last the day, if not into the middle of next week, amended Laura, checking the stacked wood that nearly filled the shed, a rather large

S. M. Cross

containment area that boasted an opening of about six feet high and eight feet wide. There had been split wood in there already and she really hadn't seen the need to chop more, but for some reason, Hank had decided more was definitely needed.

"Here, hold out yer arms," he said and then proceeded to pile the newly split pieces into her outstretched limbs. "Is that too heavy for ye?"

"No. I think I can carry it, but why didn't you just take some that was already split?"

"Ah, that. Well, ye see, there's all kinds of creepy crawlies make their home in there during the winter, and in summer, too. I didn't think ye'd relish bringing in wood and all of a sudden come face to face with a big black spider, hmm?"

The expression of horror on her face must have showed because Hank burst out laughing. "Exactly as I thought. C'mon, my brave huntress. Ye can face down a bear but a spider will be yer undoing. Let's get back inside and I'll teach ye how to make Irish soda bread. We can have some with lunch if I get a move on."

The thought of freshly baked bread had Laura's mouth watering, so balancing the wood in her arms and keeping an eye out for spiders, she went into the house and deposited the split pieces into the large metal cradle beside the hearth.

Glancing at the clock, she saw that it was still early, just after ten, and realized they'd been awake since at least seven.

"I'm never up this early when I don't have to go to work," she said as Hank loaded up the fire with more fuel and stacked the rest of what he'd brought in where Laura had placed hers.

"Oh well, then. We can always go back to bed if ye'd prefer," he said, a twinkle in his eyes.

Her stomach rumbled. Loudly. "I think I need food first," she said, rubbing her stomach.

"Right then, food it is." He quickly prepared a light breakfast of scrambled eggs and toast and then, while she ate, got out the ingredients for Irish soda bread.

"You really are going to make it?" she asked between mouthfuls of toast and jam.

"Yeah, it's one of those things from home you just can't do without for long. It's been a while but I don't think I've lost the touch."

She finished her breakfast while Hank mixed ingredients and began to knead the dough. His biceps flexed beneath puffs of flour and she marveled at the muscles in his forearm as he lifted the dough, flipped it around, and kneaded it some more. "Can I try that?" she asked, coming up behind him and peeking around his solid torso to have a look.

"Of course. I was kind of hoping ye would," he grinned. They were both in t-shirts, the fire having warmed the compact space nicely, and as she went to step in front of him, he said, "Here, let me show ye how," and took her hands in his flour-covered ones and taught her how to knead dough.

"It looked like you were really going at it but really you're being quite gentle with it," she remarked.

"The secret to good bread is to be gentle with the kneading. And to add just enough flour, not too much, not too little. The surface must feel soft. Feel that?"

She nodded and noted that the dough really did have a feel to it that could be described as soft. "Okay, so now what?"

"So now we put it in the oven, once I score the top.." He did just that, making a large "x" across the top of the mound of dough. Then, sliding it into the oven, he winked at her, saying, "Now we wait. I'll check it in about forty-five minutes or so."

"And in the meantime?"

The twinkle in his eyes brightened, the corners creased in a broad smile. "We go shower off all the flour we've accumulated." He pressed his body against her back, felt his penis hard against her butt, and had no doubt what kind of shower it would be.

Turning in his arms, she took in what she saw and began to laugh. His face was blotched with flour where he'd rubbed the back of his hand across his forehead and a smudge on his cheek told her there had been an itch there, too. He wasn't exactly covered with flour, more like he'd been dusted by some errant fairy. Glancing down her own front she saw the same telltale signs of dough and flour splotched everywhere. "Hm, I guess you're right. I'll need to throw these clothes into the wash, too. Got any spares?"

"I'm sure we can find something for ye to wear. Or maybe nothin' at all," he said, a cocky grin lighting his eyes.

Chapter Nine

They'd showered, thrown their clothes into the washing machine, and were lying sated on the bed in the aftermath of yet another glorious session of lovemaking. It had been another experience from the stuff of fairytales.

Hank had taken the soap and generously lathered it into a pile of foam that he massaged all over Laura's body and then slipped soap-covered fingers into the spot between her legs that nearly dropped her to her knees.

She'd grabbed his cock, then, wanting to take him in, but he'd held her off and so she'd played with him, much as he was doing with her. Soap was an amazing lubricant, almost as good as oil for a massage.

Face to face, the rain-head style shower generating a gentle downpour of warm water, they'd played like kids. Big kids. The kind of kids who were on a journey of discovery, of their likes and dislikes, of what each other enjoyed the most in a carnal way.

In a frenzy of activity, Hank had turned off the shower and bodily lifted Laura, carrying her to the bed, water dripping from her long, wavy hair. Plunking her down in the middle of the bed like a sack of potatoes, he'd come over her, licking water from her nipples, eliciting shrieks of delight as he went; and before she could question his antics, she'd felt him spread her legs and enter her in one swift motion. The feeling of him inside her, of being fulfilled, cherished even, nearly brought her to tears but she was in the grip of a climax that ceased all thought except that. Their shower play had brought about an intensity to their lovemaking that seemed to have trumped all before it. It just kept getting better and better.

From the bed beside her, Hank, still breathing heavily from their recent exertions, raised his head and gazed into her eyes. They were so blue, she thought, the dark ring of what could only be described as a deep navy blue enclosing a mixture of lighter and darker blues that made up the iris of his eyes. "You're eyes are the most amazing deep blue I've ever seen on anyone," she said, completely enthralled by what she saw.

"They're fair common in my family, least what I know of it," said Hank. "My da had them and so does my sister."

"And your mom?"

"Oh, yeah, her eyes were blue, too, but a teeny bit lighter. More like a blue-gray mix."

"Well, I'm glad you got your dad's eyes. They're magnificent."

He snorted his laugh. "Regardless of whose eyes they may look like, they're all mine." With that he abruptly got up, and retrieving a towel from the bathroom, laid it across her, saying, "Soda bread waits for no one."

An hour later, sated on soda bread and leftover stew, they were once again prisoners to the weather.

"I feel like I should be doing something," she said. Her back was to him, her arms were crossed beneath her breasts, and she was gazing out the front window, her perfect backside in her skintight leggings illuminated by the fire in the great stone fireplace.

"Did ye make the call in to your work?"

"Yes, thanks for the use of your phone. I left a message because no one picked up. I'm assuming they're having as much trouble getting there as I am so I just said I'd get there as soon as I could."

"Well I don't think anyone who knows where ye live is going to blame ye for not being there, at least today."

"At least," she agreed.

The phone, seeming to know it had been the subject of very recent conversation, trilled loudly from the bedroom. "I'd better get that," he told her, and hid the fact that he was hoping it wasn't Siobhan with another outrageous demand for more money.

"Hello?" he said into the mouthpiece and breathed a sigh of relief when he heard the voice identified as the local authorities, alerted by the grader operator clearing the road that there had been an accident with his truck. "Oh, yeah, I know, I was in it but was able to get out," he declared, quite satisfied that he could say that and mean it. Able to assure them of his safety, he then learned they were awaiting a tow truck to haul it out so the grader could proceed on its way to his property at the end of the road. They didn't expect to get there for at least another day, if he could hang on that long, they wondered.

"No rush. I don't think it's drivable right now anyway," he said. After a few more pleasantries and the odd joke thrown in, he hung up the phone and went back to tell Laura the news.

"That was the cops. Seems they've cleared as far as my truck…". He stopped in mid-sentence because there she was, putting on her outside gear with a determined look on her face mixed with an expression of…what? Regret? Regret at being with him? Or leaving? Which way did it go?

He didn't have long to think about it though because she spoke firmly, as if it had been planned all along when she said, "It's okay, I need to get going. Today was fun. I didn't think I'd enjoy learning to split logs or make Irish soda bread, but I did. And the bread turned out well, no thanks to my manhandling. But the fairytale is over. They found your truck, which means that as soon as I can clear my SUV out from under that snow, I can get on with the real world again.

They'll expect me back at work tomorrow, I'm sure. No excuses this time."

"But the sun is going down. You can't go traipsing through the snow on snowshoes now. It'll be dark before long." He needed her to stay. Just one more day. Didn't she know that?

"Well, I was hoping to use your snowmobile, or get you to take me home on that. Would you mind?"

Would he mind? Oh yeah, a thousand times yeah, he'd mind. But that wasn't going to take the determined look from her eye. As to the other, he had to ask. "D'ye regret our time together then?"

There, he'd said it.

Her eyes opened wide. She hesitated before speaking.

"Never mind," he said, "it was a stupid question."

"No, no, I don't regret it," she said, a half smile on her face. "I loved it, every minute. It was the kind of weekend that makes you think you've been away for a month, like a mini-vacation to the best fantasyland ever."

He nodded, unsure of what to say next. "Well, if you're determined, and I can see that y'are, I'll get me things on and take ye home. You're sure I can't persuade you to at least stay to dinner?"

"No, but thanks anyway. I just need to get stuff together for tomorrow and free my car up for the drive into town."

"Well, I can help ye with that I can. Have ye got a spare shovel?"

At her nod, he motioned her out the door, pulling on his toque as he closed it behind him. A glance back showed Figaro on the sill, watching them as they made their way to the snowmobile in the front yard.

Laura hugged Hank's body tightly as he drove his snowmobile through the dips and curves of their earlier traverse through the bush. Now, with the sun shining, even if it was late afternoon, it was a whole different world of slanted shadows one minute, blinding light the next. Efforts at seeing around Hank's body were met with too many hazards, mostly in the spray of snow from the machine's front skis.

The snowmobile bucked over some deadfall and Laura bounced into Hank's back. She clung tightly, trying to hold on, but she didn't want to. She wanted to fall off, stay behind and never go back to her old life. She wanted the fairytale to never end.

As if her thoughts provoked the incident, the vehicle bucked again, and despite her grip, she was tossed summarily into the snow.

She heard the engine gun, knew Hank was coming around for her although she couldn't see much. The snow was soft and she'd been close to being buried in it. And then Hank was looking over her, an elfish grin on his handsome face. "You okay?"

She nodded and couldn't help but grin back. Although being tossed off the snowmobile hadn't been planned, her landing was soft and she was warm, and if the truth be told, quite comfortable where she was.

"My turn," was all he said, and the glint in his eyes sparkled more than the fresh snow around them.

For a moment, Laura was completely flummoxed by his words and then she felt the zipper on her winter coveralls give, the special ones she'd had made so that she didn't have to disrobe entirely to go to the bathroom while out in the bush. The feeling was exciting, the wonder of what was to come next enticing her to play along.

The two halves of her coveralls came apart, front from back, and he flipped the front half up, then knelt before her in the snow and removed his gloves. His hands, still warm from his gloves, slid beneath her bum and pulled her leggings and underwear down her thighs. The cold air hit her nether parts and she gasped her shock at the temperature change. And then his mouth was there, kissing his way up her exposed thighs, the crotch of her clothing behind his neck, holding him to her like a sling while his mouth did wonderful things to her. His tongue, so hot against the temperature around them seared her as he licked and sucked, plunging into her depths to feast on her juices.

It was what he'd wanted to do to her the moment he saw her begin to dress to go home. He'd wanted to keep her there, never let her go; but she'd seemed frightened, ready to bolt like a doe facing a hunter. So he'd acquiesced, said he'd take her home, and make sure she was safely there.

And then Providence had provided. She'd fallen off the snowmobile in spite of the care he'd taken through the bush.

He drew his tongue across her vaginal opening, stopped to swirl it around her little nub of pleasure a few times, and then slid it inside the warmth of her. Oh, she tasted so sweet as she lifted her box toward his face and helped him go deep within, as far as his tongue would go.

He heard her gasps of pleasure, felt her body tense, and then heard his name on her lips like a wild cry into the forest as she came. He continued to push his tongue into her as far as he could until her breathing began to slow. Then, covering her pelvis with his face, he kept her warm until she came back to earth.

"Oh, my God," she yelled into the wind, "Hank, that was fabulous!"

He felt her head rise to look at him and then fall back into her snowy bed, but held there as he was by her leggings, it was too difficult to lift his head to see. Backing out from under the sling of her clothing, he gave her box one last kiss before hauling first her underwear and then her leggings back over her bum.

She squirmed and they both laughed together as he tried to straighten things out. "How does that feel?" he asked.

"What? My clothing or what you just did?"

A shrugging of his shoulders and a cocky grin was his answer.

"Then both," she laughed. "Both are just fine, thank you very much."

He couldn't help it. He leaned over and kissed her lips, delighted when she kissed him back. Whatever her earlier wish was, to be home and away from him, seemed to have dissolved in the face of their lovemaking. For lovemaking it was. He loved her, Hank knew. Had loved her all along, even though he hadn't really known her.

But he knew her now, could read her like a book even though she was a tome he'd only picked up two nights ago. Some books were like that, and she had turned out to be an edition so prized he knew he could never give her up.

Finishing their kiss, he gazed into her eyes, wishing he could read what secrets she was hiding. But there was time, he hoped, time in which he would unlock every one. "Are ye ready to go?"

She nodded and the sun seemed to leave her eyes. So, she didn't really want to go any more than he wanted to take her home. He moved off her then, cleared the snow from where it had slipped inside the opened leg of her coveralls and zipped them up.

"I think we're not far from where the truck is," he said, helping her to stand and make their way over to the snowmobile. "I'll use the road bed then and we should be at your place very soon."

"Sure, sounds good," she said, her voice flat and unemotional. Taking a moment to straighten her jacket and toque, she climbed on behind him and hugged his back. "Okay, ready."

The sun was setting quickly.

Laura hung on to Hank as before, her arms around the bulk of his jacket, but she wished more than anything they were naked in bed together. The impromptu lovemaking had been out of her realm of experience. Erik had never even thought about diving into her pants while they were out snowshoeing.

And when she thought about it, he hadn't been a very adventurous lover, either. She hadn't complained because she really didn't have anyone to compare him to. They'd married soon after high school and there had only been one boy before him. That was an affair that both had thought they wanted but had realized within about six months that it was time to move on. She had met Erik shortly after that and had eyes for him alone. Too bad it hadn't been reciprocated.

As Hank drove slowly between the trees, she remembered every minute of this day. They'd put so much into it! And who knew baking bread could be so…sensuous? He'd put his hands over hers, coming around from behind her to help her knead the dough. His bulging crotch fit into the cleft of her bum, and as they kneaded, he ground his erection against her until they could barely wait to get at each other.

By the time the loaf was ready for the oven they were covered in flour and had to shower off. And that shower with Hank was one of the best parts of the day.

C'mon, let's get cleaned up, he'd invited, and she hadn't argued.

The shower stall was large enough for two and they stripped down, piece by piece, kicking clothing off as they went. Hank's hair had its fair share of floured strands and, she imagined, so did hers.

The water was warm and the soap he used was fragrant with a scent that seemed to reflect his personality. Fun, invigorating. She remembered the feel of his hands on her breasts, fondling them as he soaped her all over. As the water washed the soap away, his mouth covered her nipples and he suckled them while he soaped her crotch, plunging his fingers deep inside her.

She wriggled her bottom at the thought, even though he'd just made her come in one of the most satisfying sexual moments she'd ever had. The only thing missing had been him inside her. She wanted him always, forever, but she wasn't so naïve now. She knew someone like him could never be satisfied with someone like her for forever and a day. He would be off as soon as someone better came along. She didn't have the confidence in herself to be able to keep him. After all, she'd loved Erik and would have done anything for him and yet he'd betrayed her. Not once, but many times over. If she couldn't see through the man she had been married to, then what chance would she have of really knowing someone like Hank?

And then there was Siobhan, whoever she was.

She hugged Hank tighter, grateful they had gained the roadbed, now ploughed neatly up to Hank's truck. The tailgate was partially visible, as was the tunnel that Hank had climbed out of. It was a wonder he'd gotten out at all.

He stopped the snowmobile and turned to look at what was left of his truck. They wouldn't really know if it could be fixed until they'd hauled it out.

"How did they know it was yours?" she asked.

"My guess is they ran the plates." He pointed to just below the tailgate where enough snow had been removed to make the letters and numbers visible. She hadn't seen it at first, the daylight was almost gone.

"I'm amazed you made it out of there alive," she said through frozen lips, mirroring her earlier thought. The temperature had dropped in cadence with the sun.

He nodded and turned the snowmobile back down the road for the mile-long trek to Laura's cabin. It wouldn't be long now, and they'd see how bad it was for her to dig out.

Chapter Ten

It's impossible, was Hank's first thought on seeing the depth of the snow in front of Laura's house. They would never get her vehicle out before morning. Not even if they were at it all night. And where would they put the snow? The grader operator wouldn't take too kindly to them putting it all back in the roadway.

He shared a glance with Laura, who had gotten off the snowmobile and was now standing in front of the wall of snow that was her driveway. It was ten feet if it was one, he thought. Maybe more. They wouldn't get that car out until spring.

Turning off the machine and coming to stand beside her, he saw the tears in her eyes.

"It's alright," he soothed, "we'll get your car out."

"I'm sorry," she apologized. "I don't know why I'm crying, I just…"

"Don't be sorry. We'll get it out. I'll call some friends with a front-end loader and they'll come and help. May not be tomorrow, though. Will ye be okay with that?"

Wiping her eyes, she sniffed and answered with a nod of her head. "I guess I'd better phone in to work again," she said.

"They'll understand," he answered her with a sympathetic hand on her shoulder. He knew she worked at one of the law offices in town as one of their research assistants, and a very good one, from what little he had heard about her. He knew because he'd asked one of the partners whose vehicle he'd fixed. The conversation was friendly. Oh, I have a neighbor that works in your law firm, he'd said. And the man had smiled politely and said what a good member of the team she was, and how nice as well. He'd then related the story of a colleague who'd broken his leg while skiing and how Laura had taken him a bouquet of flowers while he was laid up in hospital because she'd said that flowers make everyone smile.

He wasn't sure about flowers but Laura made him smile, all by herself. Hank had been interested in her since he began to hear the rumors around town. Not usually one to pay attention to them, he did to those. Snippets of conversation from people on the street or in the bar filtered through the air as he walked by, not really listening until her name was mentioned.

Perhaps it was the impression that everyone had about Erik and Laura Foster. They were the perfect couple. They were the town's version of the most upstanding Hollywood couple, and couples like that always seemed to have ghosts in the closet.

In this case, there were many ghosts. When the story came out in the local paper, Laura's husband had been caught out with no less that twelve women, most of whom were said to have spoken out against him.

To Hank's way of thinking, the guy was first class gobshite. A plonker. A real idiot. He didn't deserve a woman like Laura.

It must have taken something out of Laura for her to see their divorce splashed across the newspaper as if they really were a Hollywood couple. Her private life was laid out for all to see and she, although the victim, was made to look like an idiot, too. An idiot for not knowing what was happening right under her nose.

Hank took in Laura's distraught look, her nose red from

the cold and from crying. She'd stopped her tears but still sniffled.

"Let's take the snowmobile and make our way around to the back. We won't be able to get through this way." His words seemed to have the desired effect of distracting her from her problem. She looked up at him and smiled, her eyes still damp from her tears, but hopeful.

"You think we can get there?"

"We got out of there, didn't we?"

"Yes," she hesitated, "but a lot more snow came down afterward."

"Ah, me darlin', ye wound me with yer doubts," he drawled in his thickest brogue.

That too, had the desired effect, and smiling once again, she stepped onto the snowmobile behind him and held tightly to his back while they wound their way around to the back of the house.

"Is Figaro going to be okay? Did you leave him some food?" she asked once they were inside and were removing all their outer gear.

"Oh, yeah, he'll be fine. There's always food in his dish and water, too." He had a niggling thought in the back of his brain but it wouldn't surface. A feeling of something not quite right but at the moment, he couldn't place it and thought it must just be because he had other things on his mind. Things like the probability that Laura was not going to get her car out for a couple of days.

"Guess I should go check my messages," she said, wandering off in search of her cell phone. There was no message light blinking on her main phone that Hank could see but that made him remember his words to her about his friend with the front-end loader.

"D'ye mind if I use your phone? I'll give my buddy a call."

"Oh, sure, go ahead. I don't have any messages here I need to answer anyway."

Her voice was from the bedroom upstairs and the thought of her being in the room where they'd made love in a bed for the first time made his lad grow in anticipation. "Down, boyo," he muttered as he dialed his friend's number from memory.

Laura came down the stairs in time to see Hank hang up the phone. "Well?" she asked hopefully.

Hank was shaking his head. "I'm afraid it's not great news. He can come, but it likely won't be tomorrow although he said he'd try. This system that dropped all this snow on us was almost as bad in town as it is here. He doubts the graders will be here tomorrow, either."

"Hmm, well if it's that bad, then I guess no one will expect me for a couple of days. Good thing I've got holiday time banked because I think I'm going to be using it." Part of her felt relieved; she wouldn't have to say goodbye to Hank the Hunk quite yet. Another part of her was scared. Scared she wouldn't be able to let him go when the time came. And that was a real fear because things happened when people stayed together. You could never trust that they weren't going to drop you at a moment's notice for someone else. Much better to keep it light and enjoy it for what it was. Like a ride at the fair; when it stopped, she'd get off and keep her heart safe. But could she?

Hank was at the front door, shrugging on his jacket and pushing his feet into his boots. At Laura's querying look, he said, "I'm going to see if I can at least shovel a path through the deck down to yer car."

"A tunnel?"

"Yeah, it'll have to be," he grinned, and looked for all the world like a schoolboy heading out for a good time.

"Maybe I should see if I can rummage up some supper for us while you do that. You're going to need some food to fuel those muscles of yours," she laughed back at him.

He winked at her, opened the door, and stepped outside.

The crunch of snow beneath his feet on the wooden deck was immediately muffled once the door was closed and he got into the deeper stuff farther along.

Laura turned on the television just in time to catch the weather portion of the news. Several feet of snow had fallen over a three-day period, the announcer was saying, in which the entire town and surrounding area, which Laura knew included the mountain on which her house perched, had been blanketed, the wind that accompanied the storm making things that much worse. He went on to say that all available equipment was out but some areas would take time to clear as another system was headed their way.

Looking outside Laura saw the mound of snow that had blown up against the house. You couldn't see the road from where she was, even though the house had been built on a rise. And if more was expected, then they would have to hunker down tight until it too, had blown over.

The thought of hunkering down with Hank thrilled her right where he'd so recently had his mouth. The tingling between her legs was not to be ignored but she had promised him food, so she headed to the kitchen, promising herself that pleasure would come later.

The sausages she was cooking gave off a mouth watering aroma and she wondered how long Hank would be. Was everything okay out there?

As if her thoughts had called him in, the door opened and Hank entered, looking like an abominable snowman. Laura laughed. "That looks so much like you did the first night you came here."

"Yeah, it feels much the same. Come here, me luv, and help me off with my boots."

Laura stepped near him and he hugged her tight to his wet jacket, the clumps of snow melting onto her t-shirt and eliciting a squeal of protest from her. Hank laughed and let her go as she looked down to see her bra quite visible beneath the now damp garment. "Thanks a lot," she said, in a voice she hoped dripped sarcasm.

"Ah, my darlin', I couldn't resist. You looked so warm, stripped down to yer t-shirt and leggings and here am I, near frozen to death, don't ye know."

"Let's get this stuff off and you'll warm up soon enough." She helped him off with his snow-encrusted jacket, then picking off chunks of snow, hurled them outside the still open door. After removing his boots, they gathered up what snow chunks they could and threw them out the door as well, before closing it firmly behind them and laughing all the while.

Before she knew it, Hank's mouth was covering hers and his cool hands were sliding beneath her damp t-shirt. Her legs grew weak at his ministrations and she felt herself grow anxious beneath his touch.

An aroma of burnt sausage tickled her nose and her eyes opened in alarm. "The sausages!" She scrambled from Hank's embrace in time to rescue the meat from becoming charcoal.

"I like them like that," Hank said from over her shoulder as she turned them in the pan. "They're good and crunchy that way."

"You'd better be telling the truth or I'll be very hurt." She tried to put a wounded tone to her voice but could tell it wasn't working.

"Ah, but they're perfect like that, my sweet, especially with creamed corn."

Laura thought a moment. "I think I have creamed corn. Let me go check." She soon emerged from the pantry, a can in her hands.

Hank grinned his appreciation.

"And a feast it will be," he exclaimed, rubbing his hands together.

"So," she said as they sat down to a dinner of scorched sausages, creamed corn, and fried potatoes, "what's the verdict on the tunnel?"

Hank, finished chewing his scorched sausage with what looked like an expression of pure joy, swallowed, and said, "It'll take a while but I think I'm halfway down yer stairs."

Laura thought about it. The stairs from the deck went to a landing and then turned before going parallel to the house to where the driveway was. Each length had about eight stairs. "Did you get to the turn yet?"

"Yeah, just past it."

"What'll you do when you get to the car? It isn't like you could drive it out of there."

"Ah, well, that's the truth for sure. I'll see how fast my buddy can get here with his miracle machine and in the meantime, I'll just keep digging away."

"I have a snowblower," Laura offered, "for the driveway, I mean."

"Do ye now? And where would this snowblower be?"

She bit her bottom lip and then realized how ridiculous an idea it was. "Yeah, right. It's in the carport," she smirked.

"And a good place for it, to be sure. Just not today." He picked up her hand, kissed the back of it and winked at her as he picked up another chunk of sausage.

He seemed so sure of himself, Laura thought, watching him stuff a large forkful of food into his mouth, and that was part of what drew her to him. He didn't back down in the face of overwhelming odds against him. He got himself out of his truck when others would surely have died in there, waiting for someone else to bail them out. And as daunting a task as it seemed, he was willing to try to dig her car out.

She finished her dinner, thinking about the car. The snow above would be heavy, although the car itself was safe within the slanted roof of the carport. Because of the roof design, most of the snow had slid off into the gully on that side of the house, but there was still a good fifty feet of driveway or more before they hit the main road.

"Is it safe for you to be digging out from all that snow? I

mean, what if it caved in? You'd be buried and there would be no way on earth I could get you out."

He seemed to think about that for a moment as he chewed and swallowed. "Yeah, I'd be in a right pickle then, wouldn't I," he stated flatly, as if it were an everyday occurrence.

"Yes, well, maybe you shouldn't go back out there, just in case that's what happens."

Hank viewed Laura through half-closed lids, enjoying the last of his sausage as though it were the best he'd ever had. "Ye've a point and that's for sure," he agreed. He didn't really want to go back out there and shovel more anyway, at least not until tomorrow. And by then, maybe Greg would have his front-end loader freed up.

"I'll help ye with the dishes," he said, rising, but Laura stayed him with a look.

"No, I'm just going to put everything in the dishwasher. I really don't feel like washing them right now and you have done enough for one day."

He liked where she was heading.

"Right, then. I'll just run a bath, if that's okay with you? I could use a soak to loosen up my muscles."

She seemed to hesitate before nodding her agreement and Hank wondered if she'd be interested…if he said something…

"I could use a massage on the back of my neck and shoulders," he suggested, and knew it was the right thing because as soon as he spoke, her eyes lit up.

"I'll clear these away while you go run the tub."

He winked and left her to it while he did as she suggested.

Chapter Eleven

They made love in the tub; her big, comfortable tub that could seat two while looking through a window that had a view of the mountain behind the house. The mountain, dark against the light in the bathroom, was soon more visible once she lit candles and turned out the main light. Instantly bathed in a mellow glow, the walls ignited with each flicker of light, each movement they made sending air currents across the flames, the waxy scent of vanilla scented candles permeating the air.

"I don't have massage oil but I think this will do," she said, her voice husky as she picked up the bottle of bath oil and splashed some into her palm. Rubbing her hands together, she knelt behind him to massage his shoulders, seeking out the tight knots and kneading them away.

The feel of her nipples against his skin, tickling his back, was enough to harden Hank's flute near to bursting. Capable hands soothed the skin of his shoulders, sliding over his pectorals in front, rubbing the tips of his flat, male nipples until they were hardened little nubs. Intentional or not, her mound pressed against his back and her breasts slid up to hug his neck, one on either side like an aphrodisiac.

It was all he could take. Rotating in the oil-slicked water, he flipped her around too, his front to her back to enter her that way, her back arched, her perfect butt cheeks spread wide, and while his cock slid in and out of her box, his finger playing gently with the tight little hole of her butt.

She gasped at first.

"I'll quit if ye don't like it," he breathed into the hair by her ear.

"Don't stop," she'd purred through her moans of enjoyment, encouraging him on with slight gyrations of her hips.

He continued slowly, not wanting to hurt or frighten her.

Moments later he could feel her vaginal muscles tighten, felt her bum hole tighten around his fingertip, and knew she was ready to come. Withdrawing his finger, he pulled her hips toward him and held her while he thrust into her, felt her push against him, thrilled that she was thrusting back as hard as she could. She wanted this as much as he did.

They came together in a rush of warmth, the bathwater threatening to overflow the tub, the flickering glow of candlelight wavering madly against the night-blackened windows. The mountain beyond had since disappeared into darkness, just like the past they both fought to leave. The past, and all its pronouncements. They were no longer a divorced woman and a man trying to put his past to rest. They were simply a man and a woman, unknowingly in love.

Her bed was a sanctuary that engulfed them with its warmth. They continued their lovemaking there, wrapped in the great down duvet to keep them warm although no wrap was needed. Their actions had created enough heat between them to keep them warm for a very long time.

He kissed her shoulder as she spooned against him. "Good night, a stor," he whispered, and heard her chuckle. "What's so funny?"

"You. What does shtor mean?"

She was holding his arms about her waist, her hands clasped around his while they covered her breasts. He fingered her nipples softly.

"Ah, it's Gaelic. It means my treasure."

"And am I your treasure?" she asked into the darkness.

"Most definitely so," he assured her. "Now get some kip

because I'm going to put ye to work tomorrow."

"Kip?"

"Sleep."

"I'm going to be bilingual before much longer," she said, and he could hear the grin in her voice.

"That may be so," he said and then gave way to that certain euphoria that preceded sleep.

Lying beside him, Laura wondered how she was going to give up this man that had made such an impact on her life in such a short period of time. She wanted to stay with him forever in this fairytale existence but her head wouldn't let her. It was still in protection mode.

Why had everything happened? Why had it been Hank that had fallen into her living room that night? Why had they screwed like rabbits on the floor? She'd never done anything like that before in her life!

And then there was the trip back to his cabin. She'd never been inside it but had seen it from some of the hiking and snowshoeing she and Erik had done. She remembered his remarks when they came across it the first time as it was nearing completion. "Looks like a goddammed hippy haven," he'd remarked. Outwardly, she had mumbled unintelligibly because she really didn't agree. She thought it rustic, yes, but also very magical. There had been a purpose to its design and it fit into the forest. No, blended into the forest, the way none of the other homes did, and certainly not theirs with its huge picture windows that went from the floor to the ceiling above the loft and the light pine finishing inside and out. His cabin, she reflected, could be missed entirely if you didn't know it was there. It was private. Cute even. Kind of like a fairytale cottage in the woods.

There it was again, the thought that this was all a fairytale and would soon end. Oh, they had another day or two in which to indulge their fantasy but after that it would be back to business as usual. And then what?

She was just falling into sleep when Hank shot up into a sitting position.

"Fuck!" he exclaimed. "Oh Jaysus, no," he mumbled as he grabbed his clothes from the end of the bed where he'd tossed them earlier and started pulling them on.

"What's the matter?" Laura was alarmed; this wasn't the man she'd come to know. She'd never seen him so agitated. "Hank, what's up?"

"I didn't dampen the feckin' fire. I didn't secure the screen before I left. Something's been bugging me and I just figured out what it was."

"But it's surely okay. I mean, it's not like it was roaring or anything. And it's pitch dark out there. It's too dangerous to be heading out now, it's almost three o'clock."

"I'm sorry it is to leave ye but I have to check on it. And Figaro doesn't know how to answer a phone."

She had to smile at that. "Do you want company?"

"Nah, you stay and keep warm. I'll be back before ye know it."

"I think I should tag along. Just in case."

"Just in case?"

She nodded and scrambled to get dressed.

***

They flew through the night on the snowmobile, following the roadbed the long way around because Hank knew there wouldn't be any deadfall to worry about, nothing obstructing their passageway as he went, as fast as he'd dared with Laura behind him. He hadn't wanted her to come, hadn't wanted to be responsible for her if she fell off again because this time there would be no lovemaking in the middle of a snow bank. He was worried and knew he had every right to be. He'd been foolish, had forgotten his one main rule before leaving the house which was always to secure the fireplace first. Normally he wouldn't have left a fire going and would just rely on the backup furnace to stop things from freezing but she'd wanted to get home and there was a chance they could have dug her car out before midnight.

Or so he'd thought.

If he'd spent a minute thinking about that instead of getting back into her pants…

He could smell it before he saw the glow and knew they were too late. The front of the building, when they finally pulled up the roadway to his front yard, was fully engulfed, the window where he'd last seen Figaro, completely blown out.

A great sorrow overcame him when he thought of the cat. Had he made it out of his little escape hatch? For as much as Figaro was an indoor cat, Hank always left a window cranked open just enough should Figaro want a taste of freedom. But that window had been at the front…

He got off the snowmobile, put his head in his hands, and tried to stem the tears he wanted to cry. There was nothing to be done.

"Figaro!" he called into the night but it was hard for his voice to be heard over the roar of the fire.

Laura got off the snowmobile and stood behind Hank. She had never seen anyone in such pain, such abject misery as he cried for his cat. She didn't doubt he was upset about the house but the cat was what he seemed most upset about and she couldn't blame him.

She felt awful, herself. If she hadn't wanted to go right then and there; if she hadn't insisted on leaving in such a hurry. But she'd been scared of getting too attached to an ideal she had no right to possess, too afraid the fantasyland she'd begun to believe in would disintegrate before her eyes; and sadly, that seemed to be what was happening.

She couldn't ask him to take her back, to make this all go away, so she crouched down in the snow beside him and waited for the fire to abate. She wasn't cold. The heat could be felt where they were.

Eventually, Hank stood up and looked around for something, she didn't know what, until he found it and picked it up. It was a shovel, and he moved with a determination toward the house, shovel in hand, picking up snow as he went and hurling it through the broken window to hear it hiss and crackle, some of it evaporating before it even reached the house. And then he began running toward the back of the building, Laura hot on his heels. She didn't know why he was going back there but she had a sinking feeling it wouldn't be good.

She reached the back corner just as she saw him boot the back door in. A dark shape flew into the snow between his legs as he made to enter and he swung around, all sadness seeming to have disappeared from his voice as he cried into the darkness, "Figaro!" He chased after the cat but it had gone, taking refuge in the snowy night away from the flames. "Figaro!" he called again but Laura grabbed his arm and hung on.

"Don't chase him," she cautioned breathlessly, "he's already scared. He'll come back when he's calm, when it's lighter out."

Hank stopped, seeming to see the wisdom of what she was saying. "Alright," he nodded. "I'd best get back to firefighting then, hadn't I."

Laura shook her head. "There's nothing you can do. No tiny snow shovel can hurl enough snow inside there to stop the flames. It would be madness to try."

He thought about it, was ready to hurl more snow into the opened back door where black smoke was billowing out but then let the shovel tip rest as he leaned on the end. "Right ye are, then," he agreed, his head hung low in defeat. "Still, it's hard to see everything I've worked for all these years go up in flames because I was too stupid to remember one simple rule."

Shaking her head, she had to disagree. "It was me. My

fault. If I hadn't insisted on going right away, you would have remembered what you needed to do."

"No sense us blaming ourselves. Things happen for a reason, or so my mam always told me. Thing is, I can't quite see the reason for this."

He was upset, still trying to hold back tears, but at least he knew Figaro hadn't died in the fire. The cat was out there, hiding until it was safe to come out. She had no doubt they'd find him as long as some wild predator didn't get to him first. She took Hank's arm and led him back around to the front of the building where they watched the fire eat away at his life's work until there was nothing left but glowing embers, smoking ash, and the great stone fireplace, blackened and exposed to the cold dawn.

Chapter Twelve

They must have fallen asleep inside their cocoon of tarp they'd pulled from the shed and the snow that had fallen over them, because the next thing Hank knew was that Figaro was there, rubbing his soft, furry cheek along Hank's jaw. The stubble must have felt good to the cat because he was quite insistent on keeping it up, augmenting it with his curious purr-meow combination.

Automatically Hank's arm went around the orange beast, stroked his fur and hugged him close, grateful he had returned. He swallowed past the sudden thickness in his throat and ignored the stray hair that was intent on entering his nostril. Count your blessings, he was always taught, and if his cat being alive and restored to him wasn't a blessing, then surely they didn't exist at all.

Figaro purred his pleasure although Hank wasn't sure if it was because he'd freed him from a burning house or the cat's stomach was ringing the breakfast bell.

There was a shifting in the snow beside him and he glanced down to see Laura open her eyes just as a glop of snow dropped onto her half-opened eye. She blinked and shook it away, much as she had shaken off her fear of the fire. She had been so brave, so right in telling him not to chase after the cat, and then she'd led him away to a safe distance and knelt down in the snow with him to watch the fire finish its job. With all the snow around, it was clear the fire wasn't going to ignite the surrounding trees. It would have to thaw them first, and that only after all the snow was melted off. As hot as the fire was, trees farther away still had branches heavily laden with no sign of losing that cover yet.

They'd eventually scrounged around the shed, which was unaffected by the fire, and found some tarps to lay on the ground and cover themselves with. There hadn't been any wind, fortunately, but snow had begun to fall again and all they could do was sit and watch as Hank's lifework burned, dark ashes softly floating down, the embers still alight among the white flakes of snow. It was like a battle between good and evil. Good would eventually win out. The fire would die off, evil would be vanquished, but Hank would have lost everything.

Laura eyed the cat in Hank's arms and reached a gloved hand up to stroked the coarse fur, now rougher from being slightly scorched. Her head was leaning on Hank's shoulder, using him as a pillow. He didn't seem to mind.

"Do you think Figaro will stay inside my coat if I put him there?" she asked. "We should get back to my place so you can phone your insurance company and get something to eat. And maybe some dry clothes, too."

He laughed but there was little joy in it. "I'm afraid there wasn't much insurance on the cabin, just the bare minimum. I'd have to check the policy to see if I'm even covered for this. Oh, wait. I can't check my policy. It's in there." He indicated the smoking hunk of ash in front of them with the jut of his chin. "Humph. Well then, a call to the insurance company is surely in need. But as for dry clothes? Well, I suppose I could run around in your fluffy pink robe again while my things are in the dryer." He cast her an impish grin but she missed it, gazing as she was at the house, or rather, what was left of it.

"Yeah. I guess all your clothing went up with it, eh." At least he'd put on a different jacket to take her home with, she thought, noting the newer one he now sported, missing the tears and rents in the other one caused by his narrow escape from his truck.

They pried themselves from their cozy cocoon, dusting off the new snow as they stood. Luckily, it hadn't snowed a whole lot more, she thought, trying to see something positive in the midst of the bleak landscape before them.

"Here," he said, handing a placid Figaro over to Laura, who plucked the cat from Hank's arms and tucked him inside her coat. He squirmed at first but when Hank started the snowmobile, the cat ducked his head down in fright and Laura pulled the zipper up as high as she could.

The journey back to Laura's was slow but steady. As on their race to the cabin, Hank took the roadway and followed his previous tracks, only just visible in the new light of day. By the time they reached Laura's home, the old ones had been filled in; but as daylight now flooded the area, there was no need for worry.

They parked at the rear of her home. Laura got off the snowmobile, her arms holding the lump of a cat against her body as she walked up the back stairs into the house. Hank followed close behind. "I'll bet he's hungry," she said once inside, putting the cat down to explore his new surroundings. "I think I have some canned salmon and some canned tuna in the pantry. They had a case lot sale at the grocery store last month and I jumped on it. You know how expensive that stuff normally is," she said, rolling her eyes.

Hank nodded, watching Figaro as the cat sniffed at every little nook and cranny. "I think I can guarantee ye won't have to worry about rodents while he's here."

Laura glanced at the cat, who looked up with an inquisitive expression of his own and meowed hungrily.

She opened the can of tuna and dumped the contents into a small bowl. Figaro's nose was in it before she could empty the can and she caught the smirk on Hank's face before she could put the bowl on the floor. "What?"

"I'm just thinking that Figaro has never had it so good,"

he remarked, laughing as the cat purred his pleasure while downing the tuna in the bowl.

"Here," she said to Hank as she handed him another small bowl. "Fill this with water for him."

"Oh, right," he said, still chuckling. "Now you're really going to spoil him. I often just leave a little water in the sink for him. It makes him think he's still a hunter."

Laura tossed him a look that said that wasn't going to happen, and was satisfied when Hank did as she asked. Training had begun, she thought, and then suddenly stopped herself.

What had she been thinking! Training? Wasn't that what happened when a man and woman got married? They trained each other to adapt? To get along? It wasn't a case of making each other into something else, but to learn how to live together by taking the other's needs into consideration. Is that what she wanted?

"Would ye mind if I used your disposable razor in the shower? I feel a tad itchy and the need to scrape this hair off my face is getting the better of me."

The question was enough to shake Laura from her thoughts as Figaro downed his food. "Yeah, sure," she answered, "but take a new one from the package in the drawer. You don't need to sacrifice your face completely in order to shave."

She watched him go, casting her a wry smile before he climbed the stairs to the loft and the bedroom and bathroom beyond.

***

Hank found what he needed and disrobed, turned the shower on, and stepped into the hot water. It felt so good after being hunkered down in the snow all night. The sight of his home being consumed by fire washed from his mind under the steady flow from the tap although his soul still had trouble taking it all in. The home he'd built for himself was truly gone.

And then the tears came. Tears. He was actually crying. He'd put more love and sweat into that cabin than he'd put into anything in his life. It was his home, his haven, and he'd lost it all. First his truck, then his cell phone, and now his home. That was three, wasn't it? Didn't things happen in three's?

He heard the shower door open, turned in time to see Laura join him, opening her arms, welcoming his wet, tortured soul into her keeping. He stood beneath the hot shower and let her naked beauty comfort him, wash him, massage his tired muscles, and in the end, lead him from the shower to her bed. They made love slowly, or rather, she made love to him in a soothing, nurturing way, using the physicality of her body to relax his mind enough that he could sleep.

Her hands were like magic, rubbing the muscles of his back and neck as she sat on his bum. The feel of something warm and moist lined the length of his spine and he realized it was her tongue, gently touching, almost tickling as it moved and touched each vertebra. Other sensations, her nipples grazing his skin lightly as she moved, her fingers playing a tune along his ribs, ignited his senses and prodded his libido. He was harder than he thought possible.

She slid lower, massaged the cheeks of his butt, spreading his arse wide as she did so before leaning down to lick the base of his balls. Cool air brushed past, raising gooseflesh at the base of his spine. He wanted so badly to roll over and take her then but she wouldn't allow it. A nip on the cool flesh of his butt cheek was followed by her chuckle, throaty and warm.

Proficient hands pulled at his shoulder and he rolled at her prompt. She sat on his stomach, his penis lined against her back, wanting more than she was giving at the moment.

Sliding backward, she eased over his stiff flute and settled the length of it there in the moist cleft between her legs, rocking lightly back and forth, back and forth.

Hank closed his eyes and gritted his teeth against the powerful sensations that were nearly his undoing.

Burnished tresses tickled his nose as she rolled her tongue around one flat nipple, raising it to a little peak, stiff and moist from her mouth. The same treatment was given to the other and Hank shifted his pelvis and felt more of the moisture that leaked from her body, coating him, enticing him.

She rocked her pelvis against him, shifting her body to enclose his flute like a hotdog in a bun, covered in her juices, ready to eat.

He couldn't take any more, and before she could object, he grasped her hips firmly, tilted his body, and entered her swiftly, hearing her gasp of pleasure as she tossed back her tangled mane, damp and wavy from the shower. Spikes of pleasure coursed rapidly up and down his spine, curled into his balls, and propelled his upward thrusts.

Laura was breathing heavily herself, nostrils flared, mouth slightly opened, lips wet as her tongue quickly swiped them before pressing them together as if in pain. But it wasn't pain, it was the intense pleasure she was showing, pleasure mimicked in Hank's body.

A few more thrusts and Laura cried out, gasping her climax as Hank thrust roughly into her. Her inner walls gripped him with a ferocity of madness and then he joined her, held her pelvis against his groin as his seed pulsed deep inside. It was the most intense pleasure he'd ever known and he embraced her as she slumped over him, still breathing deeply as her body rhythm slowed from its heightened state.

He kissed her forehead where it lay cradled against him and felt her sag into sleep. His cock was still imbedded in her warmth, they were still joined, still one. Her breathing evened and he knew she'd fallen asleep on top of him.

Raising his hand to stroke her hair, he felt the damp ends on her cheek and removed them, laying the hair down her back before lifting the covers over them both. Then he, too, succumbed to sleep, not waking until the sun was slanted low through the great front windows.

Hank opened his eyes to see Laura still asleep, now beside him, her breathing steady, eyes blinking in some sort of dream. An abrupt jolt to the bed heralded Figaro's arrival, walking up the length of Hank's body, purring his happiness and contentment against his master's shaved chin. Hank stroked the cat, felt the heat-singed fur, the tips of the hair crusty instead of smooth. It had been close for this poor cat, a cat that hadn't the best start in life. But Hank had recognized a fellow stray, taken him in, and given him the best life he could.

And almost lost him. But, he admonished himself, Figaro was safe, and so was he. What was that about blessings? No more sad thoughts. No regrets. Only move forward. Life was a series of ups and downs and this had definitely been in the down classification. But no more. It was going to go up from here on in.

He sighed to himself and stroked Figaro's fur.

"Prrr-ow?" said the cat, half purr, half meow, and Hank couldn't help but chuckle. If only people had the same kind of resilience.

Laura stirred in the bed beside him, rolled over, and opened her eyes. Figaro jumped down, did his combined purr-meow again, and trotted out the door. "Is he hungry, do you think?" she asked in her sleep-roughened voice.

Hank shook his head. "No. It hasn't been so long since he ate, and to be truthful, the amount of tuna in his stomach should keep him for another day at least." And then, "Did ye sleep well?"

She nodded, stretched long, shapely limbs, both upper and lower, and let out a stifled yawn. "I don't think I ever want to get out of bed. It's so warm and so comfy."

"I know what ye mean." He eyed her for a moment, took in her relaxed state, her sleep-filled eyes and the tousled head of gold-red hair, and knew in that moment he was irrevocably in love. If she wouldn't have him, he'd have to end his life because it wouldn't be worth living without her.

"What?" she asked, in the same tone she'd used against the cat earlier.

Just then Figaro jumped on the bed, came between them and nudged them both alternatively, obviously wanting something.

"Clot-heid," muttered Hank.

"What?" she asked for the third time that day.

"Oh, I think yon moggie wants to pee. Ye don't have a litter box and he's needing to do something, to be sure."

"That poor cat!" exclaimed Laura. "But wait a minute. I never saw a litter box at your place. What did he do?"

Grinning, Hank answered, "He's toilet trained."

The look on Laura's face showed her surprise.

"I couldn't let him get eaten by wildlife just trying to do his business so I made up my mind I'd see he was civilized."

"You toilet trained him?"

"Oh yeah," he answered, nodding his head. "But I noticed ye keep yer toilet lids down, so mayhap it's what he's caterwaulin' about."

She hesitated as if she was thinking, and then, "Does he flush, too?"

Hank shook his head, his lips pursed in regret. "Nah. I tried, but he just didn't get it." With that, he threw back the covers, completely confident in his nudity, and walked into the en suite to lift the toilet lid.

As Laura lay in the bed, one arm beneath her head, the other holding the covers above her breasts, a sudden thought popped into her head. "How on earth did that cat end up with a name like Figaro? I mean, I thought that an Irishman would give the cat an Irish name, you know, like Seamus, Sean, or even Paddy. But Figaro? I remember you said something about naming him, but Figaro? Really?"

Hank crawled back into bed and snuggled up to his lover's warm, silky skin. "Ah, he told me, don't ye know?"

"No, I don't know and I think you're stringing a tale."

"Ah well, if ye must know, a neighbor I had at the time says she asked him his name, he told her, and she told me. And I swear that's the truth, so help me God." He made the sign of the cross, then reached out and pulled her to him. "So now me wee moggie's got his basic needs seen to, how about seein' to mine?"

"Really?" she asked. "You want do to that now?"

"I do, don't you?"

"You know I do," she breathed softly, closing her eyes to the onslaught of his mouth against hers. "Mm," she said as he spread her legs and eased himself into her. "Mm, don't stop."

Chapter Thirteen

It was late. The sun had gone down and they'd turned the television off after watching the late-night news. The weather forecast of clear skies to come was a relief, although they could tell the snow was still falling, however lightly.

After they had arisen from their cocoon, Laura had called her neighbor and best friend, Sarah, to get a report of how things were in town. Sarah, living across the hall in the same condo, had said that the roads were now clear but there was a buildup of snow not seen before in anyone's lifetime. She promised to keep an eye on Laura's place until her return. The news had come on shortly after that and there they were, still wide awake; they'd slept all day.

Outside, dark spots against the windowpane revealed themselves as spikey splotches of moisture from the glow of the overhead outdoor light. Through the great windows, past the snow-covered ledge and the mountain of snow on the deck, they watched the white stuff drift down, silent against the night-black sky. It was a magical view.

Lying on the couch, snuggled together in the quiet house, they could hear Figaro's purr, crouched as he was on the armrest by Hank's feet, half asleep. Laura was embraced along the length of Hank's body, her leggy limbs entwined with his. His arm was around her, his hand cupping her breast, his fingers lightly stroking her nipple to attention.

He didn't want to broach the subject but it was necessary.

In the world of yesterday, before the fire, he wouldn't have had to worry about it. It would never have come up. But this was now, he had no place to live, and he suddenly felt like a freeloader at Laura's.

"We need to talk," he said, and at his words, the spell was broken.

Laura looked up at him, her beautiful green-gold eyes stormy with questions.

He didn't waste time on trivialities. "I'm going to have to make some phone calls, get ahold of my buddy, Greg, and see if I can't bunk in with him for a while at his place."

She loved the way he said "place" as if it was "pless" and then opened her mouth, a protest on her lips, the word "but" not quite out before he continued. "I can't stay here, Laura; I need to be in town. I've no wheels, no way to get around until I either get my truck fixed or find another one." He would have said he could get a new one, but new wasn't in his budget. Until he heard from the insurance company, not much was.

She sat up, pushing herself away from him. "Well, I have a place in town. It's a small apartment, but it's home. I'd have to take Figaro there, anyway. He can't stay up here by himself all week. You could stay there, too."

While he agreed with that assessment of Figaro's status, Hank had to make her understand. "It isn't about us being together as much as it is I don't want to feel like I'm taking advantage of you, of our relationship."

"But you'd be taking advantage of Greg, so why is it okay for you to do that with him but not with me?"

He grinned at her because she was being deliberately obtuse. He knew it. "Greg's a guy. He doesn't care if I throw my things on the floor or raid his refrigerator. If I piss him off, he'll tell me. If he wants me out, he'll tell me. Besides, he owes me. He won't turn a fellow bachelor away without a pot to pee in."

She giggled. He loved it when she did that because her boobs were like globes of jelly that bounced when she laughed, making him want to taste them right then and there. His eyes roved the valley between her breasts, contained in her bra and vee-necked shirt, as if he could will them out of there with a wish.

"So I'm good enough for your cat but not good enough for you?" She was still braced on her forearms on his chest, looking down at him with those gorgeous eyes.

"Ah, ye're baiting me, ye are. I'd take Figaro with me but Greg is allergic. And I don't think Figaro likes him much. At least, the last time Greg came to visit me at the cabin, Figaro growled at him and Greg had sneezing fits. I don't think it would work."

"Figaro growled? I didn't know cats did that."

"Oh yeah, they do. Makes the hair stand up on the back of yer head if it's aimed at ye."

"Well, I'm glad he likes me, then. I wouldn't want to be growled at."

She was quiet a moment and he could tell she was thinking.

"Spit it out. What's got yer knickers in a knot?"

"Well, I don't want you to take this the wrong way, but what guarantee have I got that you aren't going to leave me now that Figaro is going to be looked after? I like him, he's a really neat cat, but I don't want to be tied down to a pet. So what guarantee have I got that you aren't going to leave me high and dry if you can't rebuild, or you have to leave, or, or, or?" She gesticulated, with her hands an ongoing wave.

"Ah, darlin', don't ye know by now that I'd never do that? I take my responsibilities very seriously, whether it's the cat or someone in my life. I'd never turn my back, never just walk away. Besides, I'd be crazy to leave someone like you."

"Someone like me?"

"Oh, yeah. You're warm, wonderful, sexy, caring, everything a man could possibly want in a woman. Why would I want to leave you?"

She wanted to ask him then about Siobhan, wanted to ask why he'd left her. Wanted to know what all that was about but it wasn't her place. Besides, she didn't want forever. So why was she suddenly so insistent that he stay with her in town? Her own duplicitous feelings were driving her crazy. She wanted, she didn't want. And she had no idea what to do about it.

He seemed to know she needed some kind of reassurance because he pulled her back to him and held her head while he kissed her deeply, sensuously. "Oh, luv, you are the best thing that's ever happened to me. And in so many ways. I'd be dead if not for you. My soul would still be yearning for something unknown if not for you. But I want to do this right. I want to take the time to get to know you and have you get to know me. I want us both to be sure before we end up living together."

Living together? This wasn't about that kind of living together, was it? She'd thought they were just talking about house-sharing with benefits. A moment of panic struck but she pushed it aside. Maybe she had read him wrong?

"Oh." She laid her head back down on his chest. "I just don't want you to go yet," she mumbled into his shirt.

"I don't particularly want to go, either; but yesterday afternoon, you couldn't seem to wait to get away from me and now you want me to stay. You need to be certain with your heart what it is you want."

"It's my fault. If I hadn't been in such a hurry to get back here, your cabin would still be there and we wouldn't be having this conversation."

"It's not your fault, darlin', and maybe not mine either except that I didn't take all the precautions I should have. It just happened. But stuff is just stuff and we're all okay, including Figaro. That's all that matters. I can rebuild, and some day I will, when I get back on my feet. Anyway, if I'm at Greg's I can do all the running around I need to. He's right in the heart of where I need to be. I don't have a truck just now. I don't know if it's drivable, or if it ever will be. There's so much I have to do and I don't know where to start. Ah, fa-a-awk," he swore, in a frustrated, pain-filled, drawn-out manner.

"What's the matter?"

"Nothin'."

She heard the roughness in his voice, sounding so close to breaking. So she didn't say anything, just put her arms around him and held him. It seemed to settle him as she felt him take a deep breath, relax a little, and kiss the top of her head.

Laura could have fallen asleep, snuggled into his chest the way she was. At times like this, it was as if she could meld her body with his, as if the lines between them could blur and become one.

He'd almost cried. She could feel it, just as she'd known when she'd stepped into the shower this morning with him. He wasn't the type to give in to his emotions, but to lose everything in the space of a couple of days had to be hard on a person. The only thing he had was his snowmobile and his cat. And the clothing on his back, she amended.

Everything else was gone. Even his bobcat that could have been used to clear her driveway was too damaged by the fire to be of use. It had been parked alongside the house where flames reached out, licked, tasted, and then consumed it in an explosive fuel-fed conflagration, leaving nothing behind but a burned-out hulk.

If he had owned anything of value, anything he'd brought from Ireland with him and left in the house, it was gone. All those things that anchored a person, gave their life a bit of color and meaning, were all gone. He would be left with his memories and that would have to do him for a lifetime because there was no rewind button and nothing but ash-covered ground to go back to.

She wanted him to stay and never leave but he'd been adamant. At first, she fought him and didn't understand why she had. This wasn't forever. He hadn't said anything about forever, but then he was talking about living together. Wasn't that akin to marriage?

Marriage? No. Not for her. Never again. She'd enjoy Hank for the time it was good but as soon as it began to sour, she'd be done and they'd part ways. And so maybe it was a good idea for Hank to be at Greg's, even though she had a place in town, too. Her place would have been cramped, because like his buddy's place, her apartment had only one bedroom. But they would share the bed, her mind argued. Even so, she countered, Hank had a presence that would make that tiny space seem crowded, and in reality, she needed to get back to earth, to discover if any of this was real because right now, it was still the fairytale.

Hank wouldn't disappear, she knew. She wouldn't be left holding the bag, or his cat. Instinct told her to believe what he said. Besides, he needed to get things done, see about his house insurance and get his truck fixed so he had wheels. She knew all that without having to be told.

And speaking of wheels, she'd still need to get hers dug out; but for the meantime, they were still here, still together, and the fairytale hadn't ended yet.

Her hand found the bulge in his pants of its own accord, as if it were on autopilot. She felt the bulge grow, harden beneath her touch, and realized she was smiling.

He responded by shifting his body beneath her, which she then took full advantage of. Her hands felt the waistline of his jeans, located the snap, and popped it open before slowly sliding the zipper down over his flute.

She'd laughed the first time she heard him call it that before he explained it was a bit of Irish slang that he used every now and then. The analogy of putting her mouth on his flute and playing him like an instrument was exactly what she

113

had in mind and she slid lower to do just that.

The velvety tip she sought was exposed enough for her to lick and watch it react. She did it again, giggled, if for no other reason than she thought it fun to watch it do that, and then as she exposed the length of him, she opened her mouth and took him in.

He inhaled beneath her and moaned his pleasure, used his hands to push his jeans past his hips. She stopped long enough to help him remove them all the way and then stripped her t-shirt off and removed her bra. The glow from the fire in the gas fireplace was all the light they had but it was all they needed. They had no fear of being seen, even though the windows were floor to ceiling. The snow was too deep, piled too high, and they were the only ones on the mountain. Add to that the fact it was almost midnight. No, they were completely alone.

As soon as she stripped herself down, she pushed him back on the sofa, noticed he'd removed his shirt while she had divested herself of her jeans and panties. They were both nude, both eager for the moment at hand.

She bent to take him in her mouth again but he'd somehow flipped her around and was stroking her butt hole with his finger, sending thrills down her spine and into the center of her core. His tongue touched her sweet spot, pushing deeply into the moisture that had gathered, and she nearly went wild with the sensation.

But it wasn't easy on the sofa. It was too narrow, too low, too…oh, she didn't know what, and so she stood, placed her hands on the back of the chair next to it, and felt him come up behind her, spread her butt cheeks, and stroke her with the tip of his penis. Her bum arched upward exposing her box as he slid inside and rode her hard. They seemed to both want it that way tonight, especially when he found her breasts, swaying in time to his thrusts, and held on, tweaking her nipples until she began to cry out her release. Then faster and harder he thrust until she felt her vaginal walls close around him, her knuckles gripping the chair back while he held her hips close and slammed into her, holding her there while his flute pulsed its music deep inside and her own heartbeat began to slow.

Her legs were shaky. If she didn't sit right now, she'd fall down; and he seemed to sense that so he hugged her from behind, his erection still inside her, and fell back onto the overstuffed pillows of the couch.

She had lost herself in him, she knew. Life would never be the same once he was gone and she suddenly felt like crying, because life wasn't fair. Just when you thought you had everything, you lost it, and for once she wanted the upper hand. It would be best if he left as he said he would, and go live with his buddy if Greg would have him. At least for a while. In the meantime, she'd keep Figaro. She never thought she'd ever own a cat, let alone enjoy one, but Figaro had grown on her. Besides, he was toilet trained.

They lay together, Hank hugging her, lightly stroking her breasts and abdomen as she lay atop him on her back. A slight movement between her legs signaled the moment when Hank's penis slipped from her body. This must be what it's like, she thought, to feel a baby slip from your body. It was a thought that had her wondering if she would ever know that feeling, and an emptiness washed over her that brought the sting of tears to her eyes.

"Got a tissue?" he asked.

Quickly swiping the moisture from her eyes with a casual swipe of her hand, she reached over to the side table where it was awkward for him to reach and pulled a couple out to hand to him. The awkward moment passed without Hank being any the wiser.

Hank held the tissue to her crotch until she took it before he cleaned himself up with a second one. That done, they remained entwined until she felt the chill of the room raise goose bumps across her body.

"C'mon, let's go upstairs," she said, sliding off him, but not really wanting to. It had been so comfortable.

"Do ye want a snack before we go up?"

"A snack? What did you have in mind?" It had been a while since they'd eaten and until he'd mentioned food, she hadn't been hungry. But now that he had…

"How about some cheese and crackers. I believe ye have a nice, tasty bottle of red to go with it. We may have a front-end loader here tomorrow to help clear up, we may not. In the meantime I think we should live while we can."

He grinned a Cheshire cat kind of grin that made his eyes sparkle with mischief so she nodded her assent. And while he uncorked the red to let it breathe, she pulled out the crackers and began slicing up a couple of different kinds of cheeses she had in the fridge. He disappeared up the stairs but then returned, just as she finished putting cheese slices on a plate.

Hank poured the wine, handed her a glass, saying, "sláinte mhaith," and then touched the rim of his glass to hers to drink deeply.

Laura sipped lightly, asking, "Shla-what?"

He repeated it slowly and made it sound like shlant-ye wa. "It means 'good health.' Just a silly Irish toast."

"It's not silly at all," she said, clinking her glass with his again and drinking deeper this time.

He picked up a piece of cheese off the plate and placed it into her mouth, then put his lips to hers, to run his tongue along the seam of her mouth as she chewed. She swallowed and opened her mouth to invite him in, felt his hand caress her bare thigh, and was aware of her nudity more than she had been earlier. "I don't think I've ever been naked in my kitchen before," she breathed after he'd kissed her well and thoroughly.

"Well, and ye should be more often," he replied. "Are ye warm enough?"

"I will be when we sit down together and polish off this feast."

"Let's take it to bed," he offered. "I'll feed ye and then we'll make mad, passionate love until dawn breaks."

"That's what I'm afraid of," she grinned, but really she was looking forward to every minute of it with him.

She followed him up the stairs, every muscle in his butt cheeks working as he took the stairs one at a time. Laura couldn't help it and leaned forward to plant a kiss on one cheek.

"Hey, no touching the merchandise," he quipped.

Temptation drew her closer but he evaded her teeth expertly, taking the last few steps quickly to place their feast on the bedside table and stay ahead of those gnashing teeth. Standing beside the bed, he gestured at the candlelit room.

Laura stopped mid-step and took the next two stairs into the room slowly, gazing about her at the glowing ambiance of so many lit candles. It was romantic, beautiful, and she couldn't hold back her indrawn breath, mouth rounded in an 'O' that expressed more than words could have.

He greeted her as if he were the host and she the guest, taking the wineglass and plate of cheese from her hands to put them with his glass next to the opened bottle of wine. Topping up her glass, he waited until she was settled in the bed and then followed her.

The room was beautiful, she thought. He'd made it into a romantic haven and it nearly brought tears to her eyes. How many more times would she take part in this ritual with him? She wanted him here, wanted this time to never end, but history had taught her better and she couldn't trust that he wouldn't turn out like Erik. After all, she'd thought Erik loved only her and no other but that had turned out to be a big lie. Her gut instinct told her that she could trust this handsome Irishman, that he was as true as his word. But he hadn't told her about Siobhan and she was too afraid to ask, too afraid that her fairytale would end.

A piece of cheese was being offered and she took it, then

took the wine he offered her as well. Sipping deeply of the crimson liquid, she felt the full-bodied wine slide down her throat and help her forget that this wasn't forever.

Hank knew something was troubling Laura but he didn't know what. It could be that she didn't want him here, or that she didn't want him to leave. He didn't know which way the wind blew. But he was here, and she seemed to like that, so for now, he was going to give her everything she could possibly want. That thought had propelled him upstairs while she prepared the cheese and crackers, and found and lit absolutely every candle there was. It turned out she had quite a few!

He placed his half-finished glass on the bedside table and set his hand on Laura's breast. Her skin was so soft, the nipple responsive as he began to play with it. She drained her glass and lay back, arms and legs akimbo, inviting him in a way he'd become accustomed to, to do what he wanted with her.

He pressed his lips lightly to hers, tasted the wine she'd just sipped, and ran his tongue along the seam of her lips. Gently, he urged her mouth open, delighted when she met his tongue with hers, felt the spearing of her fingers through his hair to hold him close.

Hank disengaged his lips, lightly kissed her mouth, and moved to plant kisses down her chin and along her jawline to her ear, where he took her lobe with its small golden earring, and tugged it gently before kissing it and leaving it behind. His mouth traveled down her neck to the hollow of her throat, where he lapped up the moisture that had formed there. His hands slid along her silk-soft skin, down to her hip to cup her buttock and caress the cheek where it joined her leg. His fingertips brushed the entry to her box and he heard her indrawn breath of pleasure.

Her nipples were puckered into little peaks from his touch, so he leaned over and kissed each one, spending time licking around them, suckling them, hearing her sighs as she became aroused again. Slowly, he made his way down her torso, laving and kissing as he went, spending time to tickle her belly button, run his fingers along the insides of her thighs, driving her to wriggle beneath his touch.

He wanted to go slow, to truly make love to her and not just leave them both satisfied. Hank wanted more for his angel of mercy, his treasure, and the Gaelic words formed suddenly in his mind as if reminding him of his roots. A stor. No, more like mo stor. She was much more to him than just a simple treasure. She was his and he wanted her to feel through his touch how much he loved her; how committed he was to her. She seemed to be afraid, although of what he wasn't certain. Maybe it was something left over from that scum of a husband she'd had; but whatever it was, he wanted to eradicate it, for now and for always.

He slid down the bed, spread her legs, kissed the inside of her thighs, then ran his tongue along the muscle, felt it stretch beneath his touch as she widened her legs, inviting him in. Her box glistened with moisture and he dipped his tongue into her nectar, felt himself grow harder and ached deep within his nads with wanting her.

Still he held off, placed his hands beneath her bum and spread her nether lips with his thumbs. Dipping his finger into the moisture that fairly dripped from her, he slid it to her butt hole, and eased the tip inside.

She raised her hips, pleaded with him as his tongue worked on her hardened nub. Her gasps were in accompaniment to her hands, reaching for him, wanting to pull him in; but he wasn't done quite yet.

Flipping her languid body over, he ran his tongue up her backside, massaging her buttock muscles and pushing her back to the bed when she would have risen on knees to allow him entry. His fingers gently massaged the muscles along her spine, around her neck, and across her shoulders before cupping her breasts to massage her there, too. Then down her back again, along her sides, the inside of her hips, chuckling when she squirmed because he was tickling her. And then along her legs to her feet, massaging the soles, kissing them when he was done and rolling her onto her back once again.

Creeping up from her toes, he laved, kissed, and massaged his way until he raised her knees to part them, exposing her box for him to lap at her juices once again.

Laura was wild with need. Hank had never taken such time before and while he had never been in a hurry to finish, he was certainly prolonging the foreplay. If he didn't take her soon, she was going to scream.

Laura's heart was racing. She wanted him inside, wanted to feel his erection as far as he could go. She wanted him buried to the hilt, to feel him take her hard all the way. And yet she was enjoying this, too, this sensual act where he was playing her body like a cherished instrument. Everything he'd done and was doing, all of it was like a symphony and she was the violin to his bow.

He played her well, knew just how to bring her along and hold her without giving her release, and then build her up again until he had her at the apex of her need. Oh, he knew how to drive her wild and she loved him all the more for it.

And then just when she thought she couldn't take any more, he slid his flute inside her and the symphony was complete. Yet still gently he rode her, let the pressure build within her and had her panting out her desire once again. She was so wet she wondered how they stayed together but Hank had her firmly in his grip.

He was so hard. Laura could feel him pressing against her core at the height of their pasion but she was so engulfed in her own pleasure, so over the top with her own climax that she almost missed the pulsating beat of his flute. Hank was emptying himself within her, taking his own release. He captured her mouth once again, thrust his tongue inside in an almost desperate rush to keep them on the high that seemed to have no limits. Stars exploded, the universe shattered, and they flew amongst the sparks they'd left behind, gently floating, languorous.

And then crashed back to earth when the telephone rang.

Chapter Fourteen

Laura slammed the receiver back into its cradle and covered her face with her hands, willing the tears not to come, but come they did. Before she realized it, she was sobbing uncontrollably.

Hank was there immediately, holding her, cradling her body with his long arms, showering her with kisses, calling her his love and some Irish words she had no knowledge of, only that they were terms of endearment. They had to be.

"What did he say?"

She didn't have to ask how he knew it was her ex-husband that had called. She was beginning to know that Hank sometimes just knew things and to leave it at that. "He said he saw us in the window. He called me names. Called us names. Horrible names. He said he had pictures and was going to share them on social media."

"Pictures? How the hell could he have pictures? We'd very little light in here and the cabin is too high up, the snow piled too high for anyone to get any kind of a shot."

He was still holding her, still caressing her back. It was comfortable, soothing. "You think he's bluffing?" Hope was a fleeting thought but it was all she had.

She could feel his head move in some sort of motion, though positive or negative, she wasn't sure.

A sigh escaped Hank's lips. "I don't know if he is or isn't but we can't fall into his trap, whatever it is. Did he want anything or was the call just to harass ye?"

Laura pulled away a little and peered into Hank's deep blue eyes, so full of concern for her. "He's only done this once or twice before, and it's usually just meant to piss me off. But this...he must know you're here with me. How would he know that?"

Hank thought a moment. "It's not a big town. Word spreads and the folks that clear the mountain road would know that you and I are the only ones up here. They know we're stranded and maybe even by now know my house burned down. It's a logical conclusion that ye'd give me shelter. You're too kindhearted not to. And he's bettin' on that's what ye did."

"You don't think he's really out there?"

"Maybe. If he's the kind of gligeen I think he is, I wouldn't put it past him. But I wouldn't worry me head over it, either. He'll do what he's gonna do and we'll just weather it." He shuffled back into the middle of the bed and pulled her close once again. "C'mere to me, luv," he said quietly.

Laura curled into Hank's embrace and dried her tears. He had touched her deeply with his body, with his heart, with his love, even though he'd never said the words. He'd told her they'd face whatever Erik had to throw at them together. He wouldn't abandon her.

Sniffing again she said, "What you did before…it was just so beautiful. No one has ever made me feel like that. Ever."

He held her close, kissed the top of her head, and rubbed his hand lightly across her back. "No one has ever brought those feelings out in me or made me feel like I could conquer the world, darlin'. No one. Until you."

She tucked his words away in her heart but she couldn't be satisfied yet. Not until the last devil in the closet was banished. "Who is Siobhan?"

She could have kicked herself for asking because immediately the mood in the room changed, became less intimate.

He sighed heavily and pushed the pillow so his head was partly raised. "I guess ye've a right to know but it's not what ye think."

"I'm sorry, I shouldn't pry."

"Nah, it's okay. Really. Siobhan is someone I knew long ago in Ireland. We had a thing for a bit but we were too young to know what we were about. I thought I fancied her and that it was returned, but after I left, I realized there'd been nothing there. We were just kids, plain and simple. And anyway, I'd fallen for a Canadian girl I'd taken on a tour through my work, and Siobhan knew that. It didn't stop her from trying to hang on, though.

"So, fast forward a few years to about three years ago. I got a phone call from her. Said she'd been looking for me and had something to tell me. She said I was a father to her daughter and it'd been okay up to then because she had a job but then the job ended and she couldn't get another one. The girl was sick and needed medicine and she didn't have enough money for that and food and rent. I know what it's like. There was never enough money for my mam to keep us in food and rent both. So sometimes we went without just to keep the roof over our heads."

"That sounds awful," Laura said, relieved that he wasn't involved with anyone else, "but you believe her about the girl? That you're her father?"

"I don't know. We had sex, but I used protection. And she would have had plenty of time to tell me before I left with Amy. The timing seems a bit off. Possible, but off."

"Did you have a DNA test done?"

"No, but she sent me a photo once. The girl looks a little like me, same dark hair and blue eyes, but that could be hundreds of kids in Kerry. The county is full of them."

"So she wants money for someone who may or may not be your child." Laura's professional mind was swinging into gear. "We could ask for a DNA sample and have it sent here and then do a match. It's one way to rule a relationship out."

"Oh, sure, that can be done. I suppose I should have had it done long ago but I really didn't think she was serious."

"Serious?"

"About taking me to court."

"Court? She's talking about taking you to court after, what…fourteen, fifteen years?"

"Close to it, yeah."

"I don't know much of anything about international law but I'd say it was a bit of a stretch. At any rate, you wouldn't have to worry until a DNA test was done. That would be a place to start." She was calmer now, focused on him rather than herself. Somehow, Erik's malicious call seemed a trifle in the face of Hank's problem.

Or what she thought of as Hank's problem. Something in her mind told her it might end up involving herself as well but it was vague, like an unseen mosquito on a hot summer night buzzing around your head without landing.

"Don't fash yerself about it. It's no matter at the moment. We've a lot of night left and I've got a lovely woman in my arms that I wouldn't trade for all the tea in China."

"You like tea that much?" she asked.

"Ah, yer a wicked wee thing, y'are, but I'll take ye anyway. Ye've bewitched me, ye have, sure and that's the truth."

"I love it when you go all Irish on me," she yawned. Stretching, she aligned herself along his body, felt his muscles relax and unconsciously rubbed her hand along his pecs. His chest was bare of hair and she curled her fingers around his nipples, massaging and enjoying the feel of him beneath her touch. If they hadn't just finished making love, she'd want to plunge in all over again; but the truth was, she was suddenly tired and wanted nothing more than to sleep.

Hank seemed to sense her mood and pulled the covers up from where they'd pushed them, enfolded her in his arms, and reached over to turn the light off. "Oiche mhaith agus codladh sámh."

"Mm," she mumbled. "I'm not sure what that means but I can guess."

"Well, no twenty questions, aye? It just means goodnight, and sleep well. I forgot to add, mo chroi."

"Mm. You, too." A smile crept along her lips, the feeling inside of her was a warm blanket and she hugged him tighter as she felt herself drift off, enveloped in his arms.

Hank held Laura close, felt her relax into sleep, and wondered for the millionth time since that fateful night how he'd ever lived without her. He loved her with a fierceness that brought out the Celtic warrior in him; wanting to protect her, shelter her from any and every storm.

He pondered their future, wondered how he could convince her of his honesty, his sincerity, and still banish the threat that Siobhan seemed to present. Was the child really his? Because if she was, then he had to step up to the plate, support her, and give her whatever he could to sustain and nurture her; give her some sort of future, although how he was supposed to do that and rebuild his life after the fire was a mystery to him. He still had only a vague idea of what his house insurance would pay and while it was a start, it would take a long time to rebuild.

Rome wasn't built in a day, he reminded himself of the old adage, and neither was his original home. It had taken him a full summer to do just the chimney alone, working after hours and on weekends, or those times when he was between jobs. The walls took another full year of building during his leisure times, the interior took another after that. Three years had gone into the building of his home, three years of working all hours, camping out until he had a roof on and then moving in so he could finish the interior. And though it was sometimes difficult to live on the mountain full time, the peace it brought him had never failed to revive him when he felt the trials of life close in on him.

And then Laura and her ex had built their cabin, putting it up in the space of one season. Hank sometimes had friends come and help with his own construction but it was nothing like the crew that built Laura's home. He'd drive by it, sometimes stop to admire it and have a quick word with one of the workers, and always, if she was outside, return the wave she'd send his way. They almost never spoke and in truth, if her husband was about, he wouldn't stop, just keep on driving to his own place farther on.

And then came the day he realized Laura was single. He was at the bar when he overheard someone talking about it, and he realized that, somewhere inside of him, a decision had been made. What he hadn't banked on was the guts needed to put a decision like that into play. What was he supposed to do? Walk up to her door and ask her out? They never seemed to meet otherwise, never walked in the same circle, and so he quit going to the bar every week, quit talking to every woman who turned his head, just stopped what he was doing and put all his concentration on how he would approach Laura and convince her that he was good enough to date her.

Money. Did it all come down to that?

He had only a basic income, dependent on when he had a contract; and at times, like recently, work was lucrative and so he had a good nest egg in the bank. But when there wasn't work to be had, the bills could pile up, and there were always bills. A part of him wondered if Laura would want him if she knew how broke he often felt, even though his bank account was proof he was doing okay.

He heard Laura sigh in his arms, felt her relax into his body as if she was a part of him, and truly, at this moment, he knew she was. She was his heart, his soul, and he knew with a certainty that he would never give her up, never let her go. Somehow he'd make her see the love they shared and convince her to stay with him. Forever.

And Siobhan? He'd figure that out later.

Taking his cue from Laura, he too sighed out his tension and fell deeply asleep.

Chapter Fifteen

Laura wasn't sure what woke her first, the beep-beep-beep of the back-up warning or the sound of the equipment itself. It was Wednesday, another day where she was supposed to be at work and unable to get there. Well, at least she'd been unable. She'd have to see what equipment was out there and were they just doing the road or had Hank's buddy shown up?

She felt a stirring and then Hank's warm breath by her ear, his lips kissing her gently as he mumbled his good morning.

She was lying on her side, spooned into him, and so she reached up and cupped the back of his head before running her fingers along his whisker-roughened cheek. "Mm, to you too," she smiled.

His hand had found the spot between her legs and Laura knew instantly that he'd found moisture there. She lifted one leg higher, felt the hard length of him jutting against her and the velvety tip with its own moisture at the entrance to its destination. And then he was sliding into her, slowly, all the while caressing her breasts, her nipples, kissing the spot behind her ear. She felt herself become aroused and shifted her butt so that he had greater access.

"Darlin'," he whispered into her ear as he moved to play with her little love button. Her breathing grew deeper, her breath came in little pants of pleasure, and when she felt she couldn't stand it any longer, her climax overtook her and Hank's body grew rigid behind her. She knew he'd waited for her, held off until she came so they could do it together. It had been such a soft, gentle loving. Much like the man himself.

They lay sated, listening to the beep-beep, before Hank finally disengaged.

"Don't get up," she pleaded, holding onto his arm as he lay wrapped around her. "Please. Don't get up."

Hank understood what she meant. This idyllic time they'd shared, the last few days of being snowed in and cut off from the world, was about to end. Had ended, if he correctly judged the meaning of the sounds coming from outside. He was as loath as she to end their tryst but the old saying of all good things coming to an end was never more apt than now. Besides, nature was calling. "I'd love to stay wi' ye like this for the rest o' my days, luv, but I seem to have a case of 'TB'."

That seemed to get Laura's attention and she opened her eyes wide. "What?"

"TB. Tiny bladder. I've got to go."

Reluctantly she loosened her grip on his arm but not before she cupped his nads and squeezed hard.

"Watch it, or I might just go here and now," he joked, pulling away from her.

"Well, serves you right for deserting me."

"Ah, darlin', if it weren't for our friends outside, I'd be jumpin' back into bed with ye right quick but I'm afraid we've no time for more shenanigans right now."

A banging on the door had Laura scrambling out of bed and throwing on her fluffy pink bathrobe. For a bit more coverage, she grabbed some plaid flannel pj pants from the drawer and quickly drew them on, stumbling as she went. Suitably attired, at least for this early in the morning, she ran downstairs and opened the door.

And then it dawned on her…someone had been able to reach the door!

A roguish grin on the fellow that greeted her on the other side of the door could only be one person.

"You must be Greg," she guessed.

"At your service. You must be Laura." He pulled off a heavy mitt to shake her hand.

"C'mon in," she invited, at a loss to say or do anything else.

"Thanks," answered Greg, pulling his mitts off and dragging his toque from his head. He had a full head of rusty-brown, curly hair that fairly sprang forth from its confinement.

Laura grinned. "I'm just about to put some coffee on. Wanna join us?"

"Uh, thanks. Maybe in a bit. Is Hank around?"

"Yeah, Hank is around," that man announced, doing up his fly as he waltzed down the stairs to greet his friend. If there had been any doubt in Greg's mind that the two had been intimate, it was now banished for good. Hank had a look on his face, still unshaven, that was akin to a cat finishing the cream. Still managing to look sleep-tousled, he shook his friend's hand vigorously.

"Ye're a sight for sore eyes, that ye are," he said, grinning the grin that had the effect of weakening Laura's knees. She was sure he didn't mean to show Greg that same grin she always likened to the forerunner of a certain activity when he was feeling particularly playful. But to Greg, it seemed, the grin was a shared code between them. Like long-lost friends, they carried on as if it had been years instead of mere days since they'd last seen each other.

"So the car is directly beneath the carport then?"

Hank nodded. "If ye get close to that, I can start peeling it away by hand."

Greg nodded, and with a quick wave to Laura, donned his toque over his wild hair, slipped on his mitts, and was out the door.

"Coffee?" she asked Hank, as the last of the water gurgled its way through the coffeemaker. She was glad for the foresight of making it the night before and setting the automatic timer.

"Of course. I'd love some. Gotta put something in my gullet before I do any heavy work out there."

Handing him a cup, she asked, "So he's close to the carport?"

Nodding, Hank answered, "He is. Come and see for yerself. He's done quite a bit up to now. I have a few minutes before I need to go out and begin shoveling the hard-packed stuff away from the entrance to the carport."

Thinking a minute, Laura said, "There's a door to the carport at the rear of the house. There's a nearly full-sized basement down there. You could access that and dig out, maybe meet Greg halfway?"

Hank gave her a look that seemed to ask why she hadn't mentioned it before. Laura just smiled, shrugged, and asked, "Do you have time for some breakfast?"

Twenty minutes later, with a bit of food in his gut and the warmth of the coffee to fuel him up, Hank began the arduous task of digging a hole toward the driveway. He was more intent on seeing how far he had to go than anything else because the wall of snow was not straight up and down. It was more like a volcano of snow that had slid beneath the carport, building up until it had filled the opening entirely. It took Hank the better part of an hour to carve a hole forward to where it broke through to the sunshine beyond, reminding him eerily of the tunnel he'd had to crawl through not so long ago. Hank felt relieved on seeing the sun, banishing his unpleasant memory, and from where Hank's digging had pushed through, Greg scooped away, now having a better idea of where the car was in relation to everything else. Hank was certain that although Greg's business was auto repair, this was one car he didn't want to have to fix. So, steadily, bit by bit, the carport was cleared, the SUV visible for the first time in days and a one-lane drive with a mountain of snow on either side of it now existing between the house and the main road.

"Wow," was all Laura could say when she looked out the window a couple of hours later. She'd finally called in to work and found out that no one was expecting her until the next day. Good, she thought, because it would take her the rest of the day to sort things out, do a laundry, and get back to reality.

The end of the fairytale was well and truly nigh.

Dressed respectably in jeans and a t-shirt, and with her face washed and her hair tied back, she wondered if she could ever get her feelings in check. However, she didn't have time to ponder them just then as Greg's footsteps could be heard on the front stairs, rendering the knock on her door redundant. Laura had a fresh pot of coffee waiting for him and a full meal. Hank, emerging from the carport up the back stairs had barely washed down a couple of pieces of toast and a splash of coffee before heading down to shovel it out and they both looked like they could use some food. In total, they'd been at it for a good three hours, maybe more.

Laura brought out the platter of fresh pancakes, bacon, and toast, poured orange juice into glasses, and with a nod, bade them sit and dive in. And dive in they did, eating as if it was their first meal in days.

"The City said they'll be up as soon as they can to finish the road up to your place," Greg said to Hank between mouthfuls. "They had a few unexpected delays, but as soon as they're cleared up, they'll be free to head up the mountain again. It's the biggest snowfall in March on record, and they're hoping it's over. Anyway, they'll be clearing out your truck soon, so I can get it into the shop and see what can be done. Once it's out of the way, they'll be able to clear the rest of the way to your cabin. Should be a piece of cake," he finished up with a swig of coffee.

Laura looked at Hank whose face had suddenly taken on the look of someone who was just remembering what they'd lost. And in reality, he was. "No rush for the road to my place," he began. Greg's expression was a cross between a cheeky retort and embarrassment at thinking what he was thinking, because Laura knew with a look that he figured Hank was moving in with her. "My place burned down."

Greg's face fell. Instantly. Whatever he'd been thinking before went out the window as he suddenly dropped his fork onto his plate with a loud clatter of metal on china. "What? When?"

"Night before last. I was bringing Laura home...we'd gone to make sure Figaro was okay and I was bringing her back here in case she could get out to go to work the next day and when I went back, the whole place was lit up like a bonfire. It was only lucky that Figaro got out. I would never have forgiven myself if he hadn't." At the mention of the big orange cat's name, Figaro rubbed against Hank's leg and did his meow-purr combination, sounding more like "pprrow," than anything else.

"Christ," muttered Greg. And then looking down, noticed the cat as if for the first time. "It all makes sense now. Jesus. Lucky thing you were here," he said, his eyes glancing at Laura.

"Yeah," she answered, sipping her coffee and thinking she wished she'd laced it with Bailey's. "I almost didn't come up this weekend because I'd heard we could have a big snow, but I didn't think it was going to be this big," she commented.

"Well, we'll see what we can do to get your truck fixed. I don't know about your house, though," said Greg, shaking his head.

"Ah, that's what I've been wanting to talk to ye about," said Hank. "I was hopin' ye'd let me stay with ye in town for a bit. Figaro is goin' to camp out with Laura but I'd be very appreciative if I could lay my head on yer couch."

Greg smirked. "Yeah, I guess you could use my couch. Gonna have to put up with the mess, though," he joked.

"I'll just add to it, if that's okay? Only I don't know how long..."

Greg jumped in before Hank could finish. "Don't worry about it. We'll get 'er done. Mi casa es su casa." He aimed a look at Laura that had a definite question in it but she wasn't up to answering.

Hank nodded, tight-lipped, and Laura knew he was choked up. It meant a lot, she could tell, that Greg would welcome him so easily because she was sure it hadn't been easy for Hank to ask.

"I can take you when I go back to town," she offered, not sure when that would be, tonight or tomorrow morning. Usually she'd go back on a Sunday night but things were so different right now.

Hank nodded. "It's not like I've a great deal to pack. Mostly the clothes on my back. I need to get to the insurance company, see what I can get for my house, and then go buy some clothes. I can't keep wearing the same things, day in and day out."

"Why not?" asked Greg with a twinkle in his eye, "isn't that what you usually do?"

It was the first time they'd laughed since the fire and it felt good, Laura thought.

A sneeze brought them back to the moment and Greg's eyes began to water. "Time to get back to work, I guess," he joked as Laura handed him a tissue.

"Pprrow," said Figaro, rubbing the length of his body against Greg's leg.

"Achoo!" Greg sneezed again as Figaro wandered off, tail in the air.

Hank saw his friend to the door while Laura began to clear up the dishes.

"She has a place in town, y'know," Greg said quietly to Hank. "You don't want to stay with her instead?"

Hank shook his head. Laura was running water in the kitchen and they kept their voices low. "It isn't right. We've already had an incident with her ex. I don't want to give him more fuel to make her life miserable."

Greg shook his head. "That asshole. Everyone knows he's been screwing just about anything on two legs. Don't know why the ladies flock to him, but they do."

"Yeah, well, mayhap they're not ladies then," Hank said, grinning.

"What did the shit-head do?" asked Greg, referring to Hank's mention of an incident.

"Ah, he phoned last night. Said he had photos of us and was going to post them on social media."

"Photos? Of…?"

"Do I have to spell it out for ye, man?"

"Uh, no. But photos here? In this place? That's almost impossible."

"Mayhap I'll be talkin' to him soon," Hank drawled.

"Right. I'll back you up," offered Greg.

"No. It won't be fisticuffs. Least ways, I'm not out for that. But he will leave her alone afterward."

"Still, call if you need me. But I'd best get back to town. See you later."

They waved at the door and Hank turned back to see that Laura had finished the dishes and was just wiping the table. It was such a domestic scene, her in the kitchen, him at the door. He could imagine himself coming in after a hard day at work to see her standing there, ready to welcome him with her arms and her body. It was enough to make tears start at the back of his eyes because he couldn't remember loving someone so much it hurt to think you couldn't spend every minute of the day and night with them.

Laura looked up and met his eyes, her smile across her face broadened, and as she put the damp cloth back in the sink, Hank came up behind her and wrapped his arms around her. "Mo stor," he began, "mo chroi…is tú moghrá." And then his mouth came down over hers and he kissed her with everything he had. Pulling her close he felt her breasts, those globes of pleasure, press up against him, felt his flute swell with wanting, and wondered if she wanted it, too.

"Mm," she sighed into his mouth. "I'd love to, right now, but we need to get organized for later. I think we should get back into town before dark, if possible."

He let her fall from his grasp and tucked an errant lock behind her ear. Her hair was falling out of its tie.

Nodding, he agreed. "Right ye are, then. We need to organize." He wasn't sure what he needed to organize, having very little with him, but he knew she would have things to do. He followed her back up the stairs to gather things for the laundry she had mentioned, and to do whatever else needed doing. As agreed on, they would be leaving before nightfall.

Chapter Sixteen

Laura lay in bed in her apartment, listening to the sounds of cars driving by, a sound she'd never really noticed before. The silence of the cabin and Hank's presence there had somehow made her feel like she'd been on vacation and she felt very alone in her bed, even though Figaro was curled up beside her. The big orange tabby had taken over the apartment immediately, claiming a spot on the back of the sofa beneath the window that overlooked the park across the street. The small balcony afforded some entertainment as the birds began to return from their winter away and feed on the tray of seeds Laura had put out for them.

For now though, Figaro was asleep, breathing deeply, almost snoring, and Laura stroked his coarse orange fur, wondering why the texture differed so much from the very soft white fur beneath his chin. Figaro stretched and snorted at her stroking before returning to deep slumber.

She couldn't sleep. Her mind kept thinking of Hank, and every time it did, she'd remember how he'd touch her, and her body would respond with wanting him like she'd never wanted anyone else. He had become an addiction she was having a hard time controlling.

The day at the cabin had gone quickly after Greg left. They'd changed the sheets on the bed, done two loads of laundry and swept the cabin from top to bottom. Although she'd wanted nothing more than to jump Hank's bones, she kept to a timetable, and when three o'clock rolled around, suggested it was time to leave.

Hank hadn't said anything, just helped her pack a few things into the SUV and then donned his winter gear. Picking up Figaro on their way out the door, they got into the car and left for town.

The first thing Hank did when they arrived at her place was to secure Figaro against his chest. The cat hadn't seen or heard traffic since he was a kitten and Hank told Laura that he was worried Figaro would become frightened and run off. So they exited the car park quickly and rode up the elevator to her apartment on the eleventh floor. Once inside, she shut the door and Hank put Figaro down. "I'll go get the other things from the car, now that I know where yer flat is, and I'll be right back up."

"Okay, I'll see that Figaro settles in okay and that the toilet seat is up." He'd met her eyes with a grin.

She was just stepping into the kitchen when she heard a knock on her door and went to answer it, thinking that Hank couldn't be back that quickly. Opening it, she said, "Well that didn't take long," and was surprised to see not Hank, but her neighbor and very good friend, Sarah.

"What didn't take long?" asked Sarah.

"Oh, nothing, it's just that I was expecting someone else," she said and felt herself blush.

"Okay, come on, you can tell me. It must be a guy."

Laura looked at Sarah, the Chinese slant to her eyes crinkled in mischief, bared, slender arms folded beneath her breasts. The outfit she was wearing was definitely something to be worn while going out. "Speaking of guys, you look you're going out to meet someone."

Sarah shook her head. "Nah, just getting out for a bit. Wondered if you wanted to come along. Fiona and I are going to go guy-hunting, see if there's any prospects. You up for it?"

"Up for what?" Neither had seen Hank exit the elevator and come up to where they were chatting.

Sarah, startled, looked at Hank and the eyes that widened in surprise took on a different look as she assessed the man now standing beside her. "Well, I guess that answers that question!" She laughed with a "See you later," and went back to her apartment across the hall.

"Who was that?" asked Hank in way of conversation as he unloaded their luggage from the car. One large duffle bag carried everything Laura needed, and since Hank had nothing, there was nothing else to bring.

"That was Sarah Chan. She's my neighbor, as you can see," indicating the door across the hall with a nod of her head, "and is one of my best friends. She was inviting me out to go prowling but I honestly didn't feel like it."

"Oh. I can go, if you'd like to go out. It's alright, I can just go over to Greg's."

"No, um, stay for dinner?" she asked, and was pleased to see his nod.

It had felt a little awkward, as if neither knew their place. At the cabin, things had been on an equal footing, an idyllic tryst where both had one goal in mind. But here, where life intruded, the rules had changed and neither seemed to understand how to go forward.

***

Dinner was a simple affair. Laura pulled out some frozen spaghetti sauce she'd conjured up a few weeks before for one of those "instant" dinners after a long day at work. Hank hadn't seemed to mind, powering into a full-sized plate with a gusto she was becoming accustomed to. But there had been no wine in the house to accompany the meal, so they'd toasted their arrival in town with a glass of water instead.

Afterward, Hank helped to clear the dishes, which were rinsed and put into the dishwasher, and then suddenly, he was at the door.

"You're leaving? Already?" Had the longing in her voice shown through? She'd meant to keep things light but the truth was, she felt close to tears.

"I think so. I should get over to Greg's before it gets late and I've also to pick up some cat food for Figaro. He can't exist on tuna, it's too dear."

She agreed on that. Tuna was an expensive dish to be feeding a cat every day and she didn't think it was the healthiest for him, either. Didn't cats need some sort of balanced meal?

But…she couldn't resist. "You don't want to stay, just a little longer?"

He stepped toward her then and put his arms around her waist but didn't pull her close. "If I stayed a little longer, I'd never leave. And ye need yer sleep. Ye've a work day tomorrow and I've a million things to wrap my head around yet."

"When will I see you again?"

He smiled, that handsome, Irish smile that lit up his whole face and made his eyes sparkle. "Ah, darlin', ye'll be seeing me tomorrow when I bring Figaro his food. What time are you home after work?"

"Five thirty. I'll be here by five thirty."

He kissed her then, lightly, but with a passion she felt all the way to her toes. He'd pulled away slowly and she tucked her head into his chest. "I wish you would stay," she whispered.

"I need to go," was all he answered before turning at the door and leaving her feeling empty. "I'll see you tomorrow, though," he promised with a wink.

Laura shut the door behind him and then felt the tears come.

It was crazy, crying for him when she'd see him again tomorrow. He was going to bring Figaro some food. He wouldn't abandon her.

Lying in bed, remembering the evening as if it were a video playing through her head, she thought how unsettled she'd felt, as if something wasn't right. How could that be when things at the cabin had been so perfect? Was it really just a fling, a time out of time with no meaning beyond enjoying themselves? Had Hank not wanted to stay because their mini-vacation was over? He'd said that if he stayed, he'd never leave, so wasn't that a good thing?

She tossed and turned in her bed, her thoughts like fireworks exploding in her brain. Every time she thought she got one thing sorted out, another appeared; and they all revolved around Hank. The trouble was, she didn't know how he felt about her, although he said some pretty nice things, mostly in Gaelic. But the one he'd translated was nice, so maybe the others were too? She knew she had feelings for him, deep feelings. Or she thought she did. Now that she was back in town, she wasn't sure about anything. Why did things have to change just because the location did? Was any of it real?

Eventually she fell asleep, dreaming of Hank and waking at six to reach for him, to make love before getting up, only to feel the empty spot beside her. Even Figaro had left during the night, likely to go explore his new surroundings some more.

***

Work had progressed as normal, although people were curious about how she fared while being stranded on the mountain. Convincing them easily that she was never worried, they soon left her to her work. But all day long she could see the glances her way, and although no one had asked, they all knew Hank had been stranded up there with her.

Finally, during the afternoon coffee break, the question was asked.

"I was really glad I was there for him," she'd answered. "He was caught in a small avalanche and had to crawl out of his truck by tunneling through to the surface. It must have been scary, not to mention cold." She had purposely left out most of the story, leaving them to fill in the details on their own and keeping it simply to the fact they each knew the other was there if they needed help.

As for the fire that they all now knew about, Laura felt easier about giving them details. Details of how they sat all night and watched it burn and were still there when the cat returned after getting over his fright, and how lucky it was for them all. She kept the snippets of how they came to be there to herself.

The end of the day couldn't come fast enough for Laura, and true to her word, she arrived home at five thirty after a quick stop at both the grocery store and the liquor store. She was hoping Hank would stay for supper and enjoy the fish she'd bought along with the nice light white to go with it.

***

He was dead tired. He hadn't slept much on Greg's couch, although it seemed comfortable enough. But he kept envisioning Laura and had spent most of the night dealing with a hard-on. He'd finally got up in the deepest part of the night, gone to the loo, and relieved himself of it. Stumbling back to the couch, he had at last fallen asleep, however fitfully.

Greg rose early to get to the garage, even though it was just downstairs. He was hoping to get Hank's truck pulled out and see what damage the avalanche had done. He didn't own a body shop, but if there was something mechanical that needed fixing, he'd do it. He said goodbye to Hank while Hank was on his second cup of coffee, waiting for the time when the cell phone shop would open. He hated being out of touch, but once the shop opened and he could get in, he recalled the look on the clerk's face when he explained what had happened to his other phone. And no, he had said to her unspoken question, he didn't have the phone with him. It was presumably still in the truck in a million pieces.

Eventually he walked out with a new phone and a few messages that had come through on his email while he was out of touch. He was about to scroll through them when he noticed he had a voice mail.

As soon as he heard the voice, he knew who had called. Siobhan's accent and the angry tone to her voice came through quite clearly. It was enough to make him want to throw the new phone through the nearest window.

Rather than call her back, he decided to think on what he had to do first. The insurance company was only doors away, so he went there to see what he could do about both his house and his truck.

"The good news is, your truck is covered. Whatever has to be done to it will be fixed. That includes body work as well as mechanical. Sorry about your phone, though. Unfortunately, that doesn't count as 'contents,' even though it was in your truck when it happened."

The insurance agent sported a wry grin and Hank had to concede she was trying. So, bad news was to follow.

"The bad news," said the pretty young thing before him, "is that you didn't have contents on your home policy. It was just the building itself."

It wouldn't be much to rebuild on, he reflected after leaving her office, but it was more than he had right now. Once the money came through, he'd be able to plan how to go forward. Rebuilding wasn't an option yet. He had to find a place to live that was affordable, buy some new clothes, and maybe rent a vehicle if he could. And as if his thoughts automatically turned to Laura, which they seemed to do these days, he had to go buy cat food and meet her at five thirty.

He glanced at his watch. Three o'clock. The mall was only a few blocks away. He could buy another pair of jeans, some t-shirts, and some socks and underwear, anything to make himself more presentable. Then he'd go back to Greg's to change and be at Laura's in time to meet her.

By five o'clock he was twiddling his thumbs, and the local establishment being only two blocks from Laura's apartment building, seemed a good place to hang out until he needed to meet her. No sense in standing around in front of her place, looking like a freeloader, even if he was dressed in clean clothes.

Sidling up to the bar, he ordered a pint and drank deeply of the pale ale set before him. It felt refreshingly good. He'd struck up a conversation with Linda, the bartender who liked to chat him up, when he saw her sigh, saw the smile leave her face, and noted the direction her gaze took. Following it, he saw Laura's ex walk through the door, case the place as if looking for a friend, and finding only Hank, walked over to join him at the bar.

Hank took a deep breath. It was going to take everything he had not to choke the man right here and now.

"Hank," said Erik, sitting down and ordering a pint for himself.

Hank nodded but said nothing, only took another mouthful of the draft that seemed suddenly to have lost all flavor.

"Hear you got caught up in the storm up the mountain," said the gligeen beside him.

"Mm-hm," answered Hank.

"Hear my ex rescued you."

"Is this leading somewhere? Because if it isn't, I'd just as soon finish up and leave."

"Seems you had yourself quite a good time up there the last few days."

Hank worked hard to not slam his pint back onto the bartop. "And what would ye be knowin' about what kind of time I had?" He didn't really want details but he was curious as to what Erik did or didn't know.

"Well, I heard they'd graded the road up there so I took a drive up. You know, curious. I mean, the road was clear, why wasn't she back here?"

"And were ye never concerned for her safety?"

"Safety? Why should I be?"

145

"Did ye never think that just because they'd got as far as her place that she still couldn't get the car out?"

Erik nodded at that. "Yeah, that's what I figured once I got there. But you know, it was such a nice cabin, I just had to look at it once again but realized I couldn't get to the front door. I tried following the snowmobile tracks around to the back but I kept punching through the snow and it was pretty deep. But I did get far enough to see what was going on. And it looked pretty intense."

"Did it now. And what would ye mean by that?"

"Oh, you know. You. Her. Doin' it."

"Really? That's interesting. I hear you got some photos. I wouldn't mind seein' them, you know, for my own sake."

"You think I'm stupid enough to show you?"

Hank shrugged. "Well, if it's on yer wee camera phone, I wouldn't suggest ye'd see much. They're probably quite dark, no one recognizable. Could be anybody, anywhere, is what I'm thinkin'."

"Well, believe me, they're recognizable."

"Oh, maybe to you, 'cause ye were there, as ye say. But I'm thinking that if ye ask yon barkeep what she thinks, I'm bettin' she'll not have any idea who they are or what they're doing. Are you a bettin' man, Erik? I've got fifty bucks on me that she can't tell ye who they are."

"And if I lose?"

"Then no sense in keeping the photos, hm? I'll watch while ye delete them. Three times."

"Three?"

Hank nodded. "Unless ye've got an older phone. At any rate, it'll be done and over with. Have we a deal?"

Erik seemed to be thinking too hard about it. Hank ordered him another drink.

A deep belch followed up Erik's last swallow as he drained his pint. To Hank's view, the man was on his way to becoming tipsy, but was he tipsy enough to be swayed? He tried again.

"About those so-called photos," he began.

"They're real," said Erik, tight-lipped and looking thirsty.

Hank bought him another and peeked at his watch. Five thirty. He'd be late, and Laura would be wondering. Ah, but it couldn't be helped. He couldn't allow whatever photos Erik possessed to run the gamut on the net. He didn't care, for himself. They could photograph him nude; he really didn't care. But Laura was different. However open she was with sharing her body with him, Hank had no doubt she wouldn't be walking down a nude beach with ease any time soon.

Erik downed the third pint. He was about to slide off his stool when Hank noted the cell phone in his back pocket. Using a technique he thought he'd long since forgotten, he bumped Erik as that man got up to announce a trip to the toilet. Mumbling an apology, he set Erik back on his feet and watched as he wove his way shakily through the tables on his way to the washroom. Once the bathroom door swung closed, Hank wasted no time.

Luck was with him. Erik didn't have a password on his phone. Better yet, it was an older phone, easy to access, and he wasted no time in searching out the phone's photos, looking for what Erik had said were top-notch pictures.

Scrolling through the few that Hank saw, he realized that Erik was not a photographer. Some phones took decent photos. Phones like his new one, which was top-notch for photos. But an old one like this, that texted, had internet capabilities and got all his email, as well as a few other attributes, did not have photos as a forte. In fact, the photos were as Hank suspected. Blurry, dark, and although you really could see that two people were together, you couldn't actually tell what they were doing. Maybe they were wearing skintight clothing… maybe they were dancing. However you wanted to describe the pictures, you couldn't exactly say for sure what you saw.

He grinned. He hit the delete button. And then he deleted the deleted photos. Quickly scanning the sent portions of the email, he noted that no photos had been sent. Hoping that there were no photos secreted away in a cloud somewhere, he was happy to see that Erik was not a member of any social media that he could tell, but he didn't have time to check the browser. Flipping through the text messages in case a photo went that way, he noted a coke deal, the dealer's handle, and an address. Interesting, he thought.

A sixth sense made him look up to see Erik, out of the loo and feeling in his back pocket, likely looking for his missing phone. As the man turned around, looking around him at the floor and tables he'd wandered through on the way to the toilet, Hank quickly placed the phone on the floor beside the bar stool and returned to his pint. Draining it, he stood up, pulling out his wallet to pay the bill.

"Hey," said Erik, "where's my phone?"

Hank called on his years after his mam had died and he was looking for employment to help him now. Years when he sometimes had to do less than reputable things in order to survive. Putting on his most bland expression, he looked Erik square in the eye, noted the other man's bloodshot eyes and constant sniffing. It was confirmation that he not only had a beer-fetish but a drug habit as well. Perfect.

"I don't know what ye mean," he said easily, pulling bills out of his wallet to pay for the drinks.

"It was in my pocket. You must have taken it when you bumped me."

Hank hadn't bargained on him remembering that. "Yeah, well, we both got up to go to the loo at the same time. I decided to let ye go first."

"Why? There's more than one in there," he slurred, pointing to the washroom.

"Yeah, but I'm a private person, don't ye know. Especially when someone likes to put private photos of other people on their devices."

Erik snickered. "Yeah. So where's my phone?"

"How the hell should I know?" said Hank, zipping his jacket up.

The phone in question suddenly rang and Erik began the search, inadvertently stepping on it before locating it.

Hank hid the smirk he felt all the way to his toes. Poetic justice. He knew what that sound meant. Erik wouldn't be using that particular phone for a while. The sound of crunching glass was just a bit too loud to ignore.

"Well, looks like I won't be viewing those photos, so ye have my apologies, but I won't be paying ye for them. Ye're welcome for the pints." He started to leave but turned at the last second. "Oh, and while we're at it, I'd suggest ye leave yer ex alone and no more blackmail shots 'cause I've some blackmailing of my own to give ye. Ye ever go near her again and ye won't be gettin' a restrainin' order. I'll let yer dealer have at ye."

Erik looked blankly at Hank, as if he couldn't make sense of what had just been said. "Dealer?"

"Snake. Well known and as bad as they come. He'll have no trouble takin' the likes o' you out."

With that, Hank nodded and walked out the door, catching Linda, the bartender, wiping the bar where he'd sat, wearing a huge grin aimed his way, and then Erik, trying in vain to get his phone to work. And noting, with a wince, exactly when that man sliced his finger as he tried to swipe the broken glass.

Chapter Seventeen

It was a quarter past six. Hank wasn't coming. The fish had curled into little canoes in the oven and she'd already gone through half the wine. Pretty soon she'd finish it off, and not even Figaro's meows could make her feel better.

She'd been had. It was just lucky that she'd decided to give the cat a treat, just in case Hank was late, and bought him a specialty cat food.

Figaro had gobbled it up and was looking for more.

And now she was sitting, wine glass in hand, waiting for Hank to arrive at her door, knowing he wouldn't; knowing that despite what he said, he was like every other guy out there. Completely untrustworthy.

The knock on her door jolted her out of her brooding. The bit of wine that sloshed over her glass when she jumped was quickly licked from the rim and the tear that was threatening was likewise dispatched before it could fall.

Standing, she straightened her clothing and tried not to run to the door. It was only a few steps.

They felt like a mile.

Opening the door, she saw Hank on the other side, a faint odor of beer emanating from him and she took a step back. "I don't think I have to ask where you were," she commented.

"Oh, ye may be able to guess where I was but not the why or the wherefore."

Standing aside, she invited him in. "Do you want some wine? I think there's some left."

"Sure, I'll split the last of it with ye. But just in case there isn't enough, I've brought ye another, and a few posies as well." From behind his back he brought out what he'd been hiding: the bottle in the bag and the posies, as he'd termed them, a fully packed arrangement of spring flowers.

She didn't want to be appeased. She wanted to be angry. She'd determined that the fairytale was over and now just wanted to be done with it all. But she couldn't. The flowers were lovely. The bottle of wine, likely a godsend. She might need it later.

"Thank you," she said graciously, feeling at odds with herself and not sure what else to say. They were so unexpected. "I'll get a vase for the flowers if you would like to pour yourself a glass." She pointed to the counter where another glass stood waiting. And then, "How did you get in downstairs?"

"Yer Asian friend was goin' out," he replied, filling his glass and topping hers off. Once the flowers were in a vase and sending their delicate fragrance around the room, they went to sit by the window, Figaro between them on the back of the sofa.

"I'm sorry I'm late," he apologized.

"That's okay. You had a lot to do," she said, realizing it was likely true. Where did someone start to put their life back together and how long did that take? His home, his truck; it was a lot to lose.

"I'm sorry, truly I am. But something very interestin' happened and I think ye'll like what I have to tell ye."

He was excited, she could tell. There was that twinkle in his eye and that bit of a grin she had come to know so well as he spoke. He'd seemed so happy while they were at the cabin that it was almost always there. She'd been happy, too, she realized, something she hadn't been for a very long time.

His grin was infectious.

"Okay, spill it. What's got you so worked up?"

Hank settled in deeper on the couch, turning to sit facing her rather than just beside her. Taking a sip of the wine, or more like a gulp, she thought, he began.

"I ran into yer ex down at the pub."

If that was all that happened, Laura mused, and if that's all he had to tell, maybe she was right to want to end things now. "And?" she coached.

"And," he took up the tale once again, "I had a wee bet with him that I'd pay him fifty bucks for the pictures but he had to prove he had them, and," he stressed, "the barkeep had to be able to tell who they were."

That sparked Laura's attention and she turned to face Hank more fully. They were now face-to-face.

Figaro opened one yellow eye.

"Seems the barkeep at the pub likes me."

Laura raised her brow.

Hank smirked and shrugged and then continued. "Okay, so she's sweet on all the guys. But this time, I was the only one in there to begin with and I was in need of a little sustenance. I'd been to the insurance company and to the bank and bought some duds."

"Yes, I can see you've got new clothes on. They're nice," Laura offered, reaching a hand out to touch the flannel surface of his newest plaid shirt. And despite her earlier feelings, she couldn't help reaching up to finger the collar and let her hand slide smoothly down his chest.

Hank took her hand in his. "There's more, darlin'." Without relinquishing her hand, he went on. "When yer ex came in, he started in on a few things but we got on to the subject of the photos right quick."

"He actually has photos?" She tightened her grip on his hand and felt the reassuring pressure in return.

"Don't get ahead of my story, it's a good one for the tellin'."

Despite her worry over photos actually existing, Laura

grinned, fully taken in by Hank's charm.

"So as I said, we had a wee bet that yon barmaid couldn't tell who it was in the photos if he'd show them to her. But the wee bugger wasn't convinced, and as he was lookin' a bit thirsty, I bought him another pint. You know the man can drink like a fish?" At Laura's nod, he shook his head as if agreeing and continued, "Well, finally, with a total of three pints in him, he suddenly had to go to the loo and that's when I saw his phone in his back pocket. I merely bumped him, his phone fell into my hand like magic, and after I straightened him up, he toddled off to yon loo." He paused long enough to take another gulp of wine.

Laura thought he must think he had beer in his glass or been so into his own story that he'd forgotten he wasn't at the pub anymore.

"Luck had it that he had no password on his phone. Nothin'. So I found his photos, got a good look at them before deletin' them completely, and then searched his sent mail but didn't see anythin'. And I don't think he has an external backup like a cloud or anythin', so I'm fairly certain I got them all. But even so, there wasn't a thing you could see. It was too dark, a couple of figures standing together. Ye couldn't tell it was us or even what we were doin'. He really thought his phone could take good photos but it's older. And it can't. Especially now."

"What do you mean, 'especially now'?"

"He stepped on it. Much as I did my own phone that night of the avalanche when I was tryin' to get out of my truck."

"And how did he come to step on it? You're leaving things out," she said excitedly.

"Oh, yeah, well, I heard the loo door swing open and saw him reach for his phone in his back pocket, only to discover it wasn't there. As he was lookin' around by the loo door for it, I quickly put it on the floor where he'd been sittin'."

"And when he came back, he stepped on it," she finished for him.

Hank's grin was ear to ear.

"If that's the phone he had when we were together, then you're right: we have nothing to worry about. It didn't even take good photos in the daytime, let alone at night."

"Ah, well, he's going to have to get another one now. I don't think he can get the old one to work."She leaned over to kiss him and he kissed her back, full on, no hesitation. Maybe it was the beer he'd had, maybe the wine—and maybe for her, too. But he wasn't going to let his treasure slip away. Relieving her of her wine glass and placing it along side his on the small accent table before them, he pulled her to him, stretching out on her sofa, and realized it was too short.

"Let's do this right," he breathed into her ear, felt her head nod, and helped her to rise. Letting her lead the way, he followed her down the short hall to her bedroom.

A bed had never looked so inviting. Leaving the light off, he strode to the large window overlooking the park and the street below and shut the blinds, then pulled the curtains across. From the dark he said, "I'm not takin' any chances of being observed with you in my arms. Maybe a hussy from the wrong end o' town but not you, darlin'."

She walked into his arms, let him start to undress her, saying, "You wouldn't want just any old hussy anyway."

"Aye, ye're right there, ye are. Ye've spoiled me."

She pulled his shirt from his jeans, and he felt her hands caress his back. Putting his lips to her ear, he kissed and laved his way around to the front to capture her mouth once more. And all the while he was removing her garments until she stood naked before him. A last fumbling with his jeans and then he was stepping out of them, his flute ready for playing like only she could.

She didn't need to be told. Her hand cupped his nads, ran slowly up and down the rod of flesh that felt like it had never been so hard before. Then kneeling before him she licked the tip, and Hank nearly lost it right then.

Holding back with what felt like a Herculean effort, he sucked in a breath, afraid to let it out as she engulfed him. Her mouth, so warm, so wet, and him so hard. He allowed her a bit of play before he pulled her up before him. "If ye keep that up, there won't be any for later," he grinned.

Leading her to the bed, he pushed her down on her back and spread her legs. The bed was high and it put her at an almost perfect height for him to lean over and place his tongue between her nether lips.

She gasped her pleasure and Hank thrust his tongue all the way inside, drinking of her juices. He could feel her passion build and so he sucked on her while his hands found her nipples and worked at them as well. In moments, he had her writhing, pleading for release; and although he wanted to wait, to prolong their lovemaking, his body was too starved for her. Climbing on top, he claimed her mouth with his, thrust himself inside her, and rode her hard until she cried out her release. Holding back just long enough to make sure her climax was well and truly on, he followed her into it, relishing in the feel of her legs wrapped around him, enclosing him there, making him feel like he'd come home.

He was just about asleep with Laura still in his arms when he heard her say, "Maybe we should have something to eat."

Hank nuzzled his face into her neck, laying her gorgeous titian-colored hair aside. "I don't want to move," he mumbled.

"Me either, really. But I'm a bit hungry. Aren't you?" Just then her stomach protested loudly.

Hank pushed himself up on one elbow. "Alright then. I supposed we'd best come up with a game plan. How about I take you out?"

"Out?"

"Yeah, unless you're really in a mood to eat the dried-up bits in yer oven. The thought was there and I do appreciate it, and after seeing them, I feel bad I was so late. So, takin' you out is the only honorable thing to do."

"Hm, I guess you're right. They don't look very appetizing now."

"It's right sorry I am but Figaro will love them tomorrow," he said helpfully.

"Okay. Out to dinner it is. I'll let you decide where we should go."

"Well, if ye don't mind drivin', and as ye'd originally done fish, how about the seafood place across town?"

Laura nodded and forty minutes later they were ensconced at the restaurant with a table over-looking the garden at the back of the building where a view of the small lake could be seen in daylight. But night had long ago descended. Snow still covered the bushes and the only exception to the very black night was the bit of water, still open, in the middle of the lake, and a beam of moonlight that could be seen reflected off the black water.

"It's pretty, isn't it?" she said.

Hank nodded his answer. He needed to tell her about Siobhan and the latest he'd heard but just then the waiter came by, bringing the wine and going through the motions of the pouring, tasting, and pouring once again before setting the napkin-wrapped bottle in the cooler at their table, leaving them alone until the food arrived.

Lifting his glass toward her, Hank entoned, "Mo chuisle, mo chroi."

She lifted her glass, touched its rim with his, and asked, "What does that mean, really?"

Hank figured he wouldn't get away without telling her and he was not very good about lying, regardless of the many times he'd had to call on that skill in order to survive. "Mo chuisle is literally 'my pulse' but often used as my darling or my love, and mo chroi is 'my heart'."

She tried pronouncing it, "Muh kishla?" At his nod she continued, "And muh kree? I've heard you say that one before."

His teeth clenched, unsure if he should tell her what the two phrases meant when put together. Literal interpretation was only one part of it. Nodding his head, he smiled. "Ye said them fairly well. I may make a calaín out of ye yet."

"Colleen? Isn't that a name?"

"It is, but it's also Irish for a young girl."

"I'm not exactly young," she quipped, raising a finely arched brow and crinkling her mouth in a comedic fashion.

"Young is relative and you're certainly not in your dotage." The look on her face made him grin even more.

Laughing, Laura looked at her glass and chewed her lower lip, making Hank wonder what she was thinking. He took her hand in his, rubbed his thumb lightly across the knuckles of her fingers. She had beautiful hands, he thought. Her skin was soft along her fingers. He never wanted to let them go. "I'd like to tell ye what it means for me to say those things to you."

She met his eyes and he wasn't sure what he saw there. "If I say those things to ye together like I did, it's a wee bit stronger than liftin' me glass to you and sayin' cheers. It's a way of tellin' ye how I feel about ye and I'm a bit worried that I've said too much."

Those expressive eyes of hers seemed to shut down and Hank's mood sank into his toes. If he'd messed this up, he was going to go jump in yon lake.

She wouldn't meet his eyes and for a moment he thought he saw her begin to tear up but there was no time to investigate that thought because just then the food arrived. As the waiter laid out the food, topped up their wine glasses and left, Laura was once again under control and Hank thought better of continuing his previous chain of thoughts. Instead, he opened up with the message he'd received from Siobhan and noted the interest Laura showed in her expression. "She's serious about takin' me to court, I think."

"What exactly did she say?"

A jumble of thoughts ran through his brain as he tried to recall exactly what her voice mail had said. It hadn't been nice. She'd been downright threatening. Grinning, he said, "I guess I'd be arrested if I ever set foot in Ireland again." It was a bit scary, he thought, to think he'd be greeted at the airport with handcuffs, and although a part of him sensed it wasn't true, he didn't have any idea of how to go forward.

But Laura did. "That's just bullshit," she said, and Hank's eyes opened wide at such a comment from her. "Well it is, plain and simple. But I have an idea. One of our partners at work is Irish. Sort of."

"Sort of?"

"Well, I don't think he was born there but he's got a ton of relatives there and goes back frequently for holidays and such. Anyway, I'll talk to him in the morning and arrange to have you come by, say, around eleven? That'll give me time to make sure he's free and if it changes, I'll call you."

"Right. And what can he do? If I've already a price on my head…"

"You don't," she said. "She's only posturing. She wants something, likely your money, and she's willing to do anything to get it."

"But what if it really is my own child?"

That made her pause a minute but his confident lady was not to be stopped. "Then we'll figure that out when we find out. But I think you need to know if she is or isn't your child before anything else and that's what Kerry can do for you right away."

"What?"

"Don't be dense. He'll arrange for DNA testing."

Hank sat back and watched as Laura dove into her food as if she'd been half starved, and in a way, she must have been. It was after nine and they were just beginning to eat.

Deciding the wisest course was to follow her lead, Hank picked up a forkful of delicate fish, very unlike what was left in Laura's oven, and let the flavor take his mind off his troubles.

Bad enough he had Siobhan breathing down his neck, he was now unsure where he and Laura stood. Did the tears he had seen standing in her eyes indicate she was upset with his declaration earlier or sentimental?

He really didn't know.

Chapter Eighteen

The next morning, Hank found himself sitting in the office of one of Laura's colleagues, a usually high-priced attorney by the name of Kerry Gallagher. But, Laura had told him, Kerry was going to make an exception in Hank's case, saying they'd discuss the fee some other time.

"Gallagher? That's a good Irish name. There's lots in County Mayo, if I'm not mistaken." Hank took the hand offered and shook it heartily, happy to come into contact with a fellow countryman.

"Yes, that's correct. County Mayo, by way of New York, Montreal, Vancouver, and now here. It only took them a hundred and twenty years to do that," Kerry joked. "Seems to me I remember my grandfather saying the family first arrived in New York in 1895 or so and made their way to Canada, settling in Montreal for a time. Came out west in the '50s, looking for warmer weather, I expect."

Okay, so not necessarily a recent countryman but an Irishman for sure. "Well, I'm a wee bit fresher than that, out of Killarney, County Kerry, about fifteen years ago. And imagine that. Laura's set me up with an Irishman with the first name of Kerry. I feel like it's a good omen for me."

"Let's hope so," said Kerry as he shuffled some papers on his desk. "Now, can I get you a coffee or something before we start?"

"Ah, no, but thanks. I've already got one here," he held up the mug Laura had given him before he entered Kerry's office.

Kerry nodded. "Okay then. So, why don't we start by you telling me about the phone call? Laura said your ex-wife called to demand money?"

Hank straightened up, resettled into the chair as his eyes went wide. "Yes, I mean, no. It's not an ex-wife, it's an old girlfriend. And she says I'm the father of her daughter. But I doubt it because the timing is off. I can't see how it can be."

Again, Kerry nodded, taking notes while Hank talked. "Why don't you give me a history and we'll put together a time line of events. By the way, you wouldn't happen to have an address for her?"

"Oh, aye, I do. This is it here. And her phone number as well," he indicated with a nod as he handed over the information.

"Excellent." Kerry took the paper, jotted the numbers into the file on his computer, and then began asking Hank about his life in Ireland, where and when he'd met Siobhan, and how he came to Canada.

They spent the next hour going over Hank's history and anything that might have anything to do with Siobhan. When they were done and Hank had looked the notes over, he had to admit it was a fairly accurate representation from the time he and Siobhan got together and when he left for Canada. And the more he analyzed it, the more he felt he just couldn't be the girl's father. "Laura said we should ask for a paternity test. Can we do that?" Hank knew it could be done, but didn't know how to go about it.

"You bet," answered Kerry. "And that's exactly what I'm going to do. Except I'm going to demand that your ex-girlfriend also have a DNA test done."

The expression on Hank's face must have clearly said he hadn't a clue as to why that would be needed.

"I can see you've got questions already. All it means is that we're going to rule out any inconsistencies. With DNA from both parents, it'll be easier to prove paternity. Or, as in this case, disprove it."

"Oh. So ye want me to take it as well, then?" Hank had off-color thoughts of jacking off in the nearest loo, using skin scrapings, or pulling out his hair by the roots.

"I do. And how we proceed will depend on on what these tests uncover. This is the address of the lab here that will do it. Just have them send the invoice and the results to me. I'll have my secretary call over and arrange it for you. Whenever you can get there will be fine, but the sooner, the better."

"Alright. But, can ye answer me this…" He waited to catch Kerry's eye before continuing, "I was wondering what I have to do for this DNA test?"

"Ah, of course. No problem. It's just a swab in your mouth with a cotton-tipped swab. That's it. No pain. No discomfort. Just a swipe around the mouth to take cells from your mucosa and bingo, you're done."

"That's it?"

"That's it."

Hank breathed a sigh of relief. And a little of regret. The simplicity of the test took all the romance out of it.

The lawyer stood, straightened his jacket, and held out his hand, indicating the door. As Hank got to his feet, Kerry said, "It only takes three days or so for results to show so I'll get the lab in Ireland to send the results back to me as soon as possible. Why don't you come in on Monday? I may have something by then."

Nodding, Hank paused at the door, "Will she go along with it, do ye think?"

Running his hand across his ring of wavy, steel-gray hair that hugged the sides and back of his head, Kerry smiled and his eyes crinkled at the corners. "She will if she wants your money."

No sooner had Hank left Kerry's office than his cell phone rang, and seeing his buddy's number displayed, he answered it. Frowning slightly, he then became excited as the conversation continued. They'd hauled his truck out of the avalanche and were bringing it into town. In fact, Greg said over the phone, they were likely at the auto body shop now. The call concluded with Hank saying, "Great, I'll be right over."

He arrived at the body shop and stood, watching as the tow truck brought his truck into the bay. It was banged up, but for all that, Hank was happy to see it. As the tow dropped the truck on its front wheels amidst a cacophony of sounds, none of them very good, Hank sighed. While his truck had been able to be towed on its two rear wheels, it was clear most of the damage had occurred toward the front of the vehicle. The cab was bent inward at the roofline and the dents along the side were not limited to just the cab. The lip of the box was bent inward as well and other dents pock-marked the sides making it appear as if many of the chunks that hit it were rock instead of snow. The windshield was smashed, though still clinging precariously to the outer frame, and Hank could see the back window where he'd had to break it in order to free himself. It was heartbreaking to see his truck in such a sorry state.

The owner of the body shop greeted Hank. "I'm surprised you got outa that alive," he remarked, leaving Hank's side and peering at the undercarriage, shaking his head. Straightening up, he checked the inside of the box, looking at the rear window, or what was left of it. "I would not have thought a grown man could crawl through there."

"Ye would if yer life depended on it," remarked Hank with a wry grin. He knew, because that's what it had felt like. He had known that if he'd been unable to get out through the window, he would have died in there. It had been a close call.

"You want my honest opinion?" The mechanic pulled out a rag, wiped his hands on it, and stuffed it back into his pocket. The rag was such that Hank couldn't tell if he was adding dirt to the rag or wiping it onto his hands.

"I do." Prepared for the worst, Hank could only cross his fingers and hope.

"I think it can be fixed. That is to say, I don't think it's as bad as it looks. The frame looks like it made it through okay but I won't know until we check it fully. Could be it's mostly cosmetic. The reason it can't be driven right now is because the whole front cab is outta whack and the front axle is broken, but once we get that off, I'll have a better idea. Come into the office and I'll get your details."

"Before I do, can I just have a peek in the cab? I think my phone is still in there."

"Oh sure, I'll just be through there," he nodded to an open doorway at the back of the shop. "Come on in when you're ready."

Thanking the man, Hank approached his truck, feeling very much like he was at the bedside of a friend in hospital whose outcome was unknown. Maybe he'd recover, maybe he wouldn't.

A lump formed in his throat. It was the best truck he'd ever had. It was his first new vehicle, everything else having been used. It had a special meaning for him and so he touched the door handle gently and tried to open it.

It wouldn't budge.

Trying a second time with a firmer grip on the handle, he only succeeded in rattling the entire vehicle.

Sentimentality aside, he put both hands on it, swore at it in two different languages, added some French he'd learned along the way, put his boot on the truck next to the door, and reefed on it for all he was worth.

The door finally gave and opened wide, creaking its protest and allowing clumps of snow to tumble out. Hank's sunglasses followed and dropped to the floor of the shop, muddy and wet. He'd forgotten they were in the truck, tucked in the front pocket of the console. Lifting them to the light, he lightly wiped the grit and moisture from the lenses and was pleasantly surprised to see they weren't any worse for wear.

Okay, one positive thing just happened, he thought. Let's keep it rolling. It took him a while to locate his phone.

Previously unable to get the data from his old phone to put on the new one, he'd felt like he was starting all over again; but although the surface of the old phone was cracked, he thought that perhaps the cell phone place could retrieve some data from it. He thought about Erik's cell phone. The crunching of that phone seemed more pronounced than his own and then the thought came to him that if he were able to get something off his phone, perhaps Erik could, too. It was a daunting thought, especially since Hank knew that the old adage was true; nothing on the internet was ever truly gone, and while he didn't know if the photos Erik took ever made it that far, there was always the chance they still existed. Time would tell.

Pocketing his cell phone and sunglasses, and finding nothing more useful in the truck for the moment, he wandered in to the body shop office. Twenty minutes later, Hank left with the keys to a loaner vehicle in his hand, a little SUV that seemed to have seen better days. But, he realized once he got in it and started the engine, the thing had guts and power, which Hank was grateful for because he had one place in mind that he absolutely had to get to.

Wasting no time, he headed for home.

The two-hour drive up the mountain went by in a flash but the sun had already reached its zenith and Hank had no wish to drive back in the dark in an unfamiliar vehicle. It would be enough to satisfy himself with a quick peek to see if anything was left after the fire. He and Laura hadn't got back to it after that final vigil.

Pulling into the end of the driveway, he saw the buildup of snow where the city's plow had stopped and the precise point where the heat of the fire had melted the rest. Out of several feet that had fallen over those few days, there was maybe only a foot left on the ground; and with the temperature warming nicely during the day, there were even some bare spots of dirt showing. As March was turning into April, the seasons were changing.

Stepping through the deeper stuff, he reached the melted areas and finally arrived at what used to be his front door. The great stone fireplace still stood to one side, blackened by soot, its broad mantel, a solid length of unpolished granite, aligned between the chimney and the fireplace itself, still as grand as it always was.

The rest was gone. He could see the outline of the building, a few timbers toward the back where, for some reason, the fire seemed to have spared them. Still, they were only fragments and not worth anything.

Or maybe they were. He could fashion things from them, he knew, if he were so inclined. A frame for a photo, a piece of art—there were many things he could use the unburnt wood for, as piecemeal as they were, but the speculation and the gathering of such artifacts would be left for another day.

He wondered how the fire started. Was the screen not there? Had Figaro knocked it over? An errant spark? He would likely never know, but in the ten years since he'd built the place, he'd never had anything close to this occur.

The smell of charred wood seemed to permeated the air still although it had been several days since it happened. But being inside the house with no walls around him made Hank feel exposed and he shuddered as a chill ran through him. If not for a lot of luck, Figaro could be among the ashes and he had to remind himself how lucky he was.

The future still loomed, unknown. That there was no more perfect purification than by fire, he knew, and would take that as a sign from above and move forward. His old life was gone. It was time to start anew. And when he thought about it, he realized that the fire had happened on Ostara, March twenty-first, the spring equinox. Some people at home called it Alban Eiler, "Light of the Earth," to celebrate rebirth and a time of planting.

He didn't need candles to light in the night, nor did he feel the need to decorate in the traditional colors of spring. All he needed was to breathe in and out, and thank God he was alive. And Figaro too, he amended.

Prayers aside, and stepping carefully over the debris, he found the remnants of his table, the chairs he'd spent what felt like a lifetime carving the backs into Celtic knots. He wondered at how some things burned completely while others did not.

As he moved toward the great fireplace, now a black yawn in the fragments around him like a hole he couldn't see into, a speck of something seemed to catch the fading sun and he bent to investigate it.

Just a glint beside the hearth, he dusted the ashes and found the small stone box with what was left of its mother-of-pearl decoration. It had held the only thing he had left from his mother, her Claddagh ring. He picked it up from inside the box, seemingly unscathed although it had been in the inferno. Somehow, the stone of the box had protected it and he fingered the smooth metal, running his fingers over its surface and remembering each symbol in turn; the hands representing friendship; the heart, which represented love; and the crown, representing loyalty. Such deep meanings in one small object. Tightening his fist around it, he wondered suddenly at the time his father had given it to his mother. Was there something he'd missed? They'd always been poor, his parents always arguing. In the end, he remembered his mother sending his father away and then crying for days afterward. He thought at the time that it was all his da's fault. Mam was the strong one, Da the joker, the one who made light of all their troubles.

Slowly, images came back to him of the look in his mam's eyes when his da held her and they weren't fighting. There had been real love there, he was certain. So why did she send him away? Had she sent him away or had he just gone?

Vaguely, another image touched him. His mother, sitting at the table when he arrived home from school one cold, rainy, blustery day. Usually, on a day like that, she'd have tea ready, or something to warm his belly. But that day, she only crumpled up the piece of paper she'd been holding and told him to look after his sister because she had to go out.

Later, he'd pulled the few pieces of unburnt paper from the fire where she'd tossed it and tried to put it back together. The handwriting was unfamiliar, and as he was still a young lad, barely ten, he'd had difficulty reading the words. "Sorry to inform you," was about all he could make out on that piece, and another had his father's name on it, or at least, part of his father's name. Maybe they were talking about another man?

Now, in the ruins of his home, he knew the truth. His father hadn't come back because he'd been unable to. Something had happened, but he didn't know what.

The ring was warm from his clenching it and he slid it onto his pinky finger as far as it would go. The silver metal gleamed in the dying light of day as a new hope burned inside him. One day he would rebuild his home, but first he had to rebuild his life.

Chapter Nineteen

Laura hadn't heard from Hank since he'd left Kerry's office, and while she wondered where he was and hoped he was okay, she knew he was not someone who needed coddling. Still, she was hoping he would call because, well, after all, she was babysitting his cat. Wouldn't that be a reason to call each day? Or had he, like she suspected in the back of her mind, decided that since the cat was looked after, he could leave?

Really, what else was here for him? She wasn't so naive to think that he would call her just because he liked her. No. She wasn't that kind of woman. Guys didn't fall all over her. They might look at her because even she knew she looked good in a bikini, but what woman wanted that kind of attention? She wanted someone who appreciated her for being her. Not someone who just wanted to use her as a sex object.

Yet what had their relationship consisted of from the get-go, she asked herself? Sex. That's all it had been.

She ignored the little voice inside her head that was ready to give her all kinds of examples to the contrary, but they'd always ended up in bed. Oh, the sex had been good and she'd really enjoyed it, but in retrospect, it was really just about the sex.

She sniffed a tear and realized she was crying. It was stupid. She shouldn't be crying over someone who just wanted her for her body. And it wasn't even that great a body. She'd long ago lost the youthful look of a teenager. She was over thirty. It was all downhill from here.

Tidying up the kitchen, she dried the last of the dishes and put them away and then decided to head into the shower. Figaro stopped at the threshold of the bathroom, leveled his nose toward the floor, and retreated to the safety of the bed once the water began running.

***

No answer. Hank hung up and pocketed his phone. There would be time tomorrow to tell her his plans. They'd have a few days before his plane took off, heading for the verdant countryside of his homeland. He was hoping he'd be able to convince her to come along but she was the one with the steady job. He could leave at any time because he'd completed all of his contracts to date. It was one of the perks of being self-employed. The drawback was that you always had to seek out other employment if there was no one left waiting in the wings.

This was one time he was happy not to have anyone banging on his door, wanting him to do some work for them. His prices were reasonable and he didn't do a lot of skimming as some contractors might, but he managed to make a decent wage and had enough set aside to last him a while. And while a trip to Ireland would eat up a couple of months' worth of that nest egg, one he would need to rebuild his home, he was okay with it, because for now, he needed to find out the answers to some very pressing questions. And without answers, what kind of a home could he rebuild?

With the weekend on his doorstep, Hank piled a few things into his loaner vehicle. His truck would take a couple of weeks to fix but he wasn't in a hurry anyway. His flight to Ireland had been booked, a rental car arranged, and all he had to do was convince Laura to go along with him. In the meantime, they had decided on a weekend up at her cabin. There were so many things he wanted to tell her, so many things he wanted her to know.

Earlier, he'd met her for lunch, and though on the surface

170

things seemed about the same, Hank felt the tension beneath as if a tidal wave was about to break. He hoped this quick side trip before he left would help put things in perspective.

***

Laura counted the minutes after lunch until she'd be able to meet Hank up at her cabin. She was still trying to figure out where things stood with him. Did he want her? Was she just an object to be played with? Their time during the snowstorm was literally a time out of time. No one and nothing had existed beyond them. But when you added the ocean to what was just a pond for two, well, it didn't take a genius to know that things would change.

Half an hour, that was all that was left in her day. She saw Kerry on the phone and wondered if he'd received anything from Ireland yet. He hadn't mentioned anything, but then he was a lawyer and Hank was his client, not her. Saying he was tight-lipped would be putting it mildly.

She scanned the document before her for the third time. Or maybe it was the fourth. She couldn't remember. She couldn't remember anything she was reading, either. Slamming the volume shut, she decided to face Kerry, demand he tell her something, anything, just to calm the anxiety that seemed to have taken hold of her this week.

Rising, she walked what she hoped was sedately to his office and knocked on the half-opened door. He glanced up, beckoned her in as he hung up the phone. A questioning look from his raised brow almost had her turning around and walking straight back to her desk but it was too late.

"I know you aren't supposed to tell me anything but…"

She'd barely got that much out when Kerry smiled. "Relax. It takes time. I've heard from the lab in Ireland, but I can't give you details until he's here. Besides, the results for comparison won't be available until at least

Monday. Are you going to see him in the next few days?"

Nodding, she admitted, "Yes. We're going to meet up at my cabin."

Kerry fiddled with the pen in his hand. "I don't need to know and it isn't any of my business, but are you serious about him?"

Laura couldn't help the smile that crept across her face and she bit her bottom lip, looking slyly through her lashes at Kerry's father-like countenance. "I don't know how much I should tell you," she offered. "I'd give you details but I honestly don't know where I stand with him."

Again, Kerry nodded. "Do you want my opinion?"

"Not really, but I sense I'm going to get it anyway."

He laughed, and reminded her of her father, happily residing on the other side of the country. "Like I said, it isn't really any of my business and you can tell me to take a hike if you want, but I think he's pretty taken with you and I don't think there's much that is going to stand in his way."

"What makes you think that?" Indecision had turned to curiosity.

"Sit down, would you? You're making me feel like a principal in school." Laura sat and when she'd quit fidgeting, Kerry continued. "He used to have a reputation with the women. I know because I used to watch him and wonder how a guy like him could get all the ladies. You know, not a millionaire, wasn't a fancy dresser, but he has charm and it didn't take much for him to walk out of the bar on any given night with a lady on his arm." He shuffled his feet beneath his desk before continuing. "And then one day it all changed. Almost overnight he stopped going to the bar, at least on a regular basis, and he stopped walking out with any young thing that walked by. Personally, I was grateful. That meant I had a better chance. At least I have some nice suits and a fancy car to offer."

"You probably wouldn't want the kind of women he got," she joked and was startled when Kerry shushed her with his hand.

"Don't debase yourself that way."

"Debase? I'm not…"

"Oh yes, you are. You have a very low opinion of yourself, thanks to your ex. But what I'm trying to tell you is that Hank only ever got the classy ladies, the ones who were independent, educated. The ones a guy like me keeps looking for and misses."

"Well, maybe if you didn't work 'til all hours of the night," she interjected.

Another raised eyebrow cut her off. He was good at that, she reflected, raising those brows in such a way as to shut anybody up.

"All I'm saying is that I wish I were him."

"Huh?"

"Go home. Get out of here. You've got a weekend ahead with someone who wants you for a lifetime. Take it while you can get it."

Laura left Kerry's office wondering what on earth had just happened.

***

He was waiting for her when she arrived at the cabin. Daylight was gone but the floor to ceiling windows shone like a beacon in the night to bring her home. As she walked in the front door, the mouthwatering aroma of roast chicken filled the air.

Putting her coat and boots away in the closet by the front door, she tiptoed into the kitchen in time to see Hank slide the chicken back into the oven and place the baster on the trivet beside the stove. He was just wiping his hands on the towel slung over his shoulder when Laura slid her arms around his waist.

Immediately, he turned in her arms, gathered her into his

embrace, and kissed her fully and solidly on her mouth.

She felt like she could have melted right then and there. Just let the world stop, she thought, right here, right now.

"You're just in time. Spuds and veggies are ready and I'm just waiting on the chicken to reabsorb the juices. A few more minutes and we can begin the feast."

Her tongue licked the bead of sweat that had collected at the base of his throat. His adam's apple bobbed as he swallowed and she heard as well as felt his indrawn breath.

"Keep that up and dinner will be late," he said.

His heart rate was beating a rapid tattoo beneath her palm.

She kissed him again. "Would that be such a tragedy?" Her leg slipped between his as she rubbed her thigh against his nads, felt his erection grow, the rod of it pressing into her belly. Rubbing her palm against the jeans material at his crotch, she sighed into his chest. "Never mind, I'm not being very polite. You spent the afternoon making dinner and here I am wanting to toss it all aside and feast on you instead."

"It would only serve me right." Hank inhaled deeply and she felt his chin rest lightly on the top of her head. "I've a great idea though," he said, setting her apart a little from him. Indicting with a nod of his head toward the back door, he smirked. "I've fired up the hot tub. It'll be ready as soon as we have our fill of food." The last was said with a whisper in her ear that sent chills to that special place between her legs.

"Oooh," she sighed, wishing that dinner was already over.

"As soon as I lay out some food for Figaro, we can eat."

That was Hank. Always thinking of his responsibilities, in this case, his cat.

His cat?

"Oh no, Figaro!"

Eyebrows raised, he asked, "What's wrong with Figaro?"

"Nothing, except that I left him back at my place," she cried. "Oooh, what kind of a cat-mommy am I that I can't even remember to bring him with me? Shit!"

"Not to worry. He won't starve overnight, I'm sure. And there's water for him, so he'll be fine."

"Are you sure?" Hank seemed so certain but she didn't feel half as sure as he obviously did.

"I'm sure. I can get Greg to go over and throw some food his way. It's no big deal."

"What do you mean, 'it's no big deal'? Greg doesn't have my key."

"Yeah, he does. I left the spare ye gave me back at his place. I'll call him later and Figaro will have a late dinner, that's all. He'll be a bit hungry but it's naught to be bothered about."

"I dunno, I just feel like crap for forgetting to bring him."

Hank laughed and brushed her hair from her face. "It's alright darlin', he'll survive just fine. C'mon, let's eat."

And eat they did. The chicken, the Brussels sprouts, the spuds. Laura wasn't sure she'd ever had such plain fare that tasted so good but Hank had a way of making the simple into the sublime.

"I think it's time," he said, topping up her wine. "The hot tub awaits."

The water was warm and steam rose into the night sky. Light from the kitchen window was the only illumination but it was all that was needed. They were naked, chest deep in water amid a snow-covered landscape, because as much as April was looming and snow in town was melting, here in the mountains it was still winter.

He pulled her into his arms, took her wine glass from her hand, and setting it safely aside, began to ravish her body, starting at the top.

"I think I've been waiting for this all day." She tilted her head back, the long titian strands of her hair floating on the water. Sometimes it felt good to be free of its weight as she leaned back into the water, thrusting her breasts into the frigid air that made her nipples pucker into little peaks.

"Mm, me too. Come sit on me." He helped her sit astride, spread her nether lips with his fingers, and slid into her. The ecstasy on her face was evident as she closed her eyes, a small smile splayed across her face. The lovely column of her throat glowed in the yellow light from the kitchen as her pert breasts lifted from the water once again, wet droplets clinging to her ruched nipples and begging to be licked off. Hank caught a drip before it left her pebbled skin, then drew the bit into his mouth, circled his tongue around it and made her sigh into him once more.

"Oh, Hank, you make me feel like nobody else exists." She was moving atop him, squeezing him with her inner muscles, riding him slowly up and down.

"Ah," he breathed in ecstasy as he suckled her hard, then abandoned her nipple to grasp her mouth with his and thrust his tongue inside to mate with hers. And all the while he let her ride him while he fingered her little bud of womanhood that told him in every way just how completely he satisfied her.

Minutes later he felt her body close around him in rapid convulsions, and immediately followed her into it as their cries split night mountain air, scaring even the wild creatures into hiding.

He was hugging Laura tightly to him, her head against his chest, light frost covering her hair and his too, he imagined. His warm breath melted the frost and he watched it for a moment to see if it would freeze again.

Giggling, she asked, "What are you doing?"

"I'm playing Jack Frost."

"What?" She leaned back to look at him, and by her expression, he knew she had an inkling this wasn't just all about having fun.

"Let's go upstairs. I've somethin' I need to tell ye."

He helped her out of the steaming tub and wrapped her warmly in a towel before wrapping himself in another.

Making the distance between hot tub and door in record time, they kept on running, him chasing her up the stairs to her squeals of delight.

Launching from the top of the landing, he landed heavily on the bed and heard it protest as the frame took the impact of his body hitting the mattress. He bounced lightly while Laura watched him and rolled her eyes.

"Was that necessary? You might have damaged the bed."

"Ah, just testin' it to make sure it's worthy of what follows."

"Humph," she mumbled and took the towel off, drying the ends of her hair with it.

"C'mere to me, luv, there's somethin' I need to say." He had half sat up, perched on one elbow, beckoning to her with his other hand.

"You kind of remind me of some sort of statue or painting, lying like that in all your glory."

"Ah, well, my glory's goin' to change pretty quick so why don't ye come and hear me out first." He waited while she sat beside him, leaning against the headboard, a pillow at her back and her knees drawn up.

"Let's get under the covers, I'm chilly," she said. And tugging at the blankets beneath her, she wriggled herself between the sheets while he did the same.

Before he began, though, Hank reached over to the bedside table and pulled open the little drawer, extracting the stone box he'd pulled from the fire. Showing her the box, he said, "I found this when I went back to check out my place. I found it in the ashes. The decoration on top is a bit damaged but other than that, it's the only thing I found that I could save."

"What a lovely little box. Oh, it's stone," she remarked, taking it from his hand and running her fingers across the top where the mother-of-pearl had been seared and burned, leaving a black stain on the stone from the glue that had held it on. "Is there anything inside? Can I open it?"

Hank felt the lump in his throat and could only nod.

As she lifted the stone lid, the small ring inside glinted in the light from the lamps beside the bed. "Oh, it's so pretty!"

"It's called a Claddagh ring, and it was my mam's."

"Oh, Hank, that's so amazing that you have this still, and pulled from the fire, no less." She went to hand it back to him but he stayed her hand.

"Here," he took the ring from the box and lifted her left hand, sliding the ring onto her finger, thrilled when it fit as if it were made for her. "It's a promise ring, and sometimes a ring given when people decide to get handfast."

"They still do that?" she asked, gazing at the ring on her finger. "Oh look, there's two hands holding a heart, and a crown on top. Do they have special meaning?"

"They do. And I want ye to know that I'm giving ye this ring because I have to go away for a while and I want ye to know I'll come back to ye. And if ye'll have me, I'd like to marry ye and be your husband."

Laura gasped as if burned. Marriage? Oh no! Anything but that. Struggling to get the ring off, her hands shaking, she choked on her words. "I can't marry you, Hank. I'll never go down that road again."

"I love ye. I'd never do what he did to ye, ye must know that."

"Please, take this back, I can't wear it." She'd finally got the ring off and was holding it out for him to take.

"No, luv, ye must keep it, and promise that ye'll give me time to prove myself to ye. I have to go away and I was hopin' ye'd come with me."

She looked at the ring in her hand, a delicate thing that had once been on his mother's hand. It must mean a lot to him, and he'd given it to her. And then his other words sank in, "I love ye," he'd said, and she wanted to believe him because she knew she loved him too. But somehow, the words wouldn't come.

"I can't leave work right now. I'm in the middle of doing some research for one of the partners on a big case she's handling. Maybe when it's over I could, but not right now."

Hank nodded and she could tell he had more to tell her. He picked up the ring where it sat on her palm and rolled it around in his hand, as if inspecting it from all angles.

"It never occurred to me that my mam only had this ring, never a wedding band, until I pulled this from the fire. The symbols, they mean a lot. Loyalty, love, friendship. But if my da loved my mam so much, why not marry her? I'd never questioned it before 'cause she wouldn't ever discuss it. Whenever I'd asked, she'd said it wasn't my business and to leave it alone. So I did, until I found this in the fire. 'Twas all of a sudden like I'd woken up and realized that there was somethin' else goin' on, only I don't know what it is. But I have to find out. And the only way I'm goin' to be able to do that is to go to Ireland. And I want ye to come with me, to see for yerself where I come from, what made me like I am. Besides, I think ye'll like Killarney, it's very pretty there. And who knows, maybe then ye'll know in your heart what I feel for you is true."

She let him slide the ring back on her finger. "What if you don't find out anything? You'll have wasted all that time and money that you could have used to rebuild your home."

"Ah, no. I can't rebuild until I've found the answers. I need to track down Siobhan and find out what's behind her schemes; what's with this girl she says is mine."

At the mention of Siobhan's name, Laura stiffened and rose from the bed, pulling on her silky bathrobe and tying the sash tightly so the knot wouldn't slip open. She wasn't sure she wanted anything to do with Hank right now.

"You know what I think?" Without waiting for an answer, she continued on, "I think that you'll find Siobhan and you'll see the girl and you'll do the honorable thing, you'll marry her to give the girl a name and a proper upbringing. And make sure they have money so they don't starve like you did. I know this because that's what you do Hank, you take care of people!"

"Aye, I do take care of the ones I love. Isn't that the way it should be?"

"What about Figaro? You're going to abandon him to go to Ireland for God-knows-how-long and who knows if you're ever going to come back?"

"I wouldn't abandon him, just like I wouldn't abandon you. I can have the cat-lady look after him so's ye can come with me."

"No, I told you, I can't go with you. Besides, he's happy at my place, I'll make sure he's okay. I guess I've just got myself a cat."

"I'll leave ye money for his food and for yer troubles…"

"He's no trouble, Hank. You're the trouble. You're the one doing this. Why can't we just go on as we have been? Why did you have to mention marriage? Weren't we fine the way we were?"

She left him in the bed and marched downstairs to the kitchen and began to make coffee. Thinking against it, she put the coffee back and reached into her liquor cabinet for the brandy. She needed something to stop the shaking inside.

"You're afraid of marriage," he said, coming up behind her.

She turned around and knew that on any other occasion she would have laughed because there he was, standing in that stupid pink bathrobe that made him look like a pink teddy bear. But inside she was quaking, and didn't know why. "You have no right to tell me what I might or might not be afraid of. It's none of your business," she ground out, knocking back the rest of the drink.

"We have somethin', you and I," he said softly. "And I mean to see this through."

"Why? What does it matter?"

"If ye don't know by now, Laura, ye never will."

Tears pricked her eyes and all she could say was, "Please leave. I'm sorry, it's very late and it's a two-hour drive back to town, but please leave. And here, take this with you." She held out the ring, forcing it into his hand when he didn't automatically take it.

Cupping it in his fist, he turned and walked away, stopping at the base of the stairs as he asked, "Do ye not feel anything for me at all, then?"

She couldn't answer that. "Just go. Please." It was so hard to stop shaking, to withhold the tears that threatened to fall.

"I'll get my things," was all he said.

She felt like a bag of shit. With a shaking hand, she poured another drink and took a swig, feeling the liquor burn its way down her throat. Brandy had been Erik's thing, not hers, but on this occasion, when she didn't know up from down, she needed something to smarten her up like a slap to the face would have done. But Hank was too much the gentleman for that.

She heard him come down the stairs but couldn't budge from her spot in the kitchen.

"I'll come back for ye, Laura. When I get this all straightened out, I'll come back for ye."

"No, you won't," she heard herself say.

Hank closed the door softly behind him and Laura drained the glass. It wasn't until she saw the lights of his car drive away in the night that she gave in to her tears, crumbled to a heap on the floor in the kitchen, and sobbed her heart out.

When the tears finally stopped, she thought of the ring he'd put on her finger, remembered the feeling of its curves, and wondered if he really meant what he said. Well, no matter, because she'd already refused his offer, and from the way she'd acted, doubted he'd ever want to be with her again. Pulling herself up from the floor, she turned out the lights and went up to bed.

Chapter Twenty

His first sight of Ireland was much like the last time he'd seen it all those years ago. Green on green hills rolled beneath verdant forests, mottled between the dull brown of winter and the new leaves of spring. The grasses were never the same from one field to the next, and if ever there was a place on earth that portrayed every green imaginable, Ireland was it.

He'd been full of hope when he left Ireland, but as one dream faded, another burned anew. Laura had surprised him. She hadn't wanted him to go and she hadn't wanted to go with him. He didn't know what kind of inner-speak she was hearing but it wasn't the truth. The truth was, he wanted her above all else, loved her above all else, but she couldn't seem to understand that. For some unknown reason, she refused to believe his intentions were pure and would rather remain alone than be saddled with another man. With him.

He couldn't blame her. Erik had bruised her just as deeply as if he'd been physically violent with her. Her soul had been scarred and he knew how that felt, somehow being thought of as disposable, first as a child by his da and then by his ex-wife. But people weren't disposable and he had to try to find a way to convince her. So maybe, he thought, if he returned to Ireland, he could settle all those questions he'd left behind.

When he thought back to how he'd tried to convince her that she'd like Killarney and that they wouldn't be gone all that long anyway, she'd argued that no one would be there for

Figaro, his orange tomcat named for a puppet in a cartoon. He hadn't realized that, until the cat lady told him. Maybe that's where his crazy friend got the idea that the cat's name was Figaro. It was really different; the cat seemed to acknowledge it and so he'd kept it. In his mind, he could see the cat-lady's child playing with a couple of toys, toys that looked remarkably like they walked straight out from a production of Pinocchio. At least the wee beast had a name. Wee?Not really. But then he hadn't known that ginger cats grew to a much larger size than other cats, another thing his cat-lady friend had told him. She should know, he thought. She owned two or three cats of her own and ended up looking after and feeding any stray that came along.

So even though he knew he could likely find someone to watch out for the cat for a couple of weeks, and even if the cat-lady was available, it burned his gut to think that Figaro would be with someone he really didn't know. It wasn't right. And for that alone, he was happy Laura hadn't come along.

When Hank first left Ireland, he was convinced he'd never go back, would never want to or need to. The land had not been kind to him, although like most memories, there was good and bad mixed together. But then his da left them destitute, his sister got pregnant and ran away, and his mam died. Why would he want to come back to a place that brought all those bad memories back?

At the time, he hadn't realized he'd need to find out the root cause of it all. He'd need to know what happened to his sister and the baby she carried. Were they a happy family somewhere? He wanted to believe that but he'd never know until he went looking. And how long that would take, he couldn't tell.

Then there was Siobhan. What game was she playing? The DNA comparison said that the girl was related to him in some way, but not to Siobhan. Kerry had talked to him on the phone, had asked him to go into the office so they could discuss the findings, but Hank was already in Ireland by the time he got the voice mail.

So if the girl wasn't related to Siobhan, then who was she and why was she with Siobhan? What was going on? Yes, he'd made the right decision. He had to come back. And this time, he was returning in a different frame of mind than when he left. He wasn't a naïve lad anymore. He was a man with a new country, a new outlook, someone who had made something of himself and had money in the bank to show for it.

The car he'd rented at the airport was a little compact model, easy to manoeuver through the narrow streets to finally pull up in front of the address he'd had for Siobhan. The row of houses was nicer than the one he'd shared with his mam and sister. These were neater, in a better neighborhood, and much better kept, although they were no bigger, he thought as he looked up and down the row of painted houses, all joined together but done up quite uniquely, each painted a different color from its neighbor. The back gardens were narrow, he knew, not any wider than the house itself, and there was only a small front garden. It was typical of the style he'd grown up in but definitely a cut above. At least this place had a front garden.

The place Hank had called home was coated with thirty-year-old paint, if it had any. They hadn't had enough money to paint and the landlord hadn't cared. Hell, sometimes they hadn't had enough money for rent and he suddenly envied the people in these homes and wondered how it was that Siobhan could afford one. Maybe she'd won a lottery or something.

Checking the house numbers, he confirmed the address; and having pulled into one of the few available parking spots along the street, he hunkered down to wait. Opening the window just a crack to keep the inside clear of condensation, he felt the fresh smell of day waft in with a hint of moisture, tickling his nostrils. He inhaled deeply, filling his lungs with the crisp, damp air. It was still early and he was hoping he'd be able to catch his quarry before they left for the day. He had no idea what kind of schedule they had, but if Siobhan had the girl there, she had to go to school at some point.

Parked as he was, he noticed immediately when the door finally opened and the teenager left for school. Not long after, Siobhan, who looked remarkably the same as when he last knew her, left as well, heading in the same direction as the girl. He told himself that he wasn't spying. He just wasn't ready to meet them yet. And although he and Siobhan had been lovers, not a twinge of excitement passed through his gut, only a kind of nervous excitement that perhaps some questions might just get answered.

Siobhan kept her head up, ignoring the breeze that blew her short, auburn hair around her face. The only difference between knowing her back then and seeing her now, reflected Hank, was the fact that Siobhan had gained a few pounds since her schoolgirl days. Or maybe it was just that she'd matured from girl to woman, that final jump to adulthood. Whatever it was, Siobhan had not changed so much that he wouldn't recognize her in a crowd.

Just as he was about to pull away from the curb to follow Siobhan, a man left the same house; but instead of walking away from Hank as did the other two, he headed straight toward Hank. The man was unfamiliar to him, but still Hank kept his head down as if rifling through some papers so as not to be noticed. He didn't want to appear as though he was waiting for something or someone.

Looking in his rear view mirror, he watched as the fellow climbed into the car parked directly behind him, and taking a good look at him, Hank knew with a certainty that he'd never met the man before. Yet something about him was eerily familiar, as if he had met him and just didn't remember. Shaking his head, he thought to himself that it must be the mysticism of the isle giving his imagination a boost. Ireland was a land steeped in lore of all kinds and the night before at the local pub had only reinforced that. Stories of ghosts and hauntings had been entertaining and he'd had his fair share of tales to add to the melee. It was newly past the spring equinox and prime time for stories to circulate once again. The weeks before and after the equinox were sure to bring out tales of adventure and misadventure and all on the theme of things that went bump in the night.

The car behind pulled away and headed into town. Curious, Hank followed, keeping at a distance so as not to be noticed. Seeing Siobhan walking briskly along, he kept his eyes on the road, his face averted as he passed her. He didn't want her recognizing him quite yet.

As Hank trailed a good length behind the mysterious man, he then passed the girl, turning onto the road toward the school. Catching a glimpse of her face in person, there was no denying that she could definitely be a relative of his. But his child? Who could say? Her nearly black hair was left free and the dark waves blew in the morning breeze, a breeze that heralded rain before long. She tugged her coat up tighter around her neck and for the first time Hank realized how thin a coat it was. She needed something heavier for weather like this, because although it was almost April, March was still upon them and today was turning out to be blustery and cold.

His attention turning back to the matter at hand, he was already making a mental list of things he needed to do. He added a coat for the girl onto the list, because if she was a blood relative, then it was his responsibility to do so.

Ahead, the car he was trailing turned off toward the Ring of Kerry and Hank followed him for a time, curious when the fellow eventually turned into a large rural property a few miles out of town. Steering the car just past the drive and off behind some bushes, Hank couldn't very well follow through the gates without being seen. But what was he hiding from? Sooner or later he'd have to meet this guy and find out his business.

Squinting through the trees, he could see a large building

beyond the grassy lea in front of it. It looked like an old manor house from years gone by and he racked his brain, trying to remember if he'd ever been there before. Two sets of mullioned windows framed the large front door with a fanlight window giving it a noble arch. Above, the second story boasted four windows, similar to those below it, beneath a sloping, slate roof.

He seemed to recall people living there at one time but that had to have been many years ago. The place had a very deserted look to it, as if neglect had been its only companion. Still, there were curtains behind the windows and he could hear sheep bleating in the distance. His mind made up, he got back in the car and made his way slowly up the long drive.

The drive was a good hundred feet of curved roadway that led to the side of the house. There looked to be an area at the front where vehicles could park, a lumpy, paved affair that sprouted grass in clumps throughout like the tufts of wool that held a child's quilt together.

Choosing to follow the road around to the side, he quickly came upon the sheep, feeding on the lush green grass in a field at the back of the place. Just when Hank thought his curiosity would never be sated as to the nature of the mystery man's business, a lorry passed him by, loaded with stone. Peering intently again, this time focusing on where the lorry was traveling to, Hank saw that there was some construction going on where an old stone wall once contained what appeared to be a walled garden.

Well, me son, he thought, nothing to be gained from gawking. May as well go find the man and see what he's about. It also occurred to him that he could pass himself off as a lost tourist if anyone asked so he continued up the length of rutted drive and parked next to some other vehicles, probably those of the workers already there.

The site was a bigger area than Hank had suspected from his first sight of it. The crumbling stone wall that housed the garden was set back from the manor house, where once a barn or other type of shed must have stood, with old beams still partially standing, weathered and broken. A big gap in the wall was being repaired where the ages and the trials of history had worn or broken down great chunks of it. The wall itself was covered with vines, newly budding with leaves of bright, spring green, thick with ancient growth beneath. At the moment, though, instead of intent on fixing the wall, much of the laborers' focus lay on the few sheep that had broken out of their large pen next to the wall and made their way into the old garden. Two people were strategizing on how to herd them back to their compound without letting them loose on the rest of the farm, while others stood around watching or calling out unhelpful tips.

Someone turned as he parked the rental, noticed him as he emerged, and approached, hands in his pockets, his neck shrugged into his collar as a brisk gust blew through. Hank braced himself. It was the mysterious man, nodding his greeting. "Somethin' I can do for ye?" He removed the cap he'd been wearing and smoothed his longish, black hair back before replacing the cap back on his head. The man pushed on it, settling it firmly, and Hank knew the effort was to keep it from blowing away in the wind.

Shrugging into his own collar, Hank said, "I noticed the work and was curious. You're putting up a new wall? That one's been down for the last three hundred years, if a day."

"And how would ye be knowin' that?" asked the mystery man.

"Oh, I grew up around these parts."

"Well, ye'd know all about what we're doing then. The old house has been designated a heritage site so the wall's getting rebuilt."

"A stone mason are ye then?" Hank's father had been a stone mason.

"Aye, like my da before me."

Hank thought that if ever there was a time in his life that he might faint, this was it. His head swam with the pieces of a puzzle floating in his brain and suddenly falling into place. It couldn't be. But it was the only answer.

"A coincidence. My own da was one as well," he said, his voice feeling less than steady.

"And you?"

"Me? A stone mason? No." No, Hank had never had the chance. His da had disappeared when he was ten. He remembered all too well his mam's tears.

"Well, if you're lookin' for work…"

"I'm not," Hank broke in. "I'm here for a much different reason. Would ye mind if we got away from the wind a bit? I think you and I need to talk."

The other man's face was stern, a look Hank remembered from his own da's features when Hank tried to pull one over on him. It was a look that said "this had better be good or else…" and Hank felt the same about this man as he did when he got that look from his da. Worried.

"Here's just as good a place as any," said the other man, adjusting his posture so he was taller, bigger. Not a good sign, thought Hank.

"Right then." Shuffling his feet, he wondered where he should start. Introductions usually helped to diffuse a potentially rough situation so that's where he began, holding out his hand for the other man to shake. "My name's Hank Mulligan, what's yours?"

"Henry O'Farrell." He reached out and took Hank's hand. "What can I do for you, now you've got that out of the way?"

The skeptical look on the man's face did nothing to ease Hank's sick feeling. They had the same first name. "Uh, I was wonderin' if ye were perhaps named for yer da?"

"I was. And it's your business how?"

He didn't want to blurt it out. The tension in the air was thick about them and all the sounds of the sheep in the garden yonder had gone quiet. A group of curious men began to form a semicircle around them. "Ye see, I'm named after me da as well. His full name was Henry Ryan O'Farrell. I have me mam's last name," he finished uncomfortably.

Henry spat on the ground. "What are ye sayin' exactly?"

"I'm sayin'…I think we're brothers."

Hank never saw it coming. Before he could react, the fist connected with his jaw and sent him sprawling. He'd never been a good fighter and liked to avoid fighting when he could because despite his height of six feet and the reach in his long, lanky arms, he was just not fast enough on his feet.

Henry came at him, ready for more. "Ye fuckin' bastard of a sonofabitch an' ye think we're related? Ye've got some gall comin' here to tell me that!" Henry stood with one fist up and the other hand beckoning. "C'mere to me, I'll brain ye. I'll show ye what I think o' the likes o' you."

C'mere to me, I'll brain ye, a classic phrase from his childhood and especially teen years when fisticuffs were a way to solve things. As soon as the words,"I'll brain ye," were uttered, you ran like the devil was chasing you because to be caught was to engage in a fight that was sure to end with your da giving you the same thing once you got home, just for getting into a fight in the first place. No, a fistfight was never a good thing, but Hank had no father or mother to run to and if he wanted to find out more from this man, then a fistfight it would be.

Hank scrambled to his feet, hands up and ready to go at Henry when a woman's voice called out. "Wisht! Both of ye. Can neither of ye see? Take a good look at yerselves, ye crazy bastards. Ye've the same da for sure!"

Neither had seen Siobhan drive up and both men halted in their tracks as she came to stand between them.

"What are you doing here?" they both asked at the same time, stunned to see her there, and then each turned hate-filled eyes upon the other for daring to speak.

"I was dropping off yer lunch, ye crazy bugger," she said to Henry. "Ye forgot it at the house and you're lucky I forgot my purse 'cause when I went back to get it, there it was next to your lunch. Mrs. Brady next door drove me here, just in time to see ye let into this 'un." She indicated Hank with a nod of her head and added, "Nice to see ye, Hank, glad you finally came. Next time, just give a knock on the door and we'll have a chat, proper like."

So much for a loving ex-girlfriend, thought Hank as she turned to Henry and thrust out her hand with his lunch in her grasp for him to take.

"I just wanted to talk," muttered Hank, his head spinning from all he was taking in, not to mention the crack on his jaw that was beginning to ache all the way up the side of his face.

"We're definitely going to talk," said Siobhan, eyeing Hank with what could only be called the angriest look of loathing he had ever seen. What on earth had he gotten himself into now?

"You, I'll see at home when yer workday is done," she commanded, pointing a sturdy finger at Henry, who by now was beginning to look like he wished he'd never laid eyes on Hank. "And you," she said to Hank, pointing at the rental parked nearby, "I imagine that's your ride? I'll take ye back to town. You're goin' to need some cleanin' up."

Hank had no wish to anger anyone any further. His head was throbbing, he wanted nothing more than a hot shower to thaw his now nearly frozen bones, and maybe a dram of good Irish whiskey to shock himself back into reality. Surely the faeries and leprechauns were having a time with him today. "It's alright," he mumbled. "I don't need help." A shaky hand took keys from his pocket but Siobhan snatched them away.

"Give them to me. You're in no shape to drive." She then went to speak to Mrs. Brady, who soon after drove away. "C'mon, get into your car. I'll take ye back to town."

Not having any other choice that he could see, Hank gave

his "brother" a last look, got a cold sneer in return, and got into the car. He wasn't sure if he wanted to face Siobhan or have another go around with Henry. At this point, it seemed he had no choice.

"I'll take ye back to my place until ye look a wee bit better. Right now ye look like ye could hurl."

"I feel like it's a possibility," he admitted. His gut felt squeamish and tight, as if he'd taken the fist there instead of his jaw.

"Well, if you're goin' to, let me know so's I can pull over."

"No, I don't think I really will, it's just…I'm still trying to digest everything I've heard."

"Ye mean Henry?"

Hank nodded. A million scenarios went through his mind, none of which made any kind of sense. "Is he really my brother?"

At first Hank didn't think she'd heard him. They were driving back to town and the countryside was quickly turning into city. Neither were talking and the only sound was from the engine as the small compact followed the narrow road back to Killarney. He was just about to repeat the question when a very quiet answer was heard above the whine of the engine. "Yes," was all she said.

It was just one word but it nearly brought tears to Hank's eyes. Holding them back and with a throat thick with emotion, the only word he could get out was, "How?"

The car slowed to turn onto the street with its tidy row of well-kept houses. "I think that's something that should come from Henry. But I'll tell ye as much as I know from the time I met him, while ye have some tea."

"You wouldn't have whiskey, would ye?"

"Sadly for you, no. Henry's a recovered alcoholic and I won't let him go down that path so I don't even keep any in the house."

"Could be a long day," muttered Hank.

Chapter Twenty-one

Rubbing a hand absentmindedly along his jaw where Henry had made contact, Hank sat in the car, wondering if he was doing the right thing. He was feeling better, at least his head had stopped spinning, but his jaw still hurt like hell. Parked outside the long row of houses, his mind going in circles, he sent a silent prayer, hoping his journey hadn't led him on a wild-goose chase. He still didn't know the truth about Emily, and Siobhan hadn't wanted to tell him. In fact, she hadn't wanted to tell him much, if anything at all. Well, tonight he'd find out. He didn't care if he got beaten to a pulp, he was going to get answers. Determination was his driving force. He hadn't come all this way to go home empty handed.

Home. Laura. How he missed her! Every thought, every minute, all of it was punctuated by the vision of her face when the sun lit up her eyes, the sound of her laughter, the feel of her body next to his. She was his home now, and with that thought, a steely determination came over him. He would find the answers he needed and then move on. Hank was done being afraid, being left in limbo because of a past he could not shake. He got out of the car and walked the short distance to the second house in the line, a bright yellow affair, cheery despite the gray sky and cold, damp wind, and strode up the short garden walk, knocking firmly on the door.

His solid rap was quickly answered by a nervous Siobhan. He had become adept at reading people over the years, and from the way she averted her eyes, he knew she wasn't happy; and if he wasn't mistaken, Henry wasn't either, if the scowl on that man's face was anything to go by. Which led him to the conclusion they'd had an argument, a conclusion that was soon confirmed.

"I told ye I didn't want him here," said Henry from his seat in front of the overly large television he'd been watching. He hadn't risen from his chair, merely cast a sidelong glance at Hank as he spoke.

"And I told ye you're going to answer his questions." Clearly, Siobhan was the one in charge because Henry merely turned his attention back to whatever it was he was watching.

"Come into the kitchen. I'll put on the kettle for some tea," she said to Hank, leading the way.

Hank nodded and followed her around the sofa that separated the sitting room from the kitchen and took a seat at the small table. He gazed around the room, noted that the wall between the kitchen and sitting room had been removed and remarked on how good it looked.

"Yeah," agreed Siobhan, "Henry did it. He's good working with his hands, he is."

"I know, quick, too," replied Hank, rubbing his jaw again, and catching Siobhan's eye, gave her a rueful smile. "If I'd known that, I would have stood farther back."

Siobhan burst out laughing, and though his back was to him, Hank could hear Henry rise out of his chair and walk toward them. He stiffened in response, waiting for whatever might happen.

"Ah, relax, mo dearthair, I was upset. I won't hit y' again. I was pissed because you'd just confirmed everythin' Siobhan had tried to tell me and everythin' I have tried to ignore since meeting yer sister. Needless to say, I don't like bein' wrong." With a jerk of his head, he indicated Hank's jaw where a bruise had formed. "Does it hurt much?"

"It's fine," Hank answered, not caring much about his chin

but worrying more about the million questions he wanted to ask. "Ye call me brother but ye don't tell me how ye know. How is it we have the same da? If ye don't mind, I'd like to know."

The kettle began to whistle and Siobhan rose to make the tea.

"'Tisn't a nice story, if ye must know. There's no rainbow with a pot o' gold at the end of it."

"I'm aware," said Hank.

Henry leaned back, accepting his cup from Siobhan and waiting while Hank doctored his own. "It may be that you can fill in some things for me as well," he offered.

"That's fair," said Hank, just wishing Henry would get on with it so he could leave.

"We lived in Inishannon and Da was often gone from home," began Henry, and as he talked, he told of a man dedicated to his craft, spending long hours on the job and sometimes weeks away at a time, going wherever the jobs were. "I'm supposing that on one of those sojourns, he met yer mam, and bein' away from home maybe thought spendin' it with a woman was far better than bein' alone. I was still in short pants when you were born. I only know that because Siobhan said you and she are of an age."

"And that makes you how old?" asked Hank, genuinely curious.

"Older than you," laughed Henry, breaking the tension that clung tenaciously about them.

"I'd truly like to know, to put things into perspective, right?"

Nodding, Henry acquiesced. "I'm thirty-seven, four years your senior."

Hank cast a quick glance at Siobhan and noticed that she'd calmed down from her earlier anxious state. It looked like they wouldn't get down to fisticuffs after all as Henry continued his story.

"Somewhere after yer birth, money around our house got tight. I recall my da saying how he had more expenses and my mam not understanding how that could be. I wasn't very old still, maybe about eight, but I'd begun to hang around Da when he was workin' nearby and he was showing me how to work the stone. I remember bein' fascinated by it, by how he could do so much with the tools he had and just his bare hands." Taking a sip of the still warm brew, he leaned back in his chair, his mind clearly on his story. "Ah, but while he was working and mam wasn't there, he'd tell me stories of a lad that looked like me and a young cailín. He said it was uncanny, the likeness between us. The old bastard never said they were his, never said he was sleepin' with another woman let alone had a family by her. And by this time, Brandon was almost four and the twins were toddlers still."

"Inishannon's not that far away," observed Hank. "Why did he not just go home?"

"Ah, he had a vision problem that prevented him from driving at night. It was a good excuse for him, I guess, easy to explain why he wouldn't be home for weeks at a time if a job was busy."

"How did your mam handle it? I know my own mam was not happy when he was gone. She was young, not well educated. Worked at a store in town so wasn't bringin' much home. When Da wasn't there, it was like she was a different person. She'd sulk for days, waitin' for the next time he'd come."

Henry cupped his hands around the teacup as if for warmth but Hank could see the man's mind was working, nodding at what Hank had said.

"Yeah? My own mam is a nurse at the hospital in Cork. She works hard, always on the go. She's independent, loves her alone time, and it may be that's why her marriage lasted and she didn't throw him out for good. I think it was rough when we were all young, but she weathered it. We had her parents around to help, too. They're still living, not too far, just down Old Head Kinsale way. Got some property in Garrettstown, close to the beach, and we used to visit on weekends and school holidays. Niall nearly drowned one year, got into a wave trying to surf and flipped the board. Good thing Brandon was there because Niall wasn't a good swimmer. Brandon grabbed him and made for shore, the two of them on the board looking like some professional stunt group. Liam went to jump on the board to join them and they all got upset and into the water again. Ciara laughed so hard I thought the cranberry juice was going to come out her nostrils!"

Although Henry's story had been humorous, Hank ignored the introduction of other family members for now. There were too many other more immediate questions to be answered.

"How did ye meet Siobhan? It's not like Inishannon is the next town over." The corner of Siobhan's lips curled up in a smile, not unlike the famous Mona Lisa, thought Hank, hiding mysteries and secret tales that you'd only know if she agreed to divulge them.

"This is where the story gets interestin'," Siobhan interjected, placing a hand over Henry's where it rested on the table.

"You want to tell him, or shall I?" asked Henry, a daring look in his midnight blue eyes.

"Oh, thanks, I'll tell the story, ye coward," she laughed, and Hank knew she was joking and loved story telling as much as the next person.

"'Twas me seein' him on the street one day, lookin' a wee bit lost that caught my eye. I was just comin' from work and was thinkin' how much he looked like you, and since I hadn't seen ye in so many years, thought maybe it was. So I started up a conversation like. Imagine the shock when he was you, but not you." Her gray eyes became round with expression.

"He had yer name, he looked identical to you, but in the end, he wasn't. We agreed to go for a pint; he was a drinkin' man in those days," she said, the smile turning into a grin as her elbow nudged Henry's arm in a familiar manner.

"And I would be still if not for you," Henry added. He looked surly but Hank had the feeling that Henry's looks often hid a gentler nature.

Siobhan grinned slyly at Henry. "Ah well, and ye might be worse off if ye still were. But don't interrupt. I let ye tell your part, now you let me tell mine."

Clearly, Hank was fortunate that he'd escaped her clutches way back when. She was nothing like Laura, and as if his mind had conjured her up right then and there, he felt himself begin to harden. Ignoring the feeling, he encouraged her to continue.

"Right y'are then," she said, pouring more tea into her cup. "Who's for more?" At a nod from both men, she filled their cups and waited, as if gathering her thoughts.

"So there we were, sittin' down to a pint, and I began to tell him of you, how I thought he was you and then he said yer name before I could tell him it. I was surprised to say the least. But it was soon straightened out, and then he asked about your sister, Meara. I couldn't tell him because I didn't know. I'd heard she'd got into some trouble. She liked her drugs and was following some plonker. What she saw in him, I'll never know. But he's the one for sure got her knocked up. Anyway, that's mostly all there is to tell," she said, "except for Emily. Only I didn't know about her then," she finished sadly.

"I knew Meara was pregnant before I left," said Hank, feeling the emotion in his throat, forcing him to clear it before he continued. "She took off that summer to go chase the fella down and wouldn't tell me his name or where she was goin'. Next thing Mam took sick and died that November and I didn't know where Meara went so I couldn't tell her."

Siobhan reached across the table to cover Hank's left hand in a soothing squeeze. "Hank, ye must know Meara's dead. She's been dead these three years past. It's why I tried to find ye and bring ye home. Ye needed to meet Emily."

Hank froze, let the news sink in, news he had known in his gut all along but hoped was untrue. He felt the tears come, the tightness in his throat clog his speech. If ever he had any thoughts on being Emily's father, they'd all just been blown out of the water. Anger so strong it bubbled out of him like a hotspring, caused him to stand. He couldn't sit just now. He wanted to hit something, to scream and cry at the wind. "Why the ruse? The threats of blackmail. Ye could have just told me!" He slammed the fist of his free hand onto the table out of frustration, making the cups and teapot bounce.

"Ye never would have come," exclaimed Siobhan, looking equally frustrated. "You were so ensconced in your new life that ye never would have come, not even to see your own kin."

"Ye never gave me the chance, did ye!" He pulled his hand away from Siobhan's, felt the tears flow anew, and swallowed hard. "Ye could have told me about Meara, ye could have said she left a daughter. I'd have come for her, I would. I maybe wasn't the kind of man that would know anything about looking after a child but I would've tried. Instead she's here and I'm only just learnin' all this."

"Don't be angry with Siobhan," said Henry. "Sit back down and I'll tell ye the rest."

Hank paced the floor, speared trembling fingers through his hair and rubbed his face with both hands, sniffing back tears, trying to get himself under control. Emily was his niece, his sister's final gift. Something of herself left behind. To a family-starved man, Hank clung to the hope that the girl would like him.

Henry waited until Hank was seated again and Siobhan handed him a tissue. Swallowing a gulp of tea, Henry continued. "It was me who found Emily first. Meara ran into me, much like Siobhan did, thinkin' I was you. Only it was in Bandon, not far from where I lived at the time. I think somehow she had figured things out, tracked me down, or maybe the family. Anyways, she'd been draggin' Emily along wi' her for years at that time. The poor kid had little schooling and naught but the clothes on her back. Emily is why I came lookin' for ye, only to find Siobhan instead. Ye see," Henry cleared his throat. If emotions were contagious, Henry was not immune. "Ye see, Meara was into drugs, heavy like. We'd come to know each other and I was tryin' to help her out. I've got younger siblings, and the thought I might have another family somewhere was interestin' to me. But it was all tangled up with anger at my da for wantin' to spend time with that other family and less time with me and the rest. And worse yet that he never had the guts to tell me. Mind, it was like to have made me want to kill him and mayhap he knew that."

"And Meara?"

"Oh, Meara." Henry swallowed hard and Hank wondered if he'd had feelings for her or if she had just been a project for him. "She was going out one night to meet a fella, she said, and would I mind watchin' Emily? I had a bad feelin' but I agreed since she said she'd be back by ten. But ten came and went as did eleven and twelve. I had no one to take over to watch Emily so I went to bed. Somewhere's around three in the mornin', the police is at my door givin' me the bad news. They found my address in her purse and not much else. Said she'd OD'd and they couldn't revive her."

Hank watched his half brother's face, saw expressions of sadness and anger cross all at once, and knew he spoke the truth. "So what happened then? How'd ye get to keep Emily?"

"I told them the truth. I was the only kin she had, as distant as it was. There was more to it—they tried to take her and put her in a home but I fought it. She was a good kid, cute. Didn't deserve to be with people she didn't know, who didn't care about her.

"Mam came to the rescue. It was her who really adopted Emily. But as she was still busy workin' and Em needed someone who was there more often, she stayed with me."

"Your mam adopted her? Why?"

"Why not? She's like a granddaughter, our da's granddaughter, eh? She's all encompassing, is Mam."

There wasn't much Hank could say to that. He wondered if his own mam would have been as gracious. And out of the blue, he wondered how it was that Henry had wandered in to Killarney. "When did you decide to come to Kerry? Didn't ye have a job in Cork somewhere?"

Henry nodded and took another sip of his brew. The last cup Siobhan poured was strong enough to melt a spoon, Hank knew, feeling the bitterness on his tongue.

Clearing his throat, Henry answered Hank's question. "Once we'd settled into a relationship, Emily and I, I thought we'd spend some time to go and look for the rest of the family. I'd learned from Meara that there was you and yer mam. I hadn't expected to hear that yer mam had passed, and I'm truly sorry for that."

Hank acknowledged Henry's words with a nod and asked, as he was genuinely curious, "Your mam is still healthy?"

Henry grinned. "Still healthy and ridin' herd on the other four, three more boys and the last one a cailín."

"I'd like to meet them one day, if that's okay?"

"One day. But one step at a time, hm?"

A sudden thought made Hank ask. "I got sent a photo of Emily's birth certificate with my name on it. Was that just a fabrication?"

Siobhan grinned. "It's amazing what ye can do with the right computer program."

He grinned at that. Not rocket science, he reflected. And

then the question that had been burning in Hank's mind finally formed. "Our da," he asked, looking his half brother square in the eye. "Is he…"

"Gone," said Henry, matter-of-factly. "Gone before I met Meara. Gone when I was still a lad, about fourteen. There was an accident with the truck that brought the stone. It broke an axle and rolled. Da was thrown from the truck and crushed by the stone. Life was hard for a while after that but Mam had a good job and so we didn't suffer overly much, just missed the wage that da brought in."

Hank was about to ask another question when Henry said, "I sure didn't miss the beatin's, though."

"He beat you, too?"

Henry looked at Hank, saying, "Humph, one more thing we have in common."

An idea occurred to Hank then and he knew that if he never asked, he'd never know. "Did he have a regular schedule when he was away? You know, did he stay away for about the same time or be away as much as he was at home?"

Henry's black brows furrowed, hiding the blue within his eyes until he had his answer. "Come to think of it, yeah, he did. Used to go away every three months or so, stay away for a couple, give or take, and then come home. Didn't seem to have any more money to show for it according to my mam."

"And when he was killed," began Hank, "was that a time when he would have left?"

As if a light had suddenly turned itself on in Henry's eyes, he looked back at Hank, a suddenly softer look as if the hard part was now behind them. "Ye might have something there, m' brother. He was headin' out of town with that load of stone, sayin' he had a chimney to build for a client down Kerry way. It's a long way to haul stone but there would have been enough for a chimney, or to repair one. He never said when he was comin' back and Mam didn't seem to care. I think she was glad of him going for periods at a time. He was a good man and a good father in some ways but he'd get to the bottom of a bottle and turn right vicious."

"That's why I won't let you drink, ye eejit," laughed Siobhan. "Ye're just like him, Henry." She ruffled his hair and Hank could see the love in the gesture as she twirled the long, wavy strands between her fingers. "God, you men and your fabulous hair. What I wouldn't do to have this on my head."

Hank laughed at her wistfulness and remembered someone else's hands running through his own dark, wavy locks.

He sat a moment as the last piece of the puzzle clicked into place and took a deep breath before he spoke. He felt the air penetrate to the depths of his lung and he let it out slowly before speaking. "Despite my own mam having told him to leave and never come back, he was going to anyway."

"I think so," said Henry. "They found a couple of things in the truck that didn't make sense for him to have there. They, or rather we, all thought that perhaps he'd been out shoppin' for gifts for us to bring us back from his travels. He sometimes did that, you know."

"I know. Meara and I often got a wee somethin', even if it was just candy."

"I can't remember exactly what all he had in there. Might have been candy but there was something there for a woman and it wouldn't have fit Mam."

Hank looked up in expectation of Henry's next words. "It was some sort of lacy thing, a negligee or somethin'. Mam wouldn't wear anything like that. She's almost as wide as she is tall. That little bit of lace wouldn't have fit past her kneecaps if'n she'd tried to pull it up." He began to laugh and Hank couldn't help but join in.

"It would have fit my own mother," he said quietly once the laughter had subsided. "I guess he loved her after all, even though she'd thrown him out."

"Oh, my mam threw Da out a few times before but he always came back and was always forgiven."

In the silence that followed, Henry reached out and clasped a meaty had on Hank's shoulder. "Welcome to the family," was all he said.

Hank didn't need to know much more than that. Somehow things had worked out that his old girlfriend had met and fallen in love with his half brother. He had a whole other family out there; Emily, whom he had yet to meet, and other siblings. Would Laura be willing...but he didn't finish the thought because the one he was most curious about was not there.

"Where's Emily? When can I meet her?"

"She'll be home directly. I asked her to stay at her friend's until seven. It's near that now."

"Did ye tell her anything about me?"

"Ye mean does she know you're her uncle? Yeah, we did. And she's excited to meet ye, but really, I just needed to know all would be well so's when she came in, we'd either be friends or ye'd have left."

Hank nodded, absentmindedly rubbing his jaw. "Understandable."

As if mention of her name had called her forth, Emily walked through the door. A great silence hung over the room as Hank stood and faced her. The clock in the kitchen ticked once for every heartbeat in his chest. His palms felt sweaty. He was light-headed, which had nothing to do with the earlier punch to his jaw.

And suddenly she was in his arms as if she'd known him all along, squeezing him as if she'd never let him go. By some will of their own, his arms enfolded her into him, his hands pressed her head against his chest, and he felt the soft, black waves of hair brushing his chin. Her first great sob was felt through his entire being, as if he was her mam come back for her. "It's alright mo chroi, it's alright."

He didn't know how long he'd been standing there, only knew when Siobhan came and put a hand on his shoulder that whatever would come, they'd laid the past to rest and all would be well.

At least, it would be on this side of the pond. A mental image of Laura flooded his mind, of the possibility that maybe, one day, they'd have a child together as pretty as Emily. And maybe he'd hold her like he was holding Emily, comforting her from whatever fears dared threaten. He'd be a knight for his wee girl if he were ever lucky enough to have one.

Chapter Twenty-two

Hank lay alone in his bed, unable to sleep, thinking of having Laura beside him once again. He imagined her waking, wondered how she was making out and if Figaro was being good. He went over their last conversation, the night he left her in her cabin, a palace compared to what he'd known in his lifetime. It hadn't ended well. Driving alone through the night into town had given him time to settle his mind on what he had to do. He'd wanted her to come with him, to discover the beauty of his homeland and to help remove the taint of the past that seemed to linger still. But she had steadfastly refused. So he'd come to Ireland, alone, with a need to find some answers to a hurt that went bone deep.

It had healed somewhat, meeting his half brother and his niece. Even seeing Siobhan again after so many years had turned out well. She wasn't vindictive after all, just trying to bring together a family where only one half knew of the other's existence.

Perhaps the most amazing part of the evening was when Henry's mother had walked in the door. Completely unexpected by anyone, she waltzed in as if she owned the place; the only announcement of her coming was a quick rap-rap on the back door before she entered.

"Oh, ye've a guest, I didn't know," she exclaimed on seeing Hank. A curious expression crossed her features.

Henry's face flushed, although his outward bearing was as neutral as could be. His features hid his every thought. The only tell-tale sign of his nervousness, besides the pinking of his cheeks, was the way he began to fidget with his teacup.

Standing, he made introductions, not leaving anything out. "Ah, Mam, this is Hank Mulligan. He's Da's son, brother to Meara, and uncle to Emily." Turning to Hank, he said, "Hank, me mam, Mrs. O'Farrell."

Hank was about to shake her hand when she pulled him from Emily's arms and embraced him in something akin to a bear hug. Her short, broad stature belied a strength in her grip as she came close to cutting off his wind.

"Never mind the 'Mrs. O'Farrell'," she said, a cheeky grin spread across a wide, pretty face, punctuating the dimples in her cheeks, "ye can call me Mam or Kathleen. Some even call me Katy."

"I'm that gobsmacked, I am," exclaimed Hank, warming instantly to Henry's mam. "I never imagined," he began, but stopped short when he felt himself tear up.

"Ah, don't fash yerself, a mhac, I imagine this is all quite new for you."

With a nod of his head, Hank acknowledged his feelings of overwhelming acceptance and only later realized she'd referred to him as her son.

Emily, his sister's child, stood in what could only be described as awe as she followed him back to the table.

"I'll put on another pot," offered Siobhan to an answering of nods all around.

The evening progressed from there. Hank had more questions answered regarding his absentee father, but was no more surprised than when Kathleen told him about his mother and how she and Henry Sr. met.

"He was down here on legitimate business, your da was," she began, "when he ran into your mam, mindin' her own business and lookin' like she hadn't eaten in a week, or so he told me. She was always skinny, was your mam, according to Henry. When I first found out about him bein' with another woman, and worse, havin' children by her, I was so angry I threw him out. 'Go to her,' I told him, 'I don't want ye no more.' But after he left, his words kept ringin' in my ears. 'But I love ye, too,' he'd said, and I didn't doubt him.

"I cried all night long, couldn't go to work the next day, nor the next, but eventually I got to missin' him and realizin' I had too many questions I couldn't answer without talkin' to him again. So I waited and wrote all my questions down because I knew without a doubt that the ol' bastard would come home eventually, tail between his legs as always.

"And one day he did. Just waltzed in the door like he'd just come from a midday walk. It was then I began askin' the questions I'd written up and he was cowed enough by then to tell all. I'd threatened him with never seein' his brood again if he didn't. And he knew I had him by his bollocks, so he began." She turned to Hank then and said, "So, is there anything you want to know?"

Clearing his throat roughly, Hank asked, "How did a chance meetin' on the street end up with them together?"

"Oh, right, I got sidetracked. Well, him seein' her there, all skin and bones and lookin' pretty despite that, well, he just took a shine to her, I suppose. He bought her some lunch and she told him that she'd left home and couldn't find work so he put her up with him for a while in the little place he kept for himself, here in Killarney."

"The place me and Meara grew up in, was it?" At Kathleen's nod, he said, "So that was why it was so small. He never meant it to be a family home."

"No, surely it was never meant for that. Y'see, sometimes he was too tired to drive so far back to Inishannon for the night, and truly, I was grateful for the place bein' here because then I knew he'd be safe. Add to that his night blindness. Anyway, there was lots of work for him here in Killarney and most of his cronies were here, folks that worked the stone like he did. It made sense, although after he met her, he was never home as often.

"So," she warmed to her story, "one thing led to another, I suppose, and she ended up pregnant and still no work. Things were beginnin' to look up then, money-wise in Ireland, but not everyone prospered. I think yer mam was just eighteen, maybe younger, when she had you and then, after that, never really worked at all except for some part-time work she found. Henry was hard-pressed to keep up with the demands of two households but I didn't care by that time. I'd written him off as my husband and we became more like business partners, sharin' a same interest but not carryin' on as if we were still married. I had a good job, after all, and he was a good father to his kids while he was home."

"Humph," said Henry from his side of the table, watching Siobhan warm his tea from the fresh pot. Clearly, thought Hank, he and his half brother were on the same wavelength, remembering the often unwarranted beatings with antipathy.

"Where did she come from, do ye know?" asked Hank. His mother had never told him, only gesturing up north.

"I don't know for sure," answered Kathleen, and Hank could see the apology in her eyes, "but there's a Mulligan family seat in Donegal; Mulligans have been there since ancient times. You could start lookin' there, if you want to know more."

From the other side of the table, Henry spoke, quietly, almost as if afraid he was going to be heard. "I know."

They all shot him a look that had surprise written all over their faces.

"Don't look so shocked," he said, as deadpan as ever. "Da used to talk to me when he was workin' outside. I'd stand and watch, always fascinated by what he could do, and while he was workin' he'd tell me things, just like I told Hank he did. It's how I knew about him and Meara before anyone else, even you, Mam." Kathleen wore a look of surprise, but if she felt anything else, Hank was at a loss to know. So, mused Hank, that was where Henry got the ability to look stone-faced when he, himself, wore his heart on his sleeve.

Henry told of a girl who survived a fire but was too young to know her mother, who had perished in the blaze. They had arrived there only recently and no one really knew them, or where they were from, according to neighbors.

Henry's voice was smooth like heated whiskey as he spoke. "They found the little girl's lunchbox in the back garden, with the name Ceilidh Mulligan inside. It had a wee toy in it…"

"A pink, stuffed pony," said Hank, breaking in.

Henry nodded. "So she had it still?"

"I remember it, although sometime when I got older, it disappeared. I don't know what happened to it."

A noncommittal shrug was Henry's response. "After that it was a series of foster homes, but she never stayed in one too long. Eventually, she ran away and the rest, as they say, is history."

"But she came from Donegal?" asked Hank.

Henry shook his head. "I don't really know. That's just where her mother died; and if there was anything found out about her family, if she had a father somewhere or grandparents, no one seemed to know and Da said she seemed even less inclined to talk about them. In any event, Da never told me more than that. O' course," he continued, eyebrows raised as if he were seeing words inside his head, "there was the investigation when we wanted to adopt wee Emily here, that turned up nothin'."

The girl blushed, her mouth curved into a delicate smile. Meara's smile, thought Hank.

"Hank," Kathleen said softly into the stillness of the room, "not everyone knows everything about their family. Ye had a mam and da who loved ye. They both did their best for you and your sister, and even if ye don't know more than ye do, isn't it enough to know ye were cared for? Loved? And thought enough of by yer da for him to travel back and forth from our family to yours every couple of months?"

Hank thought about that and it began to make sense. He hadn't realized his mam had been so young, although he saw the dates written on her chart when she was admitted to the hospital just before she died. Even then, it hadn't sunk in just how young she had been. And he had never thought to ask where she came from or how come he had no grandparents like other kids did. He recalled one boy in his class at school had no grandparents either, and he'd felt a camaraderie with the young boy as if they shared a wicked secret.

Back in his hotel room, he sighed into the night. The mountains of British Columbia seemed a very long way off, and his heart felt as empty as it ever had. He missed Laura terribly, missed her laughter, her impulsive behavior, as ribald as it often was. But more than that, he missed the softness of her and the emotion in her lovely green-gold eyes when she lay in his arms after loving.

Finally drifting off to sleep, his last thought was the hope that morning would bring some resolution to his troubled heart.

***

It was another day at the office. Hank had been gone for weeks, weeks where every day had felt like a month. Laura missed him sorely but wasn't about to give in to her feelings. It would pass, she thought. This horrible emptiness would pass, and so she buried herself in her work until Kerry pulled her into his office on a Friday afternoon, nearly four weeks after Hank had gone.

"Have a seat," he invited, "I have some news to share."

About to sit down, Laura turned abruptly and took a step toward the door.

"Hey, where are you going?" asked Kerry in a surprised voice.

"This has Hank written all over it and I don't want to hear it." She was standing, feeling defiant, anything but confident because where Hank was concerned, the truth was that she was so in love and so heartbroken, she knew she'd crack under the weight of whatever Kerry had to say. She didn't want to hear how Hank had married Siobhan. She didn't want to hear how the child really was his, or that he was never coming back after all.

The voice that brooked no argument in a court of law was in full attendance now and said, "Sit." The finger pointed at the chair before the heavy, mahogany desk where Kerry sat behind it, leaning back in his leather chair, one leg crossed over the other, ankle to knee.

She knew better than to refuse an order, even if it did sound like one you'd give to a dog. Kerry was her boss, after all, and although he was also a friend, she knew better than to argue when he took that tone.

Looking stern, Kerry unwound himself to lean steepled fingers on his desktop, and with a grim line to his mouth, said, "You must know by now that I am not a meddler in anyone's affairs. And this isn't about what you want or don't want. This is about some news you need to hear. What you do with it is up to you. Got it?"

Shakily, Laura nodded.

"Good. Now, remember before Hank left and we were waiting for the DNA comparison?" Laura nodded again. "It took a few days longer because we had to have a second one done. It's call an avuncular DNA test and it helps define relationships, not paternal, but brother, sister, aunt, uncle, etcetera. You with me?"

Again Laura nodded, feeling her heart pick up the pace in her chest.

"It turns out that if this avuncular test is accurate, the girl is Hank's niece."

"His niece? Not his daughter?" She couldn't help but feel relieved. It was awful to know that she really didn't want Hank to have a child by another woman. She wanted to be the one to bear his children, only her. It wasn't that she wouldn't have been willing to take the child in, only that she just knew the girl would always have stood between her and complete happiness with the man she loved. And refused to marry, said the voice in her head.

"The reason I'm telling you this is because Hank asked me to. He's told me the whole story, but I promised him I wouldn't tell you the rest. If you want to hear it, you need to get it from him. And since you won't answer his calls or respond to his emails, your only choice is to go pay a visit to Ireland. He's got a few more things to tidy up there and I don't have to tell you that he'd really prefer to do that with you by his side."

Tears pricked at the back of her eyes. Her heart was beating so rapidly she thought it would bounce out of her chest and her hands were too shaky to take the tissue Kerry held out for her.

"I can't," she managed to get out. "I can't."

Kerry watched the woman before him crumble. No wonder Hank loved her. If he, himself, wasn't old enough to be her father, he'd feel the same; but the truth was, she was out of his league. But that didn't stop the veil of protectiveness he wanted to cast around her.

"Laura, look at me," he commanded, and Laura, with her tear-stained face, looked back at him through glistening eyes.

"Don't be an idiot. Hank isn't Erik. Somehow you've got it in your head that Hank doesn't love you and you'll end up the same as when you were married to Erik. Well, I'm here to tell you you're wrong. You've been swooning about here for the past few weeks driving me, and everyone else, crazy with your workaholic attitude. That's not you. You work hard, yes. But you come in at nine and go home at five. Lately you've been here before I get in and I'm usually here by eight at the latest. You were right when you said I work until all hours. And suddenly so do you. While I'm sure my partners will agree that it has helped our caseload, I'm not so sure it's good for you. Hiding in work won't get him out of your heart. You need to go see him again, make sure he's what you want, and then make your decision." He pulled an envelope from the middle drawer of his desk and slid it across the blotter to her.

"So here's your plane ticket; you leave tomorrow but the return is open. Come back when you're ready. Consider it a bonus for all the extra work you've done to help us win that last case. And if I see you mooning around here any more today, I'm going to personally drive you to the airport and make sure you get on that plane."

"I can't go," she cried, disbelief and something akin to panic on her face.

"Why not?" asked Kerry.

"Figaro," she said, blowing her nose. "I can't leave Figaro. Who'd feed him?"

"Oh right, the cat. Hank mentioned him. Don't worry about him, I'll look after him. Hank said I just have to feed him and flush the toilet after he goes. Does he really do that?" he asked.

"Yes," she laughed through her tears, "he really does. It's amazing, I know. He's quite the cat. Just don't leave the lid down or he'll let you know about it."

"I'm sure he will." He looked at her, took in her eyes, puffy and red-rimmed from crying. Yet now that he'd ordered her to go, put her in a place where she felt she had no choice, she somehow seemed calmer. "So, with the cat all settled, you'll just need to give me a spare house key so I can do whatever needs to be done. Your place isn't so far from mine that I can't help you two out."

Nodding, Laura bit her lower lip in thought. "I can leave the key with Sarah, my friend across the hall. She looks after my plants for me when I go away," she said by way of explanation. "Her buzzer number is 1103. She'll be happy to help you out," she finished.

"Okay, I think I can remember that. Now go. Don't bother wasting any more of my time. I'm a busy man," he said, but couldn't help the curve to his mouth, laughing as he said it.

Laura smiled back at him and he wondered for the millionth time since she divorced her husband if he'd ever had a chance with her. Still, he recognized that life had funny twists and turns and nothing was written in stone.

Except for maybe this thing between Laura and Hank. That looked like a done deal.

And Kerry was okay with that.

Her tears finished, the tissues put away, Laura rose from her chair. "Alright, then. It seems I have some packing to do."

"Yes, you do. And don't forget to pack a raincoat."

"What?"

"It's April. It's Ireland. You'll need it."

He watched Laura go back to her desk, a smile gracing her lovely face all the way. He could tell she was smiling as she quickly tidied her desk and then, as he stood with his hands in his pockets, noted the moment when she glanced up to see him through the glass door of his office, standing behind his desk, making certain she'd do as she was told.

He folded his arms across his chest and wondered, not for the first time, why he'd let the difference in their years stop him from making any advances. If I ever meet anyone like her again… he thought, but didn't bother finishing the sentence.

Laura looked up once more, showed him a grin as broad as her face, then grabbed her purse and coat, and with a final wave, headed out the door.

Kerry picked up the phone to dial Hank as he promised he would do and then put it back down. He'd let surprise be the master of that relationship.

***

The first thing Laura did when she got home was knock on Sarah's door. Sarah, older than Laura by almost ten years, answered the knock right away.

Laura couldn't contain herself. "You'll never guess," she said, the knuckles of her fist hiding the huge grin she couldn't help.

Sarah's large, almond-shaped eyes widened in response and she urged Laura inside at once. "Come in, quickly," she invited in her very cultured British accent, "don't keep me in suspense!"

"I can't stay," said Laura, who felt as if she were standing on hot coals, "I need to go home to pack. Sarah," she breathed out, as if becoming quieter would help the pins and needles she was feeling, "I'm going to Ireland!"

"Ireland," exclaimed Sarah, "Why?" And then, "Oh, never mind. It's Hank, isn't it." A big intake of air was quickly followed with, "And he's asked you to go over there, hasn't he." She seemed as excited at the prospect as Laura did, both standing there, eyes wide with glee. "But I thought you'd given up on him?" Suddenly still, Sarah queried Laura.

The change in Sarah's tone couldn't bring Laura down. She was too excited about seeing Hank, not caring that it was Ireland. She would have flown to Antarctica if that was where he was. "I know, and I had. But Kerry just gave me some news and then he handed me this ticket and told me to leave! Isn't that fabulous?"

Sarah nodded, ignoring the buzz from her cell phone.

Hearing the phone, Laura said, "I'll go, you need to get that."

"No, I don't," said Sarah, rolling her eyes with a look of annoyance. "It's likely my parents, still trying to get me married to that fellow in Hong Kong. I absolutely refuse. I don't need them to find me a man, especially when I don't want one," she said, and Laura knew they'd been over this time and again.

Sarah's parents, elderly Hong Kong natives, wanted their daughter to marry and move back to Hong Kong, but Sarah, an independent woman with her own business as a CPA, was quite happy where she was. Away from the prying eyes of busybody parents.

At least she was laughing about it, thought Laura as Sarah made a gesture that dismissed the phone and her parents' intentions in one motion.

"Never mind me. You are going to Ireland to be with the love of your life! You are coming back, though. Aren't you?"

Laughing, Laura nodded. "Of course we're coming back. At least, I think we are. I mean, there's Figaro." As if mention of the cat brought to mind her initial purpose, she said, "And that reminds me of why I'm here. I need you to let Kerry in when he comes to feed Figaro. I'll get my spare key and bring it over to you before I go."

"When do you leave?"

"Tomorrow. Kerry wasn't taking any chances that I'd sit around and have doubts!"

Laughing, Sarah giggled out, "Oh, that's too funny. He knows you so well."

"Yeah, he does," acknowledged Laura. "So I'd best get going and pack. Will you be here in the morning?"

"Oh, yeah. You know I do most of my work from home and tomorrow I don't have any meetings until later in the day, so it's all good."

"Okay, then, I'll see you tomorrow."

"I'll be here," she finished, waving Laura out the door.

Laura stepped across the hall, inserted her key, and pushed the heavy, weighted door open and then let it fall closed behind her with a soft click. Figaro greeted her, rubbing against her leg with his usual half purr, half meow voice.

"It's not time for dinner yet, my boy," she crooned, stroking the big orange head. Crouching down beside him, she whispered in a conspiratorial voice, "I'm going to go see your dad. Figaro, I think I'm in love and I can't be without him. What am I going to do?"

The big cat merely meowed, more insistently this time, curling himself around her foot, rolling onto his back in an open invitation for a tummy rub.

"Sorry, little bud, not right now. I have to go pack." She stood and removed her coat and flung it on the chair to go in search of her suitcase when a curious idea came to her. Would Kerry find Sarah attractive? And then in the same thought, she dismissed it. Sarah would never go for anyone, least of all Kerry, who could be overbearing at times, so used to being the lawyer and having people cater to him.

Her mind back on the matter at hand and having found her suitcase, Laura got down to the business of packing.

Chapter Twenty-Three

The grueling flight was over. Laura held her stomach and thought that whatever she'd had on board certainly hadn't agreed with her because she felt as if she could be sick at a moment's notice. Once off the plane though, she began to feel better as she walked toward the immigration booths. A quick couple of questions were easily answered, her passport stamped, and she was admitted to Ireland. It was a little anticlimactic, she observed.

There had been a bit of confusion once she'd collected her bags; uncertainty as to her travel into Killarney itself. Could she catch a train, or take a bus? Kerry had said she could grab a cab but an hour and half taxi ride was surely going to be pricey.

"Excuse me," she asked, approaching the information desk, "I need to get into Killarney. Can you tell me the best way?"

"Ye've no car rental, then?" At Laura's shake of her head, the woman, a middle aged lady of stout proportions, continued in a friendly manner, pulling out brochures and pointing with the tip of her pen to the options open to her. She reminded Laura somewhat of an elderly aunt she'd had as a child, her mother's aunt if she remembered right, who was friendly to a fault. The one lingering impression Laura had of Great-Aunt Beatrice was her hair, the rusty-colored locks curled tightly into neat rows, rarely a hair out of place. Her own titian locks had come from her mother's side, although her own mother's hair was a light brown with only a few red highlights that glinted in the sun. They usually skip a generation, she'd once been told, but couldn't remember who had said that. It didn't matter because the lady before her had spread out a train schedule and was beginning to give Laura directions.

"You can get the bus into Cork right outside here. Just tell the driver where you need to go and he'll make sure you get there. It'll take you right to the train station. The train leaves every few hours; yer best bet is to reserve a seat on the 12:30 train out of Cork. See here?"

She was pointing with her pen at the glossy pamphlet before Laura. "So," she continued, her short, russet-colored hair bobbing in wayward curls about her face, "ye need to catch the one that says 'Intercity to Dublin Heuston'."

Laura gasped her objection, "But I don't want to go to Dublin."

"Ah, well, it's only the line you need to take. It gets you to Mallow, here," she drew a line with the pen, "and then you have to change trains to get the one that says Intercity to Tralee. Check the board for the right platform. It stops in Killarney, which is where you want to get off," she finished, beaming a toothy smile.

"Oh, of course. I see that now," replied Laura, hoping she was following what the woman was telling her.

"You can get first class to Mallow but after that it's only standard class. Did ye want to reserve a seat here? I'd recommend it. The trains can get pretty full, being a weekend and all."

A weekend. Laura had forgotten that she'd added a day by flying through the night. It was Friday when she left…how many hours ago? "Oh, standard is fine. I just have a small suitcase."

She paid her fare, found the bus, and after a brief waiting period at the train station, was finally ensconced for the twenty-minute ride from Cork to Mallow. After that, a quick half hour stop to find the right platform and change trains and she was finally on her way to Killarney. Her mind tried to tally the hours she'd logged in traveling to see Hank but she was too tired. Her eyes closed, her head rested against the window frame, and before she realized it, she'd slept most of the way to her destination, waking only minutes before her stop.

She jerked awake, glanced around, hoping to be able to ask someone where they were. A panicked moment held her in its grip. What if she had missed her stop? What then?

As the train rumbled along, the clack-clack of its wheels against the rails was hypnotic, enticing her to close her eyes once again. This time, she resisted and instead focused on the scenery racing by. It was all so lush!

Her eyes scanned the rail ahead as much as she could, hoping for a glimpse of some sort of sign, anything that would tell her where she was. Eventually, the train began to slow and she noted from the signage that it was pulling into Killarney. A shiver of glee ran up her spine as she realized she was really here. Really in Killarney, Hank's home. His home once upon a time, she reminded herself. Would it be his home again? Would he want to stay?

The giddiness that she first felt was slightly overshadowed by the possibility that Hank would not want to return to Canada. Well, she'd deal with it if it ever came down to that, she promised herself, and picking up her suitcase, stepped off the train into the heart of Killarney.

Kerry had given her the name of the hotel Hank was staying at and she noted during the few minutes she was awake on the train how beautiful the land could be, with its verdant countryside, ancient churches, and everything as green as green could be. Hank had been right when he said there was nowhere on earth greener than Ireland.

Noting a distinct settling in her stomach, she surmised the catnap she'd had on the train had been all she needed.

The giddiness she'd felt earlier was reasserting itself until she realized she had no idea where she was going. There was a large hotel right beside the train station but that wasn't the one she needed. Standing outside the station, the extended handle of her suitcase in her grasp, she was prepared to walk until she found it but a chance meeting saved her from herself. At least, she thought it had. The man's blue eyes smiled at her, laughing as he helped her retrieve the handbag he'd inadvertently knocked out of her grasp.

Automatically, "Oh, sorry," came out of Laura's mouth.

"No, it's me should apologize," came the reply as he handed it back to her, grinning as he left her to follow his friends.

Something nagged at her but she let it go, too wrapped up in the newness of her surroundings to process what she couldn't put her finger on. "Wait," she called, and the fellow stopped and turned, eyebrows raised in enquiry. "I was wondering if you could help me find my hotel? Tell me where it is, I mean."

The grin returned to his features and he excused himself from the group and took a moment to listen to her plea. "Of course," he said on hearing its name, "it's not far. Just to the road that way, cross it and turn left, and ye'll be there in no time." He gave her a wink and turned to join his group that seemed to be loitering as if waiting for a bus or something.

She thanked him and began walking, noting the tall, leafy trees and the signs on black iron posts, names written in Gaelic with the English translation beneath. A bird she supposed was a crow topped the post, cawing loudly as she stood looking up. Its gray hood was distinct, making her wonder if it really was a crow or some other bird that resembled them except for the gray.

As she tried to read the Gaelic, the bird flew off, startling her into turning her head and thus noting a magnificent stone church only a few minutes away. She took a moment to appreciate the beauty of it and to wonder about its history before attempting to cross the road.

Large busses were lined along the curb, likely waiting for connections from the train, she thought absentmindedly before taking a tentative step out onto the road. It didn't appear that any traffic was heading her way past the line of busses so she took another step, only to hear a warning beep-beep, before jumping back in surprise. Cursing herself for her foolishness, forgetting the traffic would be coming from the opposite direction, she scrambled back onto the sidewalk, only then noticing a set of crossing lights less than fifty feet from where she stood.

Her face felt as if it was flaming red. She was embarrassed at her own stupidity and only briefly acknowledged that she had just traveled a very long way and was undoubtedly tired. It was only natural that she would look the wrong way.

"Yeah, right," she mumbled to herself, heading toward the lights, dragging her luggage tiredly behind her. Ignoring the lure of adventure for now, she crossed the street at the lights, straightened her jacket against the oncoming breeze, and walked away from the great stone edifice. With her back to the church, she headed down the road, hoping she was going in the right direction.

She passed a parking lot on her right before crossing what looked like an alley, and then some shops and an interior decorating business that peaked her interest. Promising herself she'd check the shops later, she kept going, because as enticing as the shops were, fatigue was plaguing her and the gritty feeling behind her eyes told her just how sleep-deprived she was. Although her bag was fairly light, it was beginning to feel like she was towing a suitcase filled with bricks behind her.

Moments later, she stood in front of the hotel, coming upon it almost by accident as it was so much a part of the shops beside it that if she hadn't been looking up at the time, she would have missed the large, gold letters of its name. The broad entrance was framed in black-painted wood, glossy and impressive in its form. The interior was spacious, classy, and outfitted with furnishings fit for a royal drawing room. It was perfect.

The front desk was a large expanse of white, brightly lit and efficient in its presentation. The clerks behind the counter were smiling; someone said something funny and they laughed. It looked like a friendly place.

Spirits buoyed by both the ambience of the place and the smiles on the clerks as she approached, her happiness was soon doubled when she checked in.

"We've a room across the hall from your friend, if that would work for ye?" the clerk responded to her query of a room near Hank's. The woman's grin was infectious, making Laura return the smile as she tucked her credit card away.

Nodding her thanks, she was about to walk away when she asked if she could leave a message for her Hank. A broad smile lit the clerk's face as she quickly handed over a pen and a piece of paper.

Quickly scrawling her message, she then folded the paper and handed it back to the clerk with her thanks.

"Nay bother," the clerk grinned. At least, with the Irish lilt and laughter in the woman's voice, it certainly sounded like that. Was everyone in Ireland was so friendly?

Refusing the offer of someone to take her bag, she made her way through the elegant foyer and down the hall to the elevator, old but as classy as everything else in the hotel. It swiftly took her up to the top floor where she made her way along the corridor to the room that matched the number on her key. As she pushed the door open before her, stepped inside and looked around, an intake of breath that was held for the briefest of moments escaped into the quiet of the room.

The door closed behind her as she placed her suitcase on the stand in the closet to glance in delight at the room around her. Stepping toward the bed, she noted the green and gold décor that was so stylish and chic looking, a real treat from other hotels she'd been in. Not that any had been recent, but having traveled before, she was familiar enough with what was out there. Most of them left her feeling rather sterile, but this, this was different! Charming, with a bit of class thrown in. She stepped farther inside, inspected the bathroom, and decided that a bath would be in order before bed, it looked so divine.

Moving to the window, Laura saw that it overlooked the street in front of the hotel itself, which suited her just fine. She loved to see the comings and goings of everything, and being new to this part of the world, it was all so fascinating. Just as she was about to turn away from the view, something familiar caught her eye. Looking again, she realized it was Hank, standing on the other side of the road near something that was advertising pizza. Her heart beat madly in her chest. He didn't know she was coming, she hadn't told anyone except Sarah.

And then she saw the woman with him, knew it had to be Siobhan, and calmed herself. Her heartbeat slowed. Hadn't Kerry said something about Siobhan? She didn't think the woman was after Hank the way she'd initially thought but then why were they holding hands? And before she could rationalize that, Hank's head bent, Siobhan's face tilted upward and the pair kissed.

Deeply.

Hank's hands went to Siobhan's shoulders and Laura looked away. She couldn't bear to watch.

Sitting on the bed, she felt all the euphoria of experiencing a new and very different place drain quickly away. Exhaustion overwhelmed her and she gave way to tears that progressed quickly into heartfelt sobs of pain at all she'd lost. This was her fault. Only hers. Hank had tried to phone. He'd emailed and she'd ignored him. If she'd answered his phone calls, his emails; if she'd come when he'd asked, would the outcome be the same?

Suddenly, her stomach heaved and rolled and she held her breath, determined not to give in to another bout of nausea. She went into the washroom, wet a cloth, and washed her face, feeling better but completely exhausted. The bed suddenly held a deep appeal, so without bothering to pull the covers back, she simply flopped down on it.

Her tears lessened as she lay staring up at the ceiling. The bed was comfortable, she thought, her gaze following the patterned lines along the ceiling near the light. It wasn't a smooth ceiling but neither was it what she'd heard people call a popcorn ceiling, either. The pattern went in swirls and as her eyes followed the lines, she felt them grow heavy. She had completely tired herself out, first with the flight and then the train. And although the walk from the station was really only ten minutes, that, too, had been tiring.

And now this. Solid proof that Hank was like every other guy out there and not to be trusted. He'd lied to her. His infidelity cut her to the bone, even though she knew she'd brought it on herself.

She closed her eyes and a tear seeped out. Wiping it away with the back of her hand, she turned her face into the pillow. She was done with men, she told herself as she sniffed back the next tear. Stoically, she took in a deep breath, but no matter how stern she was with herself, her heart hadn't seemed to have heard. Another tear threatened but never came. Her body relaxed, the relief of being able to stretch out, to lie down and give in to sleep was greater than her broken heart just then, and she drifted off to sleep.

**

Hank left Siobhan at the corner as he walked across the street to his hotel. Her kiss had surprised him, and for a moment, he fell into it. But the moment was brief, a split second before his mind registered that it wasn't what he wanted. Was Siobhan offering him something? He didn't care, and so he'd laid his hands on her shoulders and set her apart from him.

"What's that for?" he'd asked, part surprise, part anger.

Siobhan had the grace to at least look as flummoxed as he felt. "Oh, nothing. I, em, I was just excited about seeing Henry's siblings and I just got carried away. I'm that sorry, I am!" she exclaimed, and Hank had to believe her.

"Well, truth be told, I'm not sorry it happened."

"Ye're not?"

His remark seemed to take her completely by surprise.

Shaking his head, he dropped his hands from her shoulders and stuffed them in his pockets. The wind blew hard against his face and he blinked to shield his eyes. "No," he said, still squinting. "I guess I'd been wondering if there was anything left between us, if we needed to get anythin' straight. But that did it." He let his voice trail off. What more was there to say?

"I see." Her downcast eyes hid whatever she was thinking and Hank recalled snippets of their conversation over lunch. She'd told him about life with Emily and shown him photographs of the girl. She'd regaled him with stories of their early days together, for as much as the girl had been through and not having a clue who her real father was, Emily was a remarkably resilient and well-adjusted person. And beautiful, thought Hank, recalling the girl's wavy, raven locks as they blew in the wind on her way to school, and the midnight blue of her eyes that had made such an impression when meeting her. His sister may be gone but she lived on in her daughter, so like her in many ways.

He was saddened that Meara had met such an untimely end, especially the way she died. It didn't have to happen that way but he didn't finish the thought. It only reminded him that Meara might still be alive if not for his da. Every time he thought about his absentee father he became angry. Recalling the many discussions he'd had with Henry, hearing Henry's side of things and finding out that his half brother had suffered as well, Hank was even less charitable with his thoughts regarding his da. He made a silent vow to himself that should he ever have a child of his own, that child would never lack for a father in its life.

Henry had proven to be much like Hank, stepping up to the plate as well and offering a home for young Emily. And now with Siobhan, Emily had a mother figure as well as the father figure Henry represented. Emily was old enough to remember what life was like with her mam, the pair of them living for the most part like unwelcome gypsies. She seemed genuinely settled where she was, preferring a life in one house, with not one, but two people she could trust enough to look after her.

Her reaction to Hank the night they first met was with him still. It gave him a warm feeling inside to think that his sister's child would come to know him and feel the love he had for her as was her right. And his, he reflected, because that's what families were all about. Love and connections. Would Laura think that, too? He wanted her so much, if she would have him, and he wanted to share his newfound family with her.

Finally, Siobhan found her voice. "There's been a lot of water under the bridge, Hank. I cared for ye, deeply, and was ever so hurt when ye left the country to go with that Canadian girl. She didn't love ye, I could have told ye that but ye wouldn't listen. That's why I cornered you that night, the night before ye left. I was hoping ye'd see that we could have something even better than what that missy was offerin', but ye'd have none of it. So I left ye to your bed and your missy." She took a deep breath as if to shake off the thoughts. "And then I met Henry and realized that the good Lord had a different plan for me. I love Henry with all my heart, as wretched as he makes me feel sometimes with his spells of anger when he yells the house down. But I know he loves me, too. And Emily. And that's worth more than a romp in the hay with you, boyo."

Even though her words held a feeling of rejection for him,

Hank couldn't help but smile. He felt the same about Laura. She was worth everything to him.

"You'd best get going if you're to meet Henry's siblings," he said, indicating the groups of people lining up at the tour buses up the street, likely having come from the train.

"Oh, they'll be waiting for me, to be sure. That's why I left the car there."

They said their goodbyes and agreed to meet later but as Siobhan walked away, Hank couldn't help but wonder if she still held a small regret that it wasn't his shoes beside hers in her house.

Then, as he had done every day for the weeks he'd been at the hotel, he automatically went to the front desk to see if anything had arrived for him. He was hoping for a letter, a message, anything, but every time he had visited the desk before, the answer was always the same, "Nothing today, sorry."

Careful to school his expression so that his disappointment wouldn't show, he was outwardly surprised when the desk clerk smiled excitedly and waved him over. "Mr. Mulligan, I've a message for ye," she'd said, waving a piece of paper in her hand. "Whatever ye've been waitin' for is here. Least-wise, that's what I think."

Taking the paper from her hand he couldn't help but wink at her and smile. Her own smile behind her half-glasses was infectious. She seemed to be bubbling over with joy.

"So ye've somethin' for me, ye say," he remarked cheerily. And then he stopped halfway through the chuckle he was rumbling through.

"Is somethin' the matter?" She was an older lady in her sixties and Hank recognized the look of concern on her face. After all, he felt like crying, but in a good way. His lady love was upstairs waiting for him.

"No, missus, somethin's very right, and I thank ye for it."

He didn't want to wait for the lift but took the carpeted stairs of the grand staircase opposite the desk two at a time, his long legs striding quickly down the hall to stop in front of her door. Taking a moment to compose himself, he knocked firmly and felt his heart race, not from the exertion of running up the stairs but from the thrill of having her near him again.

When the door failed to open immediately, he repeated his knock, calling, "Laura? Are ye there?"

The door cracked open, revealing Laura's sleep-filled eyes and something else. Had she been crying?

"Are ye alright, darlin'? Ye don't look well." Stepping inside the room and closing the door behind himself, he resisted the urge to pull her into his arms for a longed-for kiss and hug and whatever else that would lead to. But he wasn't going to be pushy. He could tell something was off. "Laura? Can I get ye somethin'?"

"Please, just go away," she said quietly, so quietly he wasn't sure if he heard her correctly. She stood there, a solid wall of resistance, her titian hair tumbling about her shoulders as if she'd just woken up from a long, deep sleep.

"Go away? I just got here. Are ye ailin'?" Whatever was going on, she wasn't making any sense. If she was here, didn't that mean she wanted him? Her note had filled him with hope. Her words, though brief, indicated she couldn't wait to see him. Why come all this way to tell him she didn't want him anymore?

"I have eyes," she said, still not making sense as far he was concerned. "I saw you with her. Outside." Her arms were crossed in front of her and the firm set to her jaw told him she was keeping her anger in check. Barely.

"Her? Oh, ye mean Siobhan?" He breathed a sigh of relief. This, he thought, was something easily explained.

"Is that who it was? I kind of figured as much." She had been standing facing him but now she sat back down on the bed and turned her back to him.

"What about Siobhan?" He didn't understand why she was still angry. It was Siobhan, no secret lover. Just Siobhan.

"I saw you two kissing. People who kiss like that aren't just casual friends."

Understanding dawned and he took a deep breath. Clearly, his lady love, over-tired and now over-wrought, needed a gentle hand. "Darlin'," he began, only to be cut off.

"Don't call me that!"

"Alright. Laura, then." This was going to take a little more effort, he thought. Sitting down in the big chair opposite the bed so he could at least face her, he took in the way she looked, tried to analyze what was going on. She was pale, he thought, with such big dark circles under her eyes. The trip must have been very difficult for her, or maybe she had a sudden case of the flu. "I need ye to know how much I care for ye, how glad I am to see ye," he began.

"So glad you're out there in broad daylight kissing another woman?" she accused. A tear escaped from her eyes to roll down her cheek and she impatiently brushed it away.

Tears? He had somehow reduced this beautiful woman to tears? "Oh, my darlin'. I never meant to hurt you with what should have been a quick peck on the cheek for an old friend. Will ye give me leave to explain?" He waited, hopeful that she would at least respond to his plea.

A nod of the head. A small one and tentative, but it was there, followed up with, "Fine."

"Right." He knew that when a woman said "fine," it was anything but, and Laura was a woman, through and through. Filling his lungs with much needed air, he jumped in with what he hoped would disarm the immediate situation. "Siobhan was goin' to the train station when I left her on the corner, to pick up my half siblings, come from County Cork. We're all going to meet up at their place later tonight. It'll be a first meetin' for me. I didn't know they existed before the other day."

"You have siblings?" The new information seemed to put a crack in the shell of armor she'd wrapped around her since he'd entered the room. Taking another deep breath, he continued.

"Half siblings. It's a long story. I'll explain it all later and it'll be clear when we go to their place."

"Whose place? I thought you said they just got in on the train."

"Siobhan and Henry are together. They live together. My half siblings have all taken the time to come over here to meet me and to have a visit for a couple of days."

Eyes damp with tears and filled with fatigue gazed up at him from her spot on the bed. She was exhausted, not just tired, now that he could see her better. The dark circles were pronounced and he wanted nothing more than to gather her in his arms and make her feel better.

"Who's Henry?"

Silly fool, he thought. He had jumped right into the middle of something he'd been a part of and which she knew nothing about. The fact that he'd told her in his emails of all that was going on and named all the players and the why's and wherefores didn't mean much if, as he now suspected, she'd never read them.

Yet there was so much he, himself, didn't seem to know. Taking the barest of moments to gather his thoughts, he tried again. "Let me back up and I'll tell ye all if you're willing to listen." His eyes met hers and he could see she was beginning to perk up. Maybe her being upset was all wrapped up with her seeing him and Siobhan kissing?

He started at the beginning, telling her how he'd found out where Siobhan lived, only to find she was living with someone and was not as destitute as she wanted him to believe. From there it progressed to meeting Emily and then of the comings and goings since then. He was feeling comfortable with his findings and wanted to convey that to her.

She fidgeted on the bed, brushing an invisible bit of something from her lap as she took in his words. However comfortable he felt about his life as it stood, it was clear she wasn't feeling the same thing.

Turning those gorgeous green-gold eyes to him, she asked, "Does that mean you're going to stay here? That you're never coming home?"

Home. How good that word sounded! He longed for the wilds of the country he lived in, the wide open spaces framed beneath majestic mountains. He longed to go home and rebuild. And so he told her, as well as he knew how.

"It means that I'm settled in here," he pointed to his chest, to the heart he could feel beginning to pound at what he was thinking. "I'm ready to go home. With you. Wherever you are, that's where I want to be. However you'll have me, that's what and who I'll be. I love ye so much I can hardly think and to have ye so close, within arm's reach, and feelin' like ye don't want me to touch ye pains me somethin' fierce. And to know you're hurting because of somethin' I've done makes me a bit crazy inside. I've never wanted to hurt ye, only wanted to love ye. And it's sorry I am to the bottom of my heart that I've hurt ye, and I'll do whatever I must to make it all right."

Was that hope burning in her eyes and a turn of her lovely lips into a smile?

Hank took it as a good sign, stood, and took the two steps to stand before her. Pulling her into his embrace, he held her close. He felt her arms go about him as she cuddled into his neck, felt her warm breath down the open vee of his shirt. It was a feeling that had him grow hard instantly. "Is tú mo ghrá," he breathed into her hair near her ear. He didn't think she needed an interpretation to understand what he'd just said.

Chapter Twenty-Four

Laura breathed in Hank's scent, the special bouquet that was his alone: a mix of manly musk and sweat that gathered at his nape. She tucked her nose behind his ear and became intoxicated, drunk on his nearness. The smell of moisture-laden air on the once familiar leathery smell of his jacket brought back who he'd been to her and who he was now. This was Hank. Her man. And as his arms came about her, as she felt his hands grasp her butt cheeks and pull her close, she knew this was right. Through the material of his jeans, she felt the hardening of that special part of him and could almost smell the musk before she exposed him to her gaze. She wanted this man, if he'd have her after all she'd done to dissuade him. And those words, though uttered in Gaelic, echoed through her heart. He loved her; he'd told her so just moments ago.

Her malady seemed to have left her, or maybe she was too focused on Hank to care. His hands were doing wonderful things to her, making her body remember. She'd missed this, she thought as she stood in his presence and felt his touch. His fingers were like feathers along her skin beneath her sweater, soft, making her shiver at their caress. How had she made it through the last few weeks without him by her side, when every day without him had felt like a life sentence?

Hank's hands tugged at the garment and lifted it over her head. Laura concentrated on his chest, on the smoothness of it beneath her hands, because while he was undressing her, she was doing the same to him.

His heart beat a steady tattoo beneath her palms in a rhythm she was innately aware of while her fingers stroked the peaks of his flat, male nipples, erect and waiting for her to twirl them much as he would hers. In fact, she felt him do just that, felt the stirrings of excitement pierce her core and realized that while she'd been checking him out, he'd removed both her sweater and the blouse she'd worn beneath it, and opened her bra.

Smiling to herself, she dropped her arms so he could slide her bra off and watched as he stood back, gazing in rapt appreciation at what he saw, and knew in that moment a wanting so deep it made her moan. The cool air ruched her nipples and sensitized her skin. Her breasts ached for his touch.

And touch he did. His fingertips, softly, lightly stroking across the surface of her nipples, puckering them until they stood high and stiff, begging for more. Laura arched into him, sucked in a breath as the first, moist heat of his tongue bathed one lucky nipple, then drew it into his mouth to appreciate it more. His mouth was hot on her fevered skin, chilled when he left the first to take in the other. Her core tightened as the moistness began to build between her legs, shifting her stance at the wet spot she keenly felt.

Feeling herself leaning back toward the surface of the bed, Laura let him guide her down on a sensation that left her drifting, like floating on air. A sensation of cool air whispered across her stomach, the knowledge that he was drawing her jeans down until all she was left with was her flimsy little bit of lacey underwear and the spot that was now saturated. As he came over top of her, she drew down his fly, flipped the snap open, and grasped his cock, all the way down to his nads, rolling them around in her hands as if she were a juggler, ready to perform.

He sucked in a breath, and she took great pleasure in that fact. He wanted her, and she wanted him, too. The realization that this was an act of love washed over her; there was more to their lovemaking than just sexual attraction. She loved him. Deeply. Like no other, and the sentiment was returned.

Laura took one look at Hank's cock, sticking out like an iron rod, its velvety tip so soft and smooth, she knew she had to taste it. Pushing him from her to help him remove the rest of his clothing, she finally had him naked beside her. A smile crept across her face, her tongue traced the outline of her lips, and she saw the recognition of what she was about to do dawn in his eyes.

Leaning over, she blew her breath lightly across the velvety head of his cock, watched it react, and saw the bead of moisture form at the tip. Resisting the urge to pounce, she opened her mouth and slowly took him inside, swirled her tongue around the tiny opening, tasted the pre-cum and took him deeper, feeling his desire transmitted in the hard muscles of his abdomen, in the flexion of the muscles along his spine, all taut with the herculean effort it must have taken for him to lie still.

She felt the softness of the tip along the roof of her mouth, tasted the salty tang of moisture that leaked out, felt the silkiness of the length of him across her tongue, and stroked along its sides.

Hank breathed deeply, moaned, and pulled himself from her. "I don't think I can take much more of that without coming, right here and now," he breathed. His voice was like a whisper, the voice of a lover, husky and warm. "My turn now," he said, before slipping that lacey bit of cloth she called underwear from her body and spreading her legs to expose her inner core to him. He bent, kissed her navel, and traced a path with his tongue to her bud of womanhood that begged for his touch.

His touch. No one else's. Just his.

He didn't disappoint her. The first touch of his tongue to her sweet spot had Laura spread her legs wider and gasp her enjoyment. His tongue, so hot in the cooler air of the room, only enhanced her pleasure.

Hank kissed her with heated lips, took her bud between his teeth and drew on it, suckled it, and brought her to the edge, thrusting his tongue deep inside, withdrawing completely before she had a chance to come.

"You bastard," she hissed, but Hank only grinned and settled himself over her, pressing that velvety tip to her entrance. He wasn't undone by her comment, she knew, and she sighed her intense pleasure at the feeling of him penetrating her, sliding gently in, filling her. She moaned her pleasure, sucked in a great lungful of air between teeth clenched in wonder, loving it the same way she did the first time it had happened. Then, it had been excitement, the discovery of something hitherto unknown but desired. Now, it was an expression of love. Still, desire was part of it, too. It was her personal nirvana and she wanted it all.

He partially withdrew before embedding himself within her once again, repeating the movement, establishing a rhythm they both knew intimately. And while his lower half was thus engaged, his hands stroked and tweaked, his lips kissed, his tongue tasted. Her breasts, her throat, her mouth, nothing was off limits.

Laura slid her hands along Hank's sides, felt the muscles of his torso bunch and relax as he moved, caressed the taut roundness of his butt cheeks and the scooped indentation where his powerful legs joined his hips, those solid pieces of bone covered in sinewy tendons and strong muscle. He was all man above her and she gloried in the feel of his skin, hot in the first flush of pending climax. The weight of his body on top of hers was familiar and comforting, and Laura knew this was where she belonged. She could no more deny him this pleasure than she could deny herself, and however rapidly his heart was beating in his chest, hers was doing the same.

Hank took a ruched nipple into his mouth, drew on it, suckled, and Laura caught the familiar scent of the shampoo he used, clinging to his hair as it tickled her nose. His teeth, teasing the nipple, sent an electric wave to her core as she lay beneath him, writhing, wanting more. As the first stirrings of her own climax begin to build, she tilted her hips to meet his thrusts, locked her legs about his waist, felt him go deeper, and urged him on. "Don't stop; please, don't stop," she breathed, and grinned when she heard a breathy reply, "I don't intend to."

"Oh, God. More. Now!" And as Hank thrust deeply, she cried out her release, felt the flush of heat across her skin, and died a thousand deaths. She thought she'd never had a climax like that before; never reached such a high before.

And right there with her was Hank, his body pulsing deep within her. Holding her tightly to him, he arched into her, his dark hair falling across his eyes like some primal, Celtic god, rigid and strong, yet ever so gentle.

As the final pulse of his desire finished, Hank collapsed on top of her, then rolled partially to the side, still embedded within her warmth. His fingers stroked the hair from her eyes and tucked it behind her ear, and in a loving gesture, he whispered ever so softly, "Is tú mo ghrá."

Entwined on the bed with him, Laura felt herself drift toward sleep, felt Hank draw back the bedding to cover them both, and pull her into his embrace to keep her warm. Although it was only midafternoon, they both slept.

***

Hank woke first, wondering for a moment where he was, taking in the unfamiliarity of the room as he gathered his thoughts. Gray afternoon light shone through the window, the sun hidden behind thick, roiling clouds. Streaks of water were drying on the windowpane, evidence of recent rain. He wondered what time it was; he was supposed to meet Siobhan and Henry around seven.

Gazing at Laura's sleeping form beside him brought his lips up in a smile, and he realized something between them had changed. Had he vanquished her fears? Spooning against her, he ran his hand along her thigh and felt her sigh against him. Her body was an addiction he couldn't fight and didn't want to. He loved her more deeply than he thought possible and he knew that should she refuse to have him, he'd never be the same. Never recover.

Yet what he'd seen in her eyes before they'd closed in sleep had given him hope. Maybe yet he could convince her he would never leave her and always be there for her?

She stirred, rolled onto her back, breasts peeking out sexily beneath the covers, and smiled at him. "What time is it?" she asked, somewhere between a stretch and a yawn.

"I don't know," he answered truthfully, raising his head to better see her, "and I don't care. I'm with you. That's all that matters." Grinning, because he knew it was true, he really didn't care. He leaned across, kissed her mouth and then kissed each nipple that dared show above the soft bed linens.

"You're amazing, Hank Mulligan. And I have something I need to say to you, and hope you'll understand."

Uh-oh, he thought. This was it. This was the part where she told him it had been fun but too bad, so sad, it was over. He braced himself to hear the words she would utter that would make him want to jump from the highest tower to end it all.

Nodding, he said, "Alright."

"Gráim thú," she said, sucking her bottom lip inward, exposing her even, white teeth in a cheeky grin.

"What did ye say?" he asked, taken by surprise. "Say it again." He needed to be certain he'd heard her right.

"Gráim thú," she repeated. "It means I…"

"I know what it means, and I love ye, too. Did ye understand when I told ye before we fell asleep?"

Shyly, she admitted, "I thought that was what you meant but when I looked it up before I came, I only found one phrase. It didn't seem too hard to remember," she giggled.

"Táim I ngrá leat, a chuisle mo chroi. Tá tú go h-álainn. An bpósfaidh tú mé." He didn't explain, just lay there beside her and watched the saucy, quizzical look she gave him.

"Okay, smart-ass, interpret."

He laughed because he knew her so well. "I said," he answered, speaking slowly and clearly so there was no chance of a misunderstanding, "and I quote…I'm in love with you, you make my heart beat…or, roughly translated, that's what it means. And then I said you're beautiful."

"Aww, that's so sweet. I think you're beautiful, too, in a manly sort of way, you Irish devil!"

He hadn't told her the last part. He wanted to save that for later. Taking a delicate earlobe between his teeth, he playfully gnawed it, swirled his tongue inside her ear, and felt her dissolve in helpless laughter, squirming beneath him to push him away. Hank wasn't done yet, though, as he pinned her arms above her head and zeroed in on her exposed nipples.

"You bastard, you're not playing fair," she swore, but the laughter was evident on her face.

Grinning, he took in her sleep-tousled look, hair sticking out in all directions like she'd just come in from a wind storm, and winked at her. "Ah, we'll have to teach ye to swear in Gaelic."

"Where did you learn Gaelic, anyway? I didn't hear much of it at all on the street or even in some of the shops I stopped in. Everyone spoke English."

Releasing her arms to rest his ear on his hand, he stretched out beside her, one hand possessively stroking her hip. "Some I learned in school, but most of what I learned was when I was working odd jobs down 'round Sneem and up a ways toward Dingle. Those places used to speak only Irish but it's changing now. Was when I was there, too, but if you went out on a fishing boat with some of the older ones, then ye'd only hear Irish, and tons of swearing as well!"

A grin split her features, lighting her eyes, "Like what?"

"Ah, like, 'póg mo thóin'."

"Hey, not so fast, say it slower so I can pronounce it."

"It's like, 'pogue muh hone'." he pronounced for her, although with his brogue refreshed from the past month back on home turf, he wondered how much she would really understand.

His answer came in the face of one tawny brow raised in obvious curiosity, begging an answer to her unspoken question.

"Kiss my arse," he grinned, "like this," and with one deft move, he had her flipped and was mock-chewing the fleshy part of her butt cheek. Her squeals and giggles would have neighbors running for aid and so he flipped her onto her back once again, took her in his arms, and kissed her deeply. It had the desired effect of calming her, and better yet, stemming the loud squeals of delight.

When he deemed her quiet enough he looked up, stroked her cheek softly, and said, "Let's get some dinner and I'll take ye to meet my siblings. Leastwise, that's what I think I'm doing. I could be startin' some great feud. Ye never know."

She smiled back at him and got out of bed.

"Another thing," he said, pulling on his clothing, "we can check ye out of this room. We won't need to keep it, do ye think?"

Laura cocked an eyebrow and smiled her reply. "Maybe not," she agreed.

***

An hour and a half later, they stood on the doorstep where Hank had stood alone not so very long ago. "Well, here we are," he said, for want of something better to say.

"Are you going to knock, or should we just send psychic messages that we're here?"

He laughed at her joke, but this was Ireland, and anything could happen.

"I'll knock," he said, and did just that, rapping solidly on the door.

Moments later, it opened to a well-lit room, a room full of people that Hank had never seen before. There were, of course, Siobhan and Emily, whom he quickly introduced to Laura, noting that Henry was nowhere to be seen just then. Then there were the rest, those that were his half siblings, people who resembled him but were completely unknown to him.

"Oh, I remember you from the train," said his lady love to one of the young men before them, surprising him with her forthright manner.

"The train?" asked Hank, turning a raised eyebrow to Laura.

"Yeah," she answered, a smile on her face, "I remember seeing them on the train from Cork except I didn't know they were on their way to see you."

"Why didn't ye just call me? I would have come and got ye."

Before she had a chance to answer, Liam introduced himself. "Liam's the name. And you must be Hank," he nodded to his half brother, "but I don't know your name, pretty lady."

"Laura," she grinned, before Hank could get a word in. He was beginning to feel like the odd man out, as if the gathering was for her instead of himself.

"I recall you as well," Liam said to Laura, in response to her remark about the train. "Ye've a strange way of talkin'," apologizing to me when it was I who made you drop your bag."

"She's Canadian," laughed Hank, as if that explained everything. He was beginning to feel more settled, having got an entire sentence out, even if it was only two words.

"Thanks," she rolled her eyes at Hank. "You are such a gentleman."

"Hullo, there," said the only woman in the room unknown to Hank. Young, petite in stature, and extending a slender hand to him, she said, "My name's Ciara, and I believe you're my half brother."

Hank shook her hand, then drew her in for a hug and a quick peck on the cheek. "Very pleased to meet ye," he said, "and this is my lady from the wilds of Canada, Laura." He grinned at Ciara, a grin that enveloped Laura as well. Laura gave him a look in return that he was beginning to know quite well. He couldn't wait to get her alone again to explore that expression more.

"And over there's the other twin, Niall. Don't let them confuse you as to who's who," Ciara continued.

"Yes, we just met Liam, but how do you tell them apart?" asked Laura.

"There's an easy way," Ciara grinned as she winked at Hank. She raised a neatly arched brow and tilted her head as if to call them over.

Hank and Laura stepped closer to listen to what Ciara had to say. She looked, Hank thought, all of about eighteen or nineteen years of age.

"Niall has the smallest birthmark behind his right ear," she said, whispering to them and indicating a spot too small to accurately detect from where Niall was standing. "Liam has a similar one, only on the other side. You can remember it by thinking to yourself, Liam has a mark behind his left ear. The double Ls make it easy to remember." She nodded smugly, and Hank thought that little hint to be very useful. The twins were identical.

Siobhan motioned Laura over, "Come and meet Henry, Hank's older brother. He's just come from work."

Hank was going to follow when Ciara's hand stopped him.

"How serious are ye over your lady?"

"Serious? Why would ye ask?" He didn't know this bit of a girl and sure didn't feel like telling her his life story. At least not the part that concerned Laura.

"Well, did Siobhan not tell ye of me?"

Hank raised a brow and thought back to everything Siobhan had said but came up blank. "What would she have said, other than you're my sister?"

"Ah, that makes sense, then. Ye see," she said continuing on, "I see things, I'm psychic, ye might say. I have a gift and there's something you should know about Laura."

Hank was confused. Psychic? Yes, he'd heard of people being psychic, but what did it have to do with Laura?

"Go on," he encouraged, his curiosity piqued.

"Ye'll take care of her? Marry her?"

He didn't know where this was going but was beginning to chafe at the riddles and questions when he thought she was going to tell him something.

Finally, he nodded, and was rewarded with a broad grin from Ciara. "Good then," she said, "that's good."

"If you're psychic, then why did ye have to ask?"

Impish green eyes, unlike the blue that seemed to be the family trait, sparkled and stared back at him, laughing. "I get things in images, and the image I had was…humorous," she said.

"That doesn't answer my question. What was your image?"

"You, Laura, being married."

Hank smiled. He wanted that to happen, and if Ciara said it would, maybe she was right. "That's nice, but not necessarily humorous," he remarked, and would have been content with that until Ciara said, "But that's not all."

"No?"

"No. She's wearin' her dress high." And then she walked away.

What the feck was that supposed to mean? thought Hank as he grasped at Ciara's arm to pull her back. "Care to explain? She's not wearin' any dress. She's wearin' jeans."

Giggling, she put her arms in front of her and mimicked

rocking a baby, at least, that's what Hank thought she meant. And the look he received as Ciara turned away was confirmation. Unfortunately, Ciara hadn't said when they would wed, so it could be a year from now. And after all, hadn't Laura said she was on the pill? A twinge of doubt crossed Hank's mind. Had Laura taken them with her to his place? Had she missed a dose? He'd heard that pregnancy could happen if the pill wasn't taken on schedule. Could it be?

Still as confused as ever, he was soon engulfed by the twins, asking questions of his life in Canada, what was it like, and when could they visit? He didn't have much of a chance to tell them anything because just then a familiar looking man burst through the back door.

"Guinness all around," he shouted, a bulky package of something in his arms.

Before the package could be opened, Siobhan called above the din, "And that'll be Brandon, Henry's next younger brother. The one who knows better than to bring alcohol in here," she scolded, looking straight at Brandon.

Brandon had the decency to look abashed but not defeated as a defiant expression was turned to Siobhan. "Well, just because he's turned into a milksop doesn't mean the rest of us must go without," he challenged, speaking of Henry.

If anyone had any doubts that Brandon was a fighter, it was soon waylaid as Henry grabbed his brother's shirt beneath his chin. Brandon, built like Hank and roughly the same age, didn't cringe beneath his brother's ire. "Go ahead. Hit me," was all he said.

The room turned silent, the tension thick enough to smell until Henry released him and brushed at the shirt to straighten it from where he'd crinkled the material. "That was just to show ye I'm still older, still bigger, and if ye ever speak to Siobhan like that again, I'll beat ye to within an inch of your life. Humph?" At Brandon's nod, Henry playfully ruffled

Brandon's hair and a collective sigh of relief went through the gathering.

"Take it outside, Brandon," said Siobhan of the stout.

"No, it's alright," soothed Henry. "I'm not so bad that I can't be around the stuff without touching it. I'll stick to cola or coffee. I'm fine with that."

"Good," said Brandon firmly as he let down the bag he was holding with a solid thunk on the table. "Here's yer bloody cola, and Guinness for the rest of us."

"He's good at providing, he is," Siobhan laughed, and from the tone of her voice, it was clear the party was on. Having already handed a cola to Henry, and Emily as well, Brandon began pulling Guinness from the bag.

A while later, with chatter all around and the makeshift party in full swing, Hank went to bring Laura another beer but noticed she still had a full one in her hand. "Do ye not like it, then?" He asked.

She smiled ruefully and handed her nearly full bottle over to him. "It's okay, just a little tough for me to take right now. I don't think my stomach is too happy about it."

He cocked his head at her as if studying her and then a small smile crept along his face as Ciara's hint at things to come settled into place.

"What are you thinking?" she probed.

"Nothin'. Nothin' at all," he said, the smile still in place. "I'd forgotten ye've just flown a long way and had a train ride as well. It's been quite the day. Let's go back to the hotel. I'd like to get up early and show ye something."

"What?"

"I'd like it to be a surprise," was all he would say. "For now, I think ye need a good night's sleep. C'mon, let's go." He reached for her hand and pulled her with him, and saying goodnight to his new-found family with a promise to get together again later the next day, they left.

***

"I'm sorry I'm being a partypooper," she apologized as they drove back to the hotel. She noted Hank's profile from the streetlights and shop lights as they passed by, the short nose so straight you could set a ruler along it, the broad cheekbones and strong chin, and best of all, the mouth she loved to kiss. His hair was curling around his face from the damp weather. He'd need a haircut soon, she thought, unless he decided to wear it long and tie it back.

As if he knew what she'd been thinking, he combed his fingers through one side to brush it out of the way, saying, "Ah, you're no partypooper. You're tired from a long trip and I don't want ye feelin' poorly. There's so much I'd like ye to see. How long before you have to head back?"

"Me? Well, I didn't know how much time I'd need or how long I'd be here, so I left it open. I was kind of hoping we'd be going back together," she finished.

Hank was silent beside her and she cursed the darkness that wouldn't let her see his face or give a clue as to what he was thinking.

They were silent then, until they arrived at the hotel. Having transferred her things into his room, Hank drew her into his arms. "Why don't ye have a nice warm bath and crawl into bed. I've got something to arrange downstairs for tomorrow but I'll be right up. I'll settle that room out, too."

Laura couldn't help but nod. The bath did look lovely, and she felt chilled from the night air. It had begun to rain again. She left him to do his errand and was chin deep in hot water when he came back in. She could hear the rustling of paper and wondered what he'd been up to.

His knock on the bathroom door was not unexpected, and as he poked his head in, she couldn't help but smile. He'd bought her a small bouquet from a shop a few doors down that was just about to close, he explained, taking the empty ice bucket from the tray on the bathroom counter, filling it with water, and placing the flowers inside it to use as a vase.

"Not perfect, but it'll work."

Laura watched him place the flowers on the bathroom countertop and thought they looked lovely. There were tulips and daffodils and other spring flowers, flowers that would only now be poking their heads out of the ground back home.

"And this, too" he held up a bulky paper bag. "I had the hotel put together a breakfast for us, so we won't need to waste a moment to be out of here. We need to get up in the wee hours so as to be there at sunrise."

Laura's expression must have shown on her face because he grinned and followed it up with, "That's okay, you can sleep in the car."

Minutes later she emerged from the bath, and while still warm, crawled into bed beside Hank, who was already there, waiting for her. As they settled down to sleep, Laura broached the subject once again. "So, will you be coming back with me?" She was suddenly afraid he'd say no, that he was going to stay in Ireland because as much as she thought the country was beautiful, at least from what she'd seen, she knew she belonged in the wilds of Canada, as Hank had put it.

"Oh, I don't know yet. There's something I must do first and depending on that…well, we'll see, I suppose."

Her heart sank. If he truly loved her, he'd be right there with her, she was sure of it, and suddenly the dark demons of doubt began to invade her thoughts.

He drew her close and settled his arm around her, kissed her gently behind her ear and along her neck and then pulled her closer to his body. She felt him sigh and fall asleep, his arm loosening the hold he had around her waist as he drifted off, and she bit her lip in worry. Had she been so blinded by seeing him again that she'd misread her feelings for him? She thought the excitement she had felt when she saw him out the window was an indication of her true feelings, but then she recalled him kissing Siobhan, and while Siobhan and Henry seemed very much a couple, did something still exist between

Hank and his ex? Was he being truthful with her when he said he'd only meant it to be a peck on the cheek for an old friend? And would that have made a difference?

She adjusted her position and felt her stomach flip. Unwilling to give in to a sensitive stomach, she closed her eyes tightly and tried to ignore the feeling. Eventually, it settled out again and with Hank's arm still resting over her waist, she fell asleep.

Chapter Twenty-Five

The soft ting-ting-ting of Hank's phone alarm woke them before dawn. It hadn't mattered because they were both awake already. Hank could sense Laura's eyes roving about the still dark room, at the unfamiliarity of her surroundings. And maybe, he thought, of the near stranger in the bed beside her. Was that part of the problem?

He'd wanted to make love to her desperately last night but even though it hadn't been late, he knew she needed sleep above all else. And then before the alarm went off, he was hoping for another chance but he sensed it wasn't the right time. Something was bothering his lady love, and as before, he'd been at a loss to know what it was. Perhaps today, after this trip, he'd be able to get her to talk, to tell him everything she was thinking.

"Are ye alright, luv? You're not still feelin' off?"

He felt her shift in the bed. "No, I think I feel okay. Maybe just jetlagged, that's all."

Leaning over her, he kissed her mouth, brushed the hair from her face, and touched his forehead to hers. In the dark, her eyes were a beacon of light, the reflection from some unknown source coming through the small gap in the bedroom drapes. "We don't have to go today," he offered, although he really wanted to do this, to finalize everything.

"No, I'd love to go and see whatever it is you won't tell me about. I'm curious."

"You're sure?"

She nodded and he could almost see her smile in the dark.

"Alright then, up ye get," he said playfully, whipping back the covers so that the chilly air caused her to gasp and grab at the covers he skillfully held out of her reach.

Not to be outdone, she launched herself at Hank, taking him by surprise, and the two of them tumbled back on the bed with Laura on top. "Oh, well, if ye'd rather do this, that's okay, too," grinned Hank. Her breasts were pressing into his chest, the warmth a fine contrast from the still cool air.

"Maybe," she said, her long, wavy locks tickling his skin.

Instinctively, his hands caressed her butt cheeks, found the cleft between, and followed it down to the moisture hidden within her folds. He grew instantly hard and knew he had to have her. "If ye want to change yer mind, ye'd best say so now."

"No. I'm not changing my mind. I want this. You. Right now."

He felt her cool fingertips grasp his flute, lead it to the sweet spot, slick and wet, and guide him in. From then on, it was Laura in control, Laura who dictated how fast he would come, and fast it was because she didn't want to wait. Pushing herself to a sitting position, she rode him well, gripping with her inner walls as she drew up, releasing the pressure as she dropped down.

Hank thought he was going to explode. Her breasts were twin peaks he held, suckled, rolling her nipples between his fingers when she pulled out of range of his mouth. And when he could no longer wait, when her muscles gripped his cock in rhythmic splendor, he gave in and let it happen. Gripping her hips, he held her in place, heard her panting her pleasure as if conscious of being in a hotel room, of people on the other side of the wall. She was usually much more vocal but Hank had no such inhibitions and let out his "Aaah," as he came, holding her to him while his seed pulsed deep inside.

Her climax receding, Laura flopped on top of him.

"Still cold?" he asked, and felt her shake her head no. "Good, 'cause now we have to get going if we're to beat the sun."

"Huh?" She sat up on top of him.

"It's a very special place, especially at sunrise." He didn't want to give it away. "Ye'd best dress warmly," was all he told her.

***

They climbed hastily into the rental car, having grabbed the bag of breakfast made the night before and the two fresh coffees in paper cups from the small coffee machine in the room. It was still dark but Hank knew they would have to go quickly if they were to make it in time.

They munched their food, two scones with butter and a smattering of jam, and drank the coffee as Hank took the road at breakneck speed. He knew the road well, having traveled it many times before, and especially just recently. He'd wanted to make sure he knew the road, knew the best way to get to the castle while it was still dark. The timing had to be perfect.

Daylight was barely a glow on the horizon before them when they came upon the ruins. Laura had been dozing for the last ten minutes but now, Hank woke her. As they got out of the car, he took her hand and pulled her quickly with him across the pasture where cows sometimes grazed, and into the shelter of the castle walls, or what was left of them.

"This is amazing," breathed Laura, her breath visible in the early morning air. The sky was beginning to lighten and he pulled her to the west side of the castle, where the sun was sure to come up through the ruins of the eastern wall. As daylight crept across the horizon, Hank waited, feeling the small box in his pocket. Hoping he'd finally understood what she was so worried about.

She was standing in front of him when the sun's first rays pierced the ancient windows of the crumbled walls. Her intake of breath as the castle began to take shape encouraged him. And then it happened: the sun, bright in a rare, cloudless day, and fully framed in a window of the ancient stone edifice, spread its rays of light into the castle's keep. Moss and ivy were a contrast to the cold, gray stone, its color an invitation to venture in.

"Watch your step," he advised, "it's still crumbling with no one to look after it. Kind of like me," he began.

"Crumbling? You? How do you mean?"

He took her to the inner wall where the sun pierced the shadows and the walls sheltered them from the ever-present breeze. Sitting her down with him on one of the wall's rocks that stood alone in the center, he put his arms around her and held her close before him. "I need to tell ye about me. To help ye understand me. I'm kind of like this old relic," he indicated the castle about them with a nod of his head. "I have my roots in this place, I'm a part of this land. And like this castle, a part of me will always be here, no matter the ravages of time or what may happen or where I might go.

"But unlike this castle, I don't make my home here anymore. I am not so married to this land that I want to stay here. I have a life in Canada, in the cabin that burned down and that I will one day rebuild. That's where home is now. And it's there mostly because of you." He caught her eye just then, the sun shining in the green-gold depths, and he looked fully at her now, noted the red and gold highlights in her hair, the faint smattering of freckles across her nose, and knew he loved her with a depth he'd never known before.

"I want ye as my own, Laura. My life, my love, my wife. I promise to stand by you, to never leave you, never make you feel anything less than the most important person in my life." He got up to stand before her, placing her on the stone seat that was still warm and dry from his body and then knelt on the wet grass, pulling the box from his pocket as he did so.

He felt her intake of breath in his soul and tried with all his might to calm her fears. Whatever happened, he had to convince her to trust him, to take this giant leap with him.

Opening the box, he withdrew the ring, let the sunlight catch the diamond and then taking her left hand, slid it onto her finger. It was the Claddagh ring, his mother's, with a diamond blazing atop the heart, as if the fingers of the two hands were cradling it. Gazing up at her face, his own hopeful and sincere, he asked the question men have asked women for centuries. "Laura, grá mo chroi, will you marry me?"

Laura began to shake and tears fell from her eyes. He was prepared to hear her rejection, and if that was what happened, then he'd have to live with it. Or die.

Instead, he saw the nod of her head, heard the laughter through her tears, and took her into his arms as she said the words he longed to hear.

"Yes, yes, oh yes," she whispered into his neck.

The next thing he knew they were hugging tightly on the ground, his coat a poor ground cover for how wet the grass was from the rain during the night. He couldn't believe it. She'd said yes when she wouldn't have done before and so he couldn't resist and had to ask.

"It wasn't you," she said. "I wanted to marry you, have wanted to for a long time. I was afraid, that's all."

"Afraid that I'd leave ye, that I'd do ye like he did?"

She nodded and he saw the tears afresh in her eyes. Pulling her atop himself so she wasn't cold against the grass, he said, "I want ye to know I am not like him. I'll never be like him. I know how fleeting life can be and how important it is that we cherish what we have with those we love. I'd never give that up." He kissed her then, and she kissed him back. And as they got up from the wet grass, he said, "I think we should get you back to town so ye don't catch a chill."

"Me," she said laughingly, "you were the one on the grass."

"Ah, well, it's just that I care about ye," he said, grinning with his secret tucked inside. He wondered how long it would be before she realized why she would sometimes feel sick, and then be fine. That day would be soon, he knew. It really was only a matter of time before other symptoms began to show.

"Hank?" asked Laura, stopping before they were very far from the ruins. She turned and looked at the high, ivy-covered walls of the castle, the majesty of the keep, even though it was ancient and crumbling, and said, "I think we should get married here, don't you?"

He looked back at the keep, at the high walls with the sun on them, and knew that she was right. The keep had lasted for centuries, protected its inhabitants, fought off weather and foes, and although it was old and crumbling, it was still a fortress to be reckoned with.

"I think that would be grand," he said, and putting his arm over her shoulder, they took a last look at the castle before returning to the car.

"Humor me a bit," said Hank as they drove. "There's one more thing I want to show ye."

Laura nodded, her smile of curiosity and adventure lighting up her face.

Hank steered the car back towards Killarney where a large Celtic cross could be seen at the top of a hill, standing like a sentry over the town. Pulling off the road they walked through a gate that seemed to belong to the house next to it, but Hank reassured her they weren't trespassing. "Public access," he said by way of explanation, and Laura eagerly followed him through. He grasped her hand, giving it a reassuring squeeze, determined to show her something he'd only recently found himself, the graves of his great-grandparents.

"This is a Protestant graveyard, not consecrated ground if you're a Catholic. She had only two children, the first being a girl that grew up to be my grandmother, the second, a boy that died in childbirth. He was buried here, with her alongside. She died hours later, unshriven, and therefore not able to be buried in a proper, Catholic graveyard. She wouldn't have wanted it anyway, so I've been told."

He shook off a pesky fly and continued. "My great-grandfather did his best to raise the young girl but soon gave the care of her over to his sister's family. The story goes that once he was certain she was in a good place, he took himself off and was never seen again. They think he took a boat out to sea to drown himself in sorrow. It's all legend, family legend, but it explains why she is buried here, and he is only mentioned on her headstone. I'll show you when we get in there," he said, speaking of the headstone. "My half-brother, Henry, had a proper stone erected a couple of years ago. They are his heritage too."

Continuing along the line of ancient graves, Hank explained the inconsistencies on some of the old headstones, and that of his great-grandmother. "What the phrases mean, the difference between 'of Killarney' and 'died at Killarney', is that if a person is from Killarney, it says so. But my great-grandfather was not from Killarney and not buried here, therefore it only says 'died at' instead of the name and the words 'of' or 'from'."

"But you said they don't know where he died," she objected.

Hank agreed. "There may be more to the story. I wasn't born yet." His blue eyes crinkled in laughter.

They were walking up the grassy lane, over the iron stile, taking care to keep clear of the stinging nettles close by.

"The leaves are harmless, but those little spikes can leave nasty blisters and festering sores if you come into contact with them. Horrible, nasty things," he commented, holding her hand as she scrambled through the deep 'V' of the stile and landed neatly on the other side. He noted her careful grasp of the rust-mottled rungs, the eyes that glanced warily at the nettles, and grinned.

Safe on the other side, they walked up the cart path toward

the hill where, on their left, stood the great Celtic cross, dark gray in the lighter gray of the pearled sky. Clouds seemed not to be moving at all though the breeze blew briskly across their faces and whipped her titian hair about like Medusa's serpents. Again he grinned. No, not serpents, just beautiful tresses.

Minutes later they came to another gate, another stile, this one with no nettles, and she clambored through it, seemingly eager to see what was on the other side.

He led her through the bluebells, hundreds of the foot-high plants spreading a blue carpet before them through a graveyard punctuated by headstones, tombstones, and the fenced off stairs to a mausoleum below one of the larger monuments. Beyond was the cross at the edge of the hill. Like a great, gray sentry standing guard over those in eternal repose, it faced toward the town, many miles from the sea and the man who'd drowned in those water's icy depths.

"If you ask anyone in town about this graveyard… if you ask them where Killegy graveyard is, most won't know. Especially people our age. Unless they've family here, they won't have heard of it."

"Is that because most of them are Catholic?" she asked, a genuine expression of interest and curiosity spread across her features.

Shrugging, because he didn't know the answer to that one, he led her from the cross and showed her other graves, told her about the people who had lived and died in the land of his birth, some he had known as a young boy.

They circled round the graveyard, trying to avoid crushing the multitudes of flowers without luck. It was impossible to step through the mass of blue without flattening the stems in their wake. He reached down and cupped his hand around a stem and pulled upwards to relieve it of the delicate petals, releasing their fragrance in the palm of his hand.

"Here," he invited, "smell these."

Her eyes told him everything he was expecting. The delicate scent brought a smile to her mouth, lips curved in obvious enjoyment. "Oh, that's so lovely," she said. "I've never smelled bluebells before. Come to think of it, I don't think I've really ever seen bluebells before."

They took a few steps and were suddenly beside an ivy covered structure, the missing door inviting them to the dirt covered floor within. It was obvious that no panes of glass had ever graced this structure, and on the wall was an engraved stone that Hank read out for her.

"This church of Killegy was built as a family mortuary chapel by Maurice Hussey of Cahirnane late colonel in the army of King James II.

"At his death in 1714 his body was borne here by his four sons and buried at midnight by torchlight."

They stood in silence for a moment before he asked her if she felt creepy in the cold depths of the stone structure. It was small, but since it was clearly meant for the soul of the individual, then it was big enough. Roughly twelve feet long and eight feet wide with a window at either end and a short doorway in the side that even Laura had to duck to get through, it was compact, if nothing else. The dirt floor was solid beneath their feet, leaving dusty footprints where they stood. At one end, beneath one of the small windows, was the rectangular, stone sarcophagus.

"Not really creepy at all. I think it's rather peaceful here," Laura answered finally.

"Oh, well. I thought I'd wait to tell you this part. A friend of Henry's has a dog that will absolutely not cross that threshold. It refuses to budge or set one foot inside and whines like the Bean Sidhes are after it if you try to coax it inside."

"Really? That's amazing. I feel nothing."

"Well, it isn't a place you want to be after dark, I can tell ye that," he grinned. "Here," taking her hand, he brought her out of the tiny structure and wove her through the grass where large stones stuck up at odd intervals. "See these three tucked close together? They are my great-great aunties, stillborn and, like my great-grandmother and her child, unable to be buried in consecrated ground. But these have no headstones because they were too poor to have any made, so they marked their graves with simple stones, just to show where they are."

Laura gazed about her, suddenly aware that many rather large stones protruded through the ground, higher than the grass. "All these stones signify people buried here, too poor to have headstones made?"

He loved the look in her eyes, part wonder, part sorrow, and she didn't even know who these people were. Nodding, he continued telling her what he wanted her to know; the reason why he'd brought her here.

"This is where I'm from. These people are my family. And while you might think it something interesting, to me it's completely amazing. This family, in this graveyard, including those people over there who I had known as a young boy, are all very real to me. I had no knowledge of family before this visit, beyond my mother and my sister. Sadly, I didn't have money for a proper grave for my mother, so she's buried in the paupers' field on the other side of town. Just a simple, white cross marks her spot."

"How sad!" Exclaimed Laura.

"It is, in some ways. But my new siblings…they showed me this place, told me the stories of my great grandparents, my aunties. It's sad about them, too, but life goes on. I'm here, with a whole new aspect to myself and my life. How can I be sad about that when I suddenly feel like I'm not alone anymore?"

"I understand. It's like you said, you're a part of this land," she commented, sniffing the pungent air where the ever-present breeze brought the faint smell of manure from a recently fertilized field. Smiling over at him, her hair whipping around her face in uncontrolled flight, she took his hand, saying, "Let's go."

With the breeze at their backs, they strolled hand-in-hand down the grassy sward, and Hank couldn't contain his grin.

They left Killegy Graveyard to its dead then, to the gray cross standing like a sentinel, piercing the canopy of trees to the great expanse of blue sky that had suddenly appeared. The graves of his ancestors remained, undisturbed and peaceful.

Chapter Twenty-six

It was as if half of Killarney had driven down to the castle to watch the wedding of Laura and Hank. Siobhan had not been idle once the couple returned to Canada after announcing their engagement, and promising them a grand wedding on their return in June, she played the wedding planner to the hilt. On the couple's last night in Killarney, they all visited the local establishment and watched with growing interest as Liam pulled out his tin whistle and then Niall reached behind the bar for his bodhran placed there for safekeeping, pre-warned as he'd been by Ciara's mention of something to celebrate. Henry's accordion seemed to have appeared out of nowhere as did Brandon's guitar. Ciara's voice rang sweet and true as the group celebrated in the local pub, a place Henry had not frequented in a very long time. But his promise to Siobhan stood fast against the teasing from the locals who recalled his earlier days when bets were to the last man standing. And it was often Henry.

"But what good is being Irish," he'd told them then, "if ye can't make fun of yerself and have a few?"

That night, the pub welcomed Hank and Laura to their midst and it was every man and woman present that night, plus a few more, that now stood on the grass before the ancient stone walls of the great castle, the green ivy covering the mottled gray sides, sparkling with recent rain under suddenly blue skies. Darker clouds loomed on the horizon but no one took them as a portent of anything but more rain.

Mercifully, the sun continued to shine as the priest made his preparations. It hadn't been easy to convince him to drive out to marry two people who he rightly stated would not be in his parish. But the argument had been followed with, "But, Father, would you rather have them live in sin?"

It was an argument that the priest couldn't win, and since he'd been visiting the pub that night with his parishioners, he simply allowed himself to be convinced it was the right thing to do, the generous donation to the parish coffers from Kerry notwithstanding. That man, pleased as ever to be present at the wedding, stood now alongside Sarah, the only Asian in the group of people and seemingly enjoying the notoriety it was affording her. She played up her exotic looks with a traditional Chinese long gown, the light weight silk heavily embroidered and flown directly from Shanghai. A talented seamstress at home in Canada, a young Vietnamese woman, had made up the dress from the pattern that Sarah's mother had decreed must be followed exactly. The seamstress had not failed. It was perfection, from the high Chinese collar to the hand-made frogs that decorated the line of silk piping from her neck, across her breasts, and down to the base of her hip where the dress then split, making for easy walking. Sexy, and in colors of green and gold, it was a little over-the-top for the wilds of Ireland, but Sarah knew she looked divine. Still, it was no finer than Laura's dress, and as Sarah was the maid of honor, Laura had thought it quite perfect and told her so.

Kerry couldn't believe that Sarah had agreed to be his date for the wedding. After he'd picked up the key to Laura's apartment so he could feed Figaro, he'd asked Sarah out for a coffee. He would have leapt tall buildings for her if she'd just say she would go out with him. So it was a shock, but a delightful one, when she'd agreed. What began as a casual meeting over coffee was beginning to look, at least in Kerry's eyes, like the next new romance of the century.

But Kerry hadn't bargained on Sarah's fierce sense of

independence. Only five years younger, Sarah had more chutzpah, as his Jewish friends would say, than ten men together. She had a strong business sense, was no nonsense when it came to juggling finances, and told him in no uncertain terms that if he were to refinance according to her strategy during the next fiscal year, he'd been sitting pretty in no time.

Kerry hadn't realized he wasn't sitting pretty and so he let her work his books and juggle things around, and used the continued contact that entailed to further his personal aim, that of making her his wife. So far, she'd resisted and they were staying in separate rooms at the hotel, but he wasn't a man to give up so easily.

And so he stood beside her, the delicate, long fingers of her hands resting easily on his arm as they followed Hank and Laura up the grassy sward to the makeshift altar inside the one intact room of the castle.

Brandon looked over his handiwork. He, his brothers, and various friends had worked like madmen the day before, constructing the alter that stood on the dirt-covered floor of the ancient keep. It was truly Celtic in design, what passed for stone appearing as though it had been there just as long as the castle.

"Ye can't use real stone," Liam had exclaimed when Brandon told him of his idea for a wedding altar, "it's too feckin' heavy. How'd ye ever move it to here, let alone construct it in time? Don't be daft, I'll talk to the special effects team on the film set and see what they can come up with." Days later, giant wood and Styrofoam pieces had arrived for Brandon to begin working with. They painted, sculpted, and attached the pieces to look like a framed doorway, completely in sync and feel with the castle wall that held it. Beneath the far window opening was the altar, the parish fineries laid out, such as the priest deemed appropriate to display. Hank had really wanted a pagan wedding but when the priest got wind of it, Hank knew he'd have to bend.

And so the wedding became a formal one, with Catholic rites and all the trappings, much to the delight of the priest. Kerry's donation seemed to have a lot of sway with him.

Liam sidled over to Brandon before the ceremony began and patted him handily on the back. "I think the special effects guys may want to borrow what ye've built for the picture we're workin' on. Ye've done a fine job. Ye may be hired," he suggested.

Brandon gazed at his brother, a man who was successfully riding the wave of actors in Ireland getting good parts in the many productions being carried out. They were very popular in places like the south and west of the island, where hills ran on forever and Macgillycuddy's Reeks, the largest mountain range in Ireland, stood like sentries before the vast glory of Killarney National Park.

"How is the film going, anyway?" asked Brandon, wondering at the varied talents his family possessed.

Liam answered with a noncommittal shrug. "Good, I guess. Not as good as this right now, though, eh?"

Niall snuck up behind his brothers and burst between them. "I haven't seen you two so friendly since God was a teenager," he exclaimed. "Admiring your handiwork?"

"Not that ye'd know anything about that, would ye now?" sneered Brandon. "Ye never showed up to help."

"I was busy," defended Niall.

"Michael's back, is he?" asked his twin.

Niall nodded and glanced back to where their mother was making her way through the deep grass. "I'd best go help Mam before she gets lost in the grass. What's two inches on everyone else is more like two feet on her," he exclaimed good-naturedly of his mother's short stature.

Brandon lightly punched his brother's shoulder before he could sneak away. "So again Michael is not going to grace us with his presence?" queried Brandon. "What kind of man is he that he's too ashamed to be seen with ye?"

Niall blushed but was otherwise unfazed by his brother's remark. He'd known since he was a young child that he was different. A "mirror twin," he'd heard himself described, exactly opposite of his brother. He was gay, his brother was straight. He was left-handed, his brother was right-handed. He was quiet and shy, his brother was bold, and a show-off if ever there was one. But with the exception of the placement of a small birthmark, his behind his right ear with Liam's behind the left, Niall and Liam were identical to a T.

"He's not yet ready to meet Mam, I expect," said Niall.

"She knows about him. About you. What's the big deal?" probed Liam.

Niall just shrugged, clearly not ready to discuss his personal situation and beginning to gain the sulky look that characterized the personality within. "I'm escorting our mother; can we not just leave it be?"

"And why is she here? Ye'd think she'd not want to be anywhere near public proof of her husband's leavin's," commented Brandon, ever donning the quarrelsome attitude.

"She told me in no uncertain terms that she was comin'. Said, and I quote, 'He's yer father's child. He needs a mam.' And since I couldn't argue with that, I brought her along." With that, he turned abruptly around and strode to where his mother was gingerly walking, picking her way up the narrow path, keeping an eye out for the extra-muddy spots, wet from recent rain.

Brandon and Liam continued toward the group forming at the front. "No prospects on your end?" asked Brandon of his brother.

"Who, me? Ye mean romantically?"

Brandon nodded. "I was thinkin' o' that actress ye introduced me to that one day. She was like to keep a man warm on any day of the week," he grinned.

"Ah, ye just want her for yerself, and ye can have her, if ye don't mind she's my leavin's," Liam joked. "Besides," he leaned over conspiratorially to whisper in Brandon's ear, "I've a much better one now." Nodding and winking, he indicated the woman standing only a few steps away, chatting with another guest and seemingly oblivious to their discussion.

Brandon ruffled his brother's hair. "You're a true O'Farrell, doing the same as our da. Just don't be sowing while you're plowing, eh?"

Liam grinned back. "It's the one lesson he taught me."

Nodding with his chin toward the wedding couple, Brandon said, "Yeah, well, I don't think our new-found brother got the message.

A quick glance at Laura's gown was not enough to give away her secret until the ever-present wind blew in a gust about her, caressing her body, swirling her dress, a pretty confection that gathered beneath her breasts and normally hung loose to the ground. But as the wind picked it up and sucked the gown to her body before blowing it out again in a rush, the outline of the baby bump could clearly be seen. She was, as Ciara told Hank, wearing her dress high.

"Ye don't think that's why he's marrying her, do ye?" asked Liam.

"Don't be such a plonker, of course it isn't. He wanted her before he got her that way. I think, mind ye, that it helped his cause since she wasn't inclined to wed him for the longest time."

"Ah, right, she'd already said yes when we got together again at Henry's a few days after she first arrived."

"True," agreed Brandon. "I recall Ciara mentioning something to that effect. You know how she often knows things before anyone else."

Liam nodded his agreement and looked toward his sister.

Ciara was standing tall and proud, every inch the Celtic woman, her clear green gaze taking in the gathering, her wild golden hair in stark contrast to the rest of the family. She followed her mother's line, a line of blonde-haired, green-eyed women that had powers beyond the norm when it came to psychic talents. Her mother could heal almost anything, which stood her in good stead as a nurse and midwife. And despite her short stature and wide hips, Mrs. O'Farrell could move with the speed of a freight train when duty called.

But Ciara did not inherit her mother's stature. None of the family seemed to have done, and instead, took their height and slim frame from their father's side. Yet the black hair, such as that that cascaded in waves down Emily's back, and the navy blue eyes that seemed to be the mark of their father's line, missed Ciara by a mile. Her eyes, a mix of as many greens as the land that surrounded them, missed nothing.

Although Ciara had envisioned this day, knew it would have sunshine and therefore encouraged the outdoor setting, she was unfortunately blind to her own future. Before her, her own path was murky, filled with the darkness of the unknown; and try as she might, she could not penetrate its heavy mantle.

A movement in the crowd caught her eye and she recognized one of the men that had helped with the altar construction. He caught her gaze and held it, and as she took in his cool gray eyes and fair hair, she slowly smiled to herself. Perhaps, she thought, but got no further.

The priest was welcoming the gathered folk, thanking them for making the trek from town while casting a sideways glance at the darker clouds to the southwest, which seemed to be moving closer. The ceremony was about to begin.

The sound of a car's automatic lock being engaged penetrated the group at the top of the hill, carried on the wind from the small parking area below. A lone figure, elegantly dressed in a gray, three-piece suit, strolled nonchalantly up the grassy sward toward the group assembled before the castle walls. His manner was sophisticated, his attitude casual. Yet something about him drew every eye.

As heads turned in curiosity, Brandon turned to look, then nudged Liam, who was busy chatting up his date. "Ssst," hissed Brandon, "tell Niall."

Liam took in the lone figure, the swarthy good looks of the man's mixed heritage, and kicked his twin in the ankle, having to stretch to reach him since he was off to the side and forward of where his brothers stood. There were no chairs; no one had thought to bring any.

Niall, feeling a sudden pain in his ankle, turned with retribution in mind until he realized his twin's intention. Suddenly, his face pinked and flushed, which had nothing to do with the stiff breeze that kept the clouds away and everything to do with the man who began searching the sea of faces for the one he was seeking.

"Michael," Brandon called, not caring that he was shouting. "Michael, he's over here." His voice carried on the wind and before long, the entire crowd was pointing to the location where Niall stood, his face as red as if it bore a fresh sunburn but smiling nonetheless.

As Michael reached Niall's side, he put his arm around Niall's waist and kissed him quickly, yet fully, on the lips.

"Change of heart?" Niall was heard to say.

"Talk later. There's a wedding trying to take place," said Michael, his hand possessively resting on Niall's very delectable rear end.

The priest cleared his throat and began the ceremony that would unite Hank and Laura.

Epilogue

Laura closed the photo album and laid it aside. Peeking in the bassinette, she barely heard the soft sounds of breathing from her infant son over Figaro's loud meow.

"Hungry, kitty?" she asked the great orange beast as he wove his way through her legs, purring his way beside her as she made her way to the kitchen.

She hadn't noticed that Hank had followed the cat in and started as his arms came around her.

"All's well in here?" he inquired, kissing her neck as he held her close against him.

"Well, it would be if you'd let me feed your cat," she admonished, trying to scoop the food from the tin. Figaro was still winding himself in and out of her legs and meowing hungrily while Hank hadn't given up on her nape where he'd lifted her hair to lave her with kisses.

"I'd just as soon the wee beastie starve so I can get some attention."

Just then the newest member of the family began to make himself known, causing Laura to raise an eyebrow at her husband. "Your turn. I've been with him all afternoon."

"Yeah, well, you have the equipment, I don't," he quipped, gazing at Laura's breasts that had begun to leak, darkening the front of her outfit.

"Ah, dammit," she swore, gazing at her breasts with dismay, "that's at least the second time today."

Hank never let it faze him. Putting the now full bowl of food down for Figaro, he grasped Laura's shirt at the hem and lifted it off over her head. His eyes zeroed in on the milk-soaked pads in her bra, and licked his lips.

Laura pushed him away. "No, you don't. This is for your son," she said, enjoying the fact that she had one over on him. He would never deny his son anything, especially not his meal.

Just then the voice from the bassinette yowled in earnest and Laura left Hank standing in the kitchen.

Minutes later, while she was settled in the rocker with the baby at her breast, Hank sank down on the couch next to her. They had sold Laura's one-bedroom condo and bought a small house in town with a back yard and three bedrooms. The bonus of a playroom downstairs and a swimming pool outside made the purchase one they couldn't resist.

After their wedding, they'd come back to Canada to their lives as they'd been, and began to re-build Hank's Irish cabin. Only this wouldn't be the same little one-bedroom cabin in the woods. This one was going to be their home away from home.

"What are you thinking?" asked Laura as she pried her son's lips from her nipple in order to burp him.

"I was thinking as how I'd like to trade places with my son," joked Hank.

"Sorry, try again."

"Okay. Then I'd like to have the work on our house up the mountain done."

Having received a good healthy belch from her three-month-old son, she placed him on her other breast and looked at Hank. He was still the handsome man she'd fallen in love with, still full of Irish charm and devil-may-care outlook. He was her everything. There wasn't anything he wouldn't do for her, or she for him. And now, with their son in her arms, she knew she'd move heaven and earth to make this the perfect life for them all.

So she came up with the only idea she had. "Why don't

you see if Brandon will come over and help you? He could use a job and it would keep him out of trouble," she suggested.

"Yeah, it'd like to keep him out of trouble but it would also be a whole lot of trouble for me to have him here. I'd like to kill him, I would, and he's not even here."

"Why? What has he done now?"

"See? See what you've just said? 'What has he done now?' end of quote."

A smile crept across Laura's face. She couldn't help it. "So, what aren't you telling me?"

"Ah, it's no bother. Nothing that a good cuff wouldn't cure. And I'm sure Henry will pay for the bloke's boat."

That got Laura's attention. "What boat?"

"The one in Portmagee. He 'borrowed' it, to take some people over to Skellig Michael where they did some filming. Liam's pissed because now his name has been muddied in the affair. Everyone thinks Liam gave Brandon the scoop on the island, and now with the environmentalists all on board with saving it from people, Brandon's just dug the knife in and twisted it. He's opened a big can of worms and if I don't see his name in print for all the wrong reasons, I'd be surprised."

"Well, he'd certainly be out of the news here. There isn't a reporter for miles around who knows anything about the skelligs," she said truthfully.

Hank nodded his agreement. "While that may be true, there's a whole lot more trouble he could get into, I'm thinkin'."

"Like what?" She gazed at the baby in her arms. He'd stopped suckling and was trying hard to stay awake.

"Like the good-looking women in town. Do you know, I think his preference might be two at a time?"

That got Laura's attention. "How on earth would you know that?"

"Seems a cat fight ensued whilst he was otherwise engaged down Kinsale way. The third didn't like the other two."

"Third?" Her eyes widened in question.

Again Hank nodded. She'd heard him right. "Seems the woman got wind of him bein' with someone else but didn't realize the 'someone else' was actually 'others.' Plural. I guess once the door opened at her knock, she barged in and hauled the one out of the way, which got the first one, who'd answered the door thinkin' it was room service or something, in the fight to stop her from spoilin' their fun. By the time they got the third one out of the room and security called, the entire hotel was awake and everyone in on the story. I think it'll be a while before Brandon shows his face there again."

Laura was trying hard to stop her shoulders from shaking while she tucked the receiving blanket around her now-sleeping son and laid him back in his bassinette.

"Oh, that's too funny," she said, still giggling. "How embarrassing!"

"For Brandon? No, I don't think so. He thrives on notoriety."

"Hmm," she commented. And then gazing at the sleeping infant, said, "I think we're okay for at least half an hour." She removed her bra with the soaked pads, and spreading her arms as she stood facing Hank, watched as his eyes widened in expectation. "Come with me," she invited, holding out her hand and nodding toward the bedroom. "I think I'm horny."

Hank didn't need to be asked twice.

THE END

ABOUT THE AUTHOR

The daughter of an Air Force family, and therefore an extensive world traveler, Ms. Cross has been writing since the age of fifteen, creating stories around the places she has lived and visited. After writing an editorial column for a newspaper for fifteen years, she is now retired and living in Canada's north with her children, grandchildren and an assortment of cats and dogs.

DOUBLE TAKE

You'll be thrilled to read the next installment in S. M. Cross's O'Farrell Legacy series. *Double Take* is now available from Lumau Publishing: A ribald tale of Hank's twin half brothers, Liam and Niall, mirror images of each other and completely opposite in every way.

DOUBLE TAKE
Book Two of
The O'Farrell Legacy

By S. M. Cross

Chapter One

Niall felt Michael's hand on his arse, soft, caressing. Even through his dress pants, the warmth soothed and comforted. Or should have. But they were out in public, in a field before a great ruin of a castle in County Kerry, and a long way from Killarney where it all began, there to witness the marriage of Niall's half brother, Hank, and his Canadian bride, Laura, in holy matrimony.

The weather held fair, and was expected to according to Ciara, his younger sister who had, as many old people used to call it, "the sight." These days, people just said she was psychic. And she was. She'd predicted this wedding, this day, and said that if they all got together and had an early wedding, the rain wouldn't spoil it at all. So far, so good.

His identical twin brother was in attendance as well. Liam, the outgoing twin, the one who laughed and joked and dangled life from his little finger the way local fishermen played with a fish on a line. Nothing was too good for Liam. He had the world by the tail. An actor and a lady's man, he was the one who didn't care what people said, who thrived on rumor and innuendo. His photo was front page news, his movies made headlines. He was Ireland's hero, and he knew it. And loved it.

Not so Niall. The less people knew of him, the better. He was uncomfortable to the extreme in public and having his brother's picture plastered in the news in whatever media was being viewed, was bothersome to him. He neither wanted nor looked for attention from anyone, and so he stood, uncomfortable and edgy, feeling Michael's hand on his arse.

"I thought you said ye'd never attend," he whispered hoarsely to Michael, ignoring the massage of Michael's fingers through the fabric.

"I had second thoughts," said Michael, his cultured English accent pouring into Niall's ears like a good whiskey. Smooth, intoxicatingly deadly. "Let's go inside."

They followed the family into the castle, to the one room that still remained with four walls and a ceiling. Hank was already standing at the altar they'd built, waiting for his bride.

Michael bent to say something in Niall's ear but was quickly shushed. "They're about to begin," Niall said.

Michael straightened, his hand once more straying to Niall's arse, his thumb hooked into the back pocket, almost concealed beneath the edge of Niall's jacket.

Niall shifted, felt Michael's hand cup the globe of his arse and shifted again. The hand stayed. A look was exchanged, Michael winked. And so Niall stood, with Michael's hand caressing his arse and the multitude of folk, there to witness Hank and Laura's wedding, also witnessing the possessiveness with which Michael claimed Niall. The only blessing was that everyone was standing in very close quarters, because no one had thought to bring any chairs. It was an old castle, and they were in the only complete room; a room with a dirt floor and stone walls with niches where candles were lit and where mirrors had been placed to reflect the candles' glow a hundred-fold. The effect had been staggering and the old ruin seemed to glow with new life.

The room being small, any folk who could not squeeze in looked in from windows vacant of any coverings, or from the doors at either side of the room where entrance and egress to other parts of the castle occurred. Niall felt lucky that only a few people would see the familiarity with which Michael possessed him in public.

Michael. A truly different sort. They had met at a conference in Amsterdam a few years back; had been working for the same computer software company, Michael in London and Niall in Cork. Over the past year, though, Michael had relocated to Ireland, to be closer to Niall, and while the company wouldn't recognize spousal relocation in their case, Michael was prized enough by the company to be re-hired in Cork to work alongside Niall. Neither of them worried too much about working in the same office, they just wanted to be together after work.

At least Niall thought they did. He was never sure where Michael was concerned. Michael, who was much more confident than Niall in his body, his looks, his sexuality. He was used to standing out in a crowd, him with his mixed Arabic-English background. His swarthy good looks turned many heads, usually female. But those in the know would never mistake his masculinity as a tidbit for feminine wiles. Michael was as gay as they came.

Niall, also gay, was not so comfortable. Raised in a staunch Catholic family of four boys and one girl, he remembered always identifying with his younger sister, wishing he could play with her toys, and later on, watching the boys she went out with as she got older. He didn't care what they wanted of her. He only thought they might be interested in himself.

Ciara was now a young woman, and he and Liam young men. Liam could get any woman he wanted. Both of them possessed the full head of black, wavy hair and midnight blue eyes that seemed to be a trait within the family, inherited from their father. The only one who'd missed those attributes was Ciara. She had taken their mother's coloring, the blonde hair and clear emerald eyes of the fey folk. Even though their mam had no psychic ability beyond a mother's intuition, it was said that in generations past, there were a few that were that way, and Ciara was one of them.

The priest had concluded the ceremony, the bride and groom kissed, and Michael turned Niall's face toward him and planted one full on his mouth.

Niall pushed him off, "Cop on," he scolded, but Michael only grinned.

"You're the finest looking man here," he said, his fine English accent so different from the chatter around them. Hank and Laura were walking out of the room and its make-shift altar that Liam had contrived with help from the design crew of the set of his latest film. His brother had connections, and no mistake, thought Niall.

Brandon, another brother, second oldest only to Henry, had pitched in to help. Brandon had been offered work by the men that delivered the altar and helped set up, but Brandon had only grinned and declined. It seemed he had a better gig going on over in Kinsale with surfing, women, and something about taking tourists around. It was a craic gig, he'd said, and too good to give up in order to work for someone else where the women were maybe scarce.

Liam watched the crowds go off to enjoy the luncheon after the wedding. He was proud of himself and of his brothers for helping to get the altar set up and turn the castle's one complete room into a make-shift chapel, ready for the wedding. He'd cajoled and bugged the design team to help him out by building an altar out of scrap materials. It looked like stone but was mostly plywood, Styrofoam and a lot of paint. Hank and Laura hadn't wanted a wedding at any of the churches in Killarney; they'd almost refused a Catholic wedding at all. Hank wanted a pagan wedding. Laura hadn't cared. She was carrying their child and stated that, really, she just wanted it over and done with and legal in two countries, Ireland and Canada.

Liam had wanted to do it just for fun; to have the old castle look like something out of a medieval movie, with knights and damsels and all the trimmings.

And so he had. By hook and by crook, literally, for they'd borrowed more than one piece from the production's properties house and re-created a religious sanctum for Hank and Laura. Liam couldn't have been more pleased. The best part was that his brothers had been involved. Niall had hung back but even he had come up with his own touch at the end. The mirrors behind the candles reflected light from the deep niches in the stone walls, niches that were once used as storage cupboards, likely for dishes, hundreds of years ago. It was a magical effect and Liam was happy with his brother's contribution. Niall didn't often think of such things. He was entirely unemotional, in Liam's eyes.

The woman on his arm, a supporting actress with a substantial role in the film, put her arm around him. "Let's go," she whispered huskily, and Liam was inclined to agree. He'd hired some buddies from the set to stop by before nightfall to gather up the bits and pieces that belonged to the company and since it was now mid-afternoon, he knew they would be there within the next hour or two. In the meantime, his little actress would provide plenty of entertainment. He teased her when they first met, calling her Sine of the Jungle. But Miss Sine Maguire was no joke. She was as foxy as they came, a tall, copper-haired woman with luscious curves that Liam was curious to find out if they were all hers or not. He was pretty sure they were.

Sine had giggled at the jungle joke when he met her, telling him she'd heard it before and rolling her eyes in a tolerant fashion. Liam didn't care, rarely a phrase came out of his mouth these days that wasn't a quote from some film or play he'd been in.

His success as an actor was ramping up. Over the past month he'd been seen and photographed with no fewer than five women. Intimacy hadn't been a part of any of those relationships but one read through the tabloids would provide the reader with enough innuendo to draw an entirely different conclusion.

Instead, Liam had been watching Sine Maguire, and had been doing so for a long time now. He'd first come across her in an American film, but then she dropped off the radar for a while and shown up in Ireland. He didn't care how she got there; had in fact been quite impatient to get to know her, and so had followed her around once she arrived on set, waiting for an opportunity to ask her out. While outwardly chasing the previous five females, he had set his sights on her alone. He could have asked the leading lady to be his date at his half brother's wedding, and very nearly did. But Sine's arrival changed all that.

After the ceremony, everyone filed out of the castle to linger on the grounds and partake of the food and beverages that had been brought in, picnic style, for the event. Liam led Sine to the tables and grabbing two plates, soon had them filled. While Sine carried two mugs of ale, he led her round to where some blankets had been spread and chose one in the shelter of the castle walls, away from the wind coming in from the sea.

He fed her, let her take food from his fingers and was surprised when she held on to one lean digit, sucked the juices off and let him slide it from her mouth to watch her lick her lips afterward. He was suddenly very glad she'd consented to spend the night with him.

And then it was time to toast the bride and groom and cut the wedding cake, and so they all stood around while Henry, as best man, and Sarah, as the Maid of Honor and Laura's best friend from home, said their speeches, and encouraged the couple to kiss each time the gathering urged them to do so.

Liam wasted no time during such episodes to join in, turning Sine's heart shaped face to his to kiss the lips that seemed to cry out for it.

Niall, feeling Michael pull him into a hug, shrugged off his lover's touch. He was not an exhibitionist like his famous brother, and the fact they were twins, which made his life more observable to the masses, convinced an introverted personality such as his to vigorously shun public displays of affection. Michael was not put off, he knew. There would be all the time they needed, later.

The crowd began to file out of the castle and down to the small parking lot at the base of the hill after the cake cutting ceremony. Friends helped load the excess into the large van they'd rented and soon Hank and Laura were on their way, leaving the rest to party or go home as they chose.

Later that night, the rest of the family all met up at the pub in Cahersiveen that boasted a large taproom with plenty of room to dance, if a band was in attendance, or just to gather round the tables in the center or the trestles at the room's edge. The place was hopping when they got there, and Liam noticed his twin, gaining more than his fair share of attention. He was used to that. Used to having himself and Niall confused by the masses who wanted an autograph and sometimes more, although right now, Liam's head had been shaved for the production they were still shooting. His normal locks might be absent but that didn't throw the crowds off much. They simply gathered around Niall instead.

Niall seemed to be handling it well enough, although one keen look told Liam that his brother was flaming, no doubt about it. And Michael, Niall's love interest, wasn't far behind.

They were kind of cute to watch, thought Liam. Michael was all over Niall like a sailor on shore duty and Niall, for once, was letting himself go, acting as if it was an everyday occurrence. They held their heads together when talking, seated at the bar. Michael would slide his hand down Niall's arm in a possessive manner and Niall had his hand on Michael's knee. He expected them to kiss any moment now.

Sine sidled up to him. "Let's get a drink," she said, and then thrust her breasts out in front of her like spotlights on a stage and waltzed over to the bar to order. She noticed Michael first and did a double take. How could she help it, thought Liam? Michael was a looker whether you knew he was gay or not. But then she spotted Niall and the double-take doubled. He really hadn't had time to introduce her to anyone before the wedding, and afterward…well…

Liam only shrugged. What could he say? He didn't feckin' care. She was with him, and Niall was certainly no threat, nor Michael, so he followed her to the bar and ordered their drinks. Before long, a trio of fellas came in and set up lights, mics, amps, the whole bit. The pub would soon be rocking!

***

The hotel room was dark and unfamiliar. Niall held his head to stem the solid thumping of his brain against his skull. Any minute now, his stomach contents would decide to leave. Maybe if he just laid there and didn't move…

"What's the matter?" came the voice at his side.

"Shhh," hushed Niall. "M'head's about to blow off."

A chuckle came from the darkness. "Hmm, had a bit too much, did you?"

"Don't tell me ye don't feel a thing," Niall replied through gritted teeth.

The chuckle repeated itself. "Well," said Michael, "let's just say that I can hold my liquor better than you."

"I don't bloody drink," exclaimed Niall, then wished he hadn't. His head hurt when he moved, and unfortunately, talking meant you had to move something.

"Tell me something I don't know, boyo," he laughed.

"Don't 'boyo' me," Niall snarled, regretting his action. "Just shut up. Just feckin' shut up."

Michael's hand ran along his thigh. "Let me give you a massage," he offered. "It'll help. Trust me. You'll soon forget all about your aching head."

"Mm," was Niall's answer.

The bed shifted and Michael turned sideways to begin his ministrations of his lover's body. Niall lay still, letting Michael have his way.

Warm hands kneaded the tense muscles at his shoulders until they finally began to relax against Michael's ministrations. Niall was on his side, Michael half astride him, just below his arse. He could feel his lover's nads, settled between his legs, touching his own; felt the erection that he knew he'd soon enjoy. The insides of his thighs tickled in expectation.

Niall shifted his body, and a strong hand slid down his side, caressed his buttocks and cupped his nads, rolling them around in his fingers like dice in a game. He felt his lover's kisses, warm and tender, down the length of his body, seeking out all those sensitive spots, just like Michael knew he liked. Michael's hand was splayed across his belly, taut with desire, to slide upward across the bare skin of his pecs, tweaking nipples ripe for rolling between strong fingers.

Niall felt his hips begin to move; his own erection was

primed and ready. Michael's hands shifted, stroked his lad as Niall pressed into Michael's palm, hearing his lover's words, breathing warm and tender into his ear. "Soon, luv. Soon."

Fingers traced a line between the globes of his arse, worked his anus, felt it soften beneath his touch. Headache or not, Niall knew he wanted Michael just then, just that way.

A towel appeared out of nowhere and Niall realized that Michael must have planned this interlude while he was still passed out. Then, a touch of lubricant, cold, then suddenly warm. And then pressure as Michael entered him, slowly, deliberately, filling him. Hands engulfed Niall's flute, stroking, gripping. Niall lay beneath Michael, feeling the passion engulf him, taking over his being so that everything disappeared except for the dark man who rode him and the delicious sensations he was feeling.

Michael's thrusts became intense and Niall grabbed a fistful of sheet, gritting his teeth in pleasure. Very soon, he knew, they would both be fulfilled.

A moment more, then Michael's breathing hitched, his gasps sounding like someone in pain but it wasn't pain, Niall knew, it was the way Michael sounded just before he came. Then suddenly the room and everything in it disappeared and all Niall saw was the blackness and the stars exploding like fireworks behind his eyes. Awareness of every nerve in his body intensified, coalesced in his nads as the twin balls tightened, then let loose in the heat of a climax, both men panting their completion in each other's arms.

Michael had been right. He hadn't thought about his headache the whole time.

END OF EXCERPT

Double Take, *the exciting second instalment of S. M. Cross's O'Farrell Legacy series is now available.* www. smcross.net

IRISH AND IRISH SLANG
Usage and Pronunciation

a chroi	(uh kree) my heart
a mhac	(uh wak) my son
a stor	(uh shtor - like 'store' with an 'h added) my treasure
An bpósfaidh tú mé?	(on bohs-ee thoo may) Will you marry me?
banjaxed	broken, usually irreparable
bean sidhe	banshee – In Irish folklore, the Bean Sidhe (woman of the hills) is a spirit or fairy who presages a death by wailing.
black stuff	Guinness
bowsie	thug, scumbag, wife-beater
box	vagina
boyo	boy, lad
cáilin	(colleen) girl
chipper	a place for burgers or fish 'n chips
chubbed	erection
Claddagh	a design on a ring, of two hands clasping a crowned heart between them
clot-heid	(clot-hade) cloth head - another word for idiot, more Scottish than Irish but used all the same
cop on	smarten up, leave off, settle down, etc.
craic	(crack) fun
eejit	idiot
fáilte	(FAHL-cheh) welcome - also the National Tourism Development

	Authority
fella	your guy, partner/husband/ boyfriend
flange/fanny	women's genitals
flute	penis
gabh transna ort fhéin	(gave tras orth hayn) go fuck yourself - literal - 'go sideways on yourself'
Garda/Gardai	police, also called shades
Gligeen	stupid person
gobsmacked	surprised
gonch	underwear
Gráim thú	(ghraw hoo) I love you
grá mo chroi	(yraw muh kree) Love of my heart
hoer	(Dutch) whore
horned up	horny
Is tú mo ghrá	(Is too moh Greah - the eah like in "yeah") I love you
jammered	stolen
jarveys	men who drive the jaunting cars
kip	sleep
lack	girlfriend
lad	penis
langer	multiple meanings – in the books it is sometimes used as a term for penis, as are 'lad' and 'flute'
loo	toilet
manky	dirty, flithy, disgusting
mo cáilin	(muh colleen) – my girl
mo chroi	(muh kree) my heart
mo chuisle	(muh kishla) my pulse
mo dheartháir	(Muh ghrih-hawr) my brother
moggie	cat
nads/clackers	gonads; balls

neddy   idiot, fool

Oiche mhaith agus codladh sámh (EE-hyeh WY(h) ogg-uss KOLL-oo SAA-oo) good night and sleep well

pennyboy   menial worker

plonker   country bumpkin, slow on the uptake

póg mo thóin'   (pogue muh hone) kiss my ass

poot   (Dutch) homosexual man

ráicleach/raaklochk (rack lock)   slut

shandy   beer mixed with another drink - lemonade, ginger ale, etc.

skank   untrustworthy, low-life criminal type

sláinte   (slawnt-ye) health

sláinte mhaith   (slawnt-ye wa) good health

Striapach   whore

Tá tú go h-álainn.(TAW too guh HAW-linn) you are beautiful

Táim I ngrá leat (TAW-im ing graw let) I'm in love with you

thick   extremely stupid ('brick' is also used)

wankers/gormless   idiots